Artful Dodging: The Torpedo Factory Murders

by

M. S. Spencer

Artful Dodging: The Torpedo Factory Murders

COPYRIGHT © 2016 by Meredith Ellsworth

Cover Art by *Kristian Norris*

The Wild Rose Press, Inc.
PO Box 708
Adams Basin, NY 14410-0708
Visit us at www.thewildrosepress.com

Publishing History
Previously published by Secret Cravings, 2012
First Crimson Rose Edition, 2016
Print ISBN 978-1-5092-0876-0
Digital ISBN 978-1-5092-0877-7

Published in the United States of America

Archie waved and walked on

without turning around. Milo took the stairs two at a time to the third floor. The serpentine halls and studios were unlit, and she shook off the sensation of menace smoldering in the gloom. *For heaven's sake, Milo, don't be a sissy. Everyone's gone home.* She opened the door that led up to the tower office used by the Friends of the Torpedo Factory. Wide windows opened onto the waterfront from the stairwell. As she watched, the lamps on the boardwalk dimmed, leaving only the tiny lights twinkling along the ornate iron railings of the sternwheeler named the *Cherry Blossom.* The cabin cruisers and launches in the marina bobbed at their moorings, lifeless except for an open powerboat at the far end. A lantern danced in its stern, flickering on and off like a tiny buoy. No light shone from the rest of the buildings, not even the Chart House. *That's right, it closes early on Monday.*

She reached the fire door and pulled out her key. The little room, only about ten by ten, lay in darkness. Usually the city lights let a bit of illumination into the room, but someone had pulled the blinds across the bay windows that looked south and north. She tripped over some stacked chairs and bumped into the worktable that filled the middle of the room. Backing up, she fumbled for the switch, flipped it, and screamed.

Praise for M. S. Spencer

"*ARTFUL DODGING* is a hot read—a mystery with a plausible, tantalizing romance that literally had me at 'hello'…This is a tale told by an author full of humor, wit, and a sure hand for shaping both believable characters and an engaging narrative. Yes, a must-buy."

~*Erin O'Quinn*

~*~

"*ARTFUL DODGING* is a well-crafted tale with the perfect mix of unique characters, intrigue, passion, challenging relationships and conflicts…Spencer's characters are so real, it's easy to get drawn into their lives. About the time you think you've figured things out, she throws in a curve or two to keep you guessing."

~*Mark Love*

~*~

"[Spencer's] books are tightly written, her characters well-drawn, and she keeps me guessing who did it right up until the end—which is difficult to do…"

~*Rochelle Weber*

Dedication

To My Play Group:
Artists Each and Every One

Chapter One

Milo checked her watch. The storm showed no signs of letting up. *Why the hell didn't I bring a hat?* A woman tripped on the cobblestone sidewalk outside the bar and dropped her umbrella. She toyed with the idea of darting out of O'Connell's and grabbing it, but the man who had been standing in the doorway for the last fifteen minutes blocked her path.

Tony edged around him to reach her seat in the cozy little window nook. "Another Jack D, Milo? Might as well. No letup in sight."

"Sure. But give me something to nibble on. I still have to drive home."

The bartender backed out past the man, who made no move to get out of his way. Milo frowned. The fellow appeared oblivious to the fact that his position inconvenienced everyone. At first she had assumed he was waiting out the rain, but his body language spelled expectant. Every minute or so, he would poke his head out and look up and down King Street. For lack of anything more exciting to do, she fell to observing him. The top of his head brushed the doorjamb, making him about six feet three inches. His bulk didn't jibe with his height, though. She guessed him to weigh in at maybe one hundred seventy-five pounds stripped. He was undeniably her type—lean, trim, tall, clean-shaven— none of that painted-on, five-o'clock shadow male

1

celebrities sported nowadays. *And old enough, for once. Maybe forty?* She could only see his profile at the moment, which revealed thick black hair curling over his ears, slices of silver gray relieving the dark waves at the temple, a straight nose, moderately rosy—from drink or the cold?—and a forceful chin. Without warning he pivoted, and Milo caught the full impact of a deeply masculine face right in the kisser. *Whew.* Even with the Armani suit, definitely *not* gay.

He tapped the toe of a highly polished Gucci loafer with impatience and pulled out a pocket watch. By this time, Milo had dropped all pretence and openly scrutinized the man. He thrust the watch back in his pocket with a scowl and spun around toward the bar, almost colliding with Tony. He took Milo's glass from the startled bartender. "Thanks, just what the doctor ordered."

Milo lifted a finger in protest. Tony looked at her, and the man followed his gaze. Eyebrows raised in surprise, he held up the whiskey. "Er, I take it this isn't for me?"

She tried to come up with a flip response, but his rich baritone rattled her.

Tony stepped between them. "Yes, sir, that drink belongs to the lady. May I get you something?"

The man didn't answer. He stared at Milo more or less the way she was staring at him. Flustered, she plopped back down on the narrow bench, barely avoiding an embarrassing slide to the floor. He continued to stare. She resisted the impulse to pat her short, fawn-colored ringlets, which always appeared tousled no matter what she did, and blinked. He blinked back.

Finally she blurted out, "Would you care to join me?"

He shook his head as though to clear his mind. "Forgive me—I've never seen such lovely eyes...I mean, eyes that color...I mean...sorry. What would you call them? Mahogany? Bronze?" His admiring gaze did wonders for Milo's mood, which took a decided uptick.

"I just call them brown. But thank you."

"I'm sorry about purloining your drink. May I buy you a freshener in restitution?"

"I guess so. Er...did you want to sit down?"

"I'd better not. I'm waiting for someone."

"Oh." His plight, though not unexpected, depressed her. Of course Armani man had a date. *He probably always has a date, even during Lent.*

Tony brought another glass. The man paid him, then hesitated as though reconsidering. "You know, she *is* awfully late. Since you're right in the window seat with a commanding view of the entrance, may I be allowed to change my mind and sit here until she arrives?"

Ulp. "Not at all." *Good—got that out without stuttering.*

"Thanks." He pulled a low barrel stool next to the bench and clinked her glass. "Cheers."

They sipped their whiskies in companionable silence while the rain pummeled both the sidewalk and the pedestrians with barely concealed antagonism.

After a few minutes, Milo decided her heart had settled down sufficiently to ensure a quaver-free sentence. "I'm Milo Everhart." *And I'm Gorgeous George. You don't mind if I seduce you, do you? No, wait—he didn't say that. I did. Hopefully in my head.*

"Um, I didn't catch your name?"

"Tristram Brodie. Pleased to meet you."

Not much for conversation, but that could be a plus. *What, what, what can I say to keep him here?* "Your shoes, they're…er…highly polished." He turned astonished eyes on her. "I mean, are you in the military by any chance?"

His lips turned upward, then opened to reveal perfect white teeth as he let out a belly laugh. He puffed, "How did you know?"

Milo didn't want to tell him how she knew. She still found it nearly impossible to speak Michael's name. More than a year had passed, but the grief stabbed as sharply as it had the day she answered the door to see Lieutenant Colonel Murray, a look that said it all on his compassionate face.

"I've known some Marines in my life." Her voice tripped over the words.

"Well, you're right. I am a Marine. Retired." He lifted a shoe and admired his reflection. "I guess spit-and-polish is the one habit you never break."

"You seem too young to be retired." Better to keep the questions focused on him.

"Thanks for thinking forty is young."

Yesss.

He smiled at her, his green eyes twinkling. "I enlisted at eighteen, the day after graduating high school. It was either that or juvie."

Milo checked out his bearing, his suit, and his starched white shirt. "You don't look like a dropout."

He grinned. "I clean up good. Impressed the Marines so much they sent me to college."

"What for? I mean…" Milo concentrated on her

4

drink, hoping Brodie wouldn't bristle at her grilling.

"Why did they pay for my college degree? They needed at least one officer who could write multiple unappreciated, unread reports in proper English. I pushed a lot of paper."

"Where were you assigned?"

He put his glass down. "You really want to know?"

Milo surprised herself by nodding. She really did want to know.

"I shuttled around Europe inspecting the Marine Security Guard detachments at U.S. embassies. Found some great dives."

"You never saw any action?"

He shook his head. "The only serious issues I dealt with involved tourists seeking sanctuary because they'd run out of money. Oh, and once I watched a training exercise in Iraq…from the safety of a Seahawk helicopter." He sighed. "Not that I didn't want to fight, you know. I applied once a month for combat duty. My general told me dress blues fit me better than fatigues." He smiled at her. "But enough about my glorious past. What—"

"There you are, Tristram! I've been wandering all over O'Connell's looking for you!" A statuesque brunette leaned over the table, her bosom within grazing distance of Milo's cheek. A wide, black, patent leather belt cinched her fuchsia Albert Nippon suit tightly, pushing the D cups breathlessly up and almost over her silk camisole. Three-inch heels clicked impatiently on the floor.

Brodie stood hastily. "I've been here for half an hour, Ursula. Where were you?"

She swung an arm encased in silver bangles around

to point, her voluminous Louis Vuitton purse nearly decking Tony. "I came in the other entrance. I've been upstairs—*waiting*—for you." She pressed her crimson lips together and turned back to Milo. Her voice dropped and her eyes narrowed. "And you are?"

Milo's hand rolled into a tight fist while she struggled to keep her elbow from connecting with the woman's solar plexus. As if he sensed her thoughts, Tristram laid a gentle but surprisingly firm palm on her shoulder.

"This is Milo Everhart. She was gracious enough to let me sit here while I waited for you. Why don't you thank her?"

The question seemed to throw Ursula. "Thank? Her?"

As she floundered, Tristram spun her around, winked at Milo, and marched his date through the bar to the dining room. Milo gazed after them, the shock of losing him too great for words. *Wait. Losing him? Am I out of my mind?*

The rain had stopped. Milo paid Tony and rose to leave. As she pulled on her ancient duffle coat, she noticed that she still wore the artist's smock she'd had on at the studio. She caught a glimpse of her face in the mirror. A large smudge of tailor's chalk zigzagged across her face. Worse than that, it constituted her only makeup. No wonder he'd looked at her so oddly.

She trudged back to the parking garage, found her Subaru, opened the moon roof so she could see the stars, and drove home.

"Pinkie! I'm home! *Ooph. Must* you wallow underfoot like that? I could have broken a leg." Milo picked up the tortoiseshell cat that lay stretched out to twice her natural length on the carpet and carried her to the sofa. She pushed aside the unread newspapers, needlework catalogues, and cracker crumbs, and sat down. Pinkie struggled to escape until Milo had settled into an uncomfortable position, then proceeded to flop heavily on her mistress's lap, purring.

"I'm not going to pet you for long. I'm hungry." In response, the cat began to knead, penetrating the thin jersey of her mistress's paint-stained trousers. Milo looked down. *Oh my God, I'm wearing the double knit pants.* The ones that added twenty pounds to her butt. That, and no makeup, not to mention the muumuu of a smock. *Sigh.* Milo gently disengaged the cat from the frayed cloth while her gloom deepened. *Not that it matters. I'm sure what's-his-name didn't notice. Not with Dragon Lady on his arm.* Before she could slap her own forehead, the telephone rang. Pinkie scattered, and Milo pulled the cell phone from her pocket.

"Milo? Where have you been?"

"Oh, hi, Tekla. I rode out the storm in O'Connell's."

"Nice work if you can get it. Are we still on for tomorrow?"

Milo sighed inwardly. She had three canvases to finish before Christmas, not to mention the needlepoint stocking for Isabel's baby, but she had promised her best friend they would walk in the annual Old Town Alexandria Scottish Walk. *I need the exercise anyway.*

"Of course. When and where do we gather?"

"In the Safeway parking lot at the corner of Royal and Wilkes. Ten-thirty. The parade is supposed to last until one o'clock, so we can grab lunch somewhere afterwards. Make sure you layer—weather channel says

7

it will be nippy. Now where did I put that tartan coat for Sparky?" Tekla's voice faded.

"Tekla? Are you still there?"

Milo heard a crash and a curse followed by a yelp. "I'm here—I tripped over the damned dog."

Milo chuckled. "You mean the light of your life, right?"

"Whatever. I'll see you tomorrow." The phone went dead.

Milo pulled out the last two pieces of the anchovy pizza she'd ordered three days before, turned on the news, poured a glass of wine, and snuggled under the fake fur throw on the sofa. Pinkie—tired of begging from the floor—jumped onto her lap, jettisoning both Milo's supper and her drink. Not for the first time Milo wished she'd gotten a hamster instead. Then a thought spilled in. *He said my eyes were lovely. What color did he call them? Mahogany?* She fluttered her lashes and lapsed into a smile.

****

"I'm freezing, Tekla! Tell me again why we're doing this?"

Her companion unwound two heavy scarves from her face and replied crossly, "We're doing it for the dogs. You know that. The Miniature Schnauzer Rescue League needs donations, and showing them off is like free advertising." She picked up a fidgety ball of gray and white fluff covered in a plaid wool coat and thrust it at Milo. "How can you say no to this? *Hmm*?"

Milo dutifully scratched the dog. "Yes, well, Sparky is a dog among dogs. Although I think you're a bit disingenuous putting him in a Scottish coat."

"Germans don't have tartans. Anyway, when in

Rome…"

"Do as the Scots do?" Milo's amusement warmed her face.

"Yes. Now stop picking on poor Sparky." Tekla looked up. "There's Luisa with that horrid Airedale of hers. Finally we can move out! Come on, Milo. Remember to use the Queen's wave."

Two hours and at least one frostbitten toe later, they had almost reached Market Square and the end of the agony. Milo had long since lost touch with her feet and could only pray they were doing their thing. The crowds were sparser here—the spectators quickly heading to restaurants before the marchers could commandeer all the tables. Tekla hadn't said a word for the last two blocks—most likely in order to save her breath—and, thankfully, even Sparky had ceased his infernal yapping.

Milo peered down the street, checking for lines at the Warehouse Bar & Grill, when she caught sight of a vaguely familiar form on the corner of King and Fairfax. He wore a long, dark, woolen coat and a plaid scarf. Movie star looks. Milo caught her breath. *Oh my God, it's that guy from O'Connell's. What was his name? Tristram Brodie.* Even his name sounded like a movie star's. And that scarf—her tartan, a Douglas, for sure. Tristram waved madly at her, grinning.

As Milo raised her hand, she noticed a befurred woman next to him. *Ursula.* She indicated the coat with her chin and muttered to Tekla, "I can't believe it—is that raccoon? Where do these people come from?"

Ursula pretended she hadn't noticed Milo and slipped one suede-gloved hand through Tristram's arm. Her Cari Bourquin cloche hat dipped as she whispered in his ear.

Milo closed her eyes. "Come on, Tekla. Let's go get a hot toddy."

Her friend rubbed her mittens together and dropped the leash, giving Sparky the opportunity to sniff the Airedale's private parts. Tekla snatched up her dog and slanted a venomous look at the innocent victim. "I guess we'd better snag a table while there are still some to be snagged."

They wandered down King Street. Lines snaked out into the street in front of the Wharf, O'Connell's, even Landini Brothers. They turned left on Lee Street and a few blocks later nipped inside Bilbo Baggins just before a minivan dropped off its load of Goodwin House seniors. A nice fire chortled in the upstairs dining room, and they sank gratefully into the padded chairs.

"Three hot buttered rums, please."

The waiter, long in tooth and short of temper, said, "We don't serve alcohol to dogs here, lady."

Tekla's brilliant black eyes flashed. "How dare you imply I'd feed my dog liquor? Two of the rums are for me, you…"

Milo caught her before she said enough to ruin their dining experience. "Thank you, and could you bring us some of your delicious blue cheese chips as well?"

When he'd stalked off, the two women unwrapped various bits of clothing. Tekla shook out her long black hair and blew her nose while Milo took a moment to survey the room. She stopped mid-sweep at a table in the window. *Brodie.*

At that moment he caught her eye, stuck a thumb

up, and grinned. He stood and wended his way through the tables toward her. "We've got to stop meeting like this. Milo, isn't it?"

Milo was too busy asking herself questions to reply—*Did I brush my teeth this morning? Is my hair clean? Did I remember to put on mascara?*

Tekla spoke up. "Yes, this is Milo Everhart. I'm Tekla Spirikova. And you are?"

"Tristram Brodie. Pleased to meet you. I saw you two marching in the parade. You must be frozen solid."

Tekla picked Sparky up. "I had my dog to keep me warm. Do you...er...like dogs, Mr. Brodie?" She fluttered her fake eyelashes so violently one of them detached itself.

"Love 'em. I used to foster dogs when I lived down near Charlottesville." His quick response—and the fact that he ignored the dangling lash—pleased Milo. He scratched Sparky's ears, endearing himself to the entire table. "Now I just watch the Westminster Dog Show and mope."

"Do you live in the city?"

Thank you, thank you, Tekla. Please, God, may I have my voice back before he decides I'm a good candidate for institutionalization?

"Old Town. Lee Street, at the top of Windmill Hill Park. I can walk down to the Torpedo Factory and waterfront any time I like. It's great."

"The Torpedo Factory!" Tekla's voice rose and her Russian accent thickened. "Milo and I both have studios there. You should come visit them. Mine's the one with the magnificent bronze bear at the door."

"That's fascinating. What—"

"Me too." Milo was too proud of herself for

11

managing to spit out a full sentence to worry about cutting Tristram off. "I mean, I love Old Town. I mean, I live in Old Town too." *Wipe that drool off your chin, Milo.* She glanced around, almost hoping for the dreaded Ursula to appear.

He took the revelation of her mental deficiency in stride. "You do? What part?"

"Er…um…north side—near the power plant."

He wrinkled his nose. "Boy, is that place a dump. I suppose we need to put them somewhere, but they could at least paint it something other than dirty gray. I wonder if we could enlist some graffiti artists…"

Milo found herself on the verge of defending the most hated building in Alexandria when she heard a bloodcurdling voice. *Ursula has entered the building.*

"Why, Tristram, honey, didn't you get us a table?"

Ursula swirled up, enveloping Sparky with her fur coat. The little schnauzer promptly helped himself to a mouthful and began to chew. Tekla detached her pet while Ursula hissed and brandished a magenta fingernail at him. The dog settled down, but directed a baleful eye at his mistress. Tristram could only offer an apologetic face to the two women as Ursula swept him back to the window seat.

Tekla sipped her rum. "Tristram Brodie, huh? Sounds like a movie star. *Looks* like a movie star. Where did you pick him up?"

"I didn't. Obviously. He's with Gloria Steinem over there."

Her friend stared thoughtfully at the couple. "Number one, he doesn't really care for her. Number two, she doesn't really care for him. Which means he's either rich or powerful or both. And judging by his clothes, he's both. I suggest you let him continue to flirt with you."

"And how do I do that? I don't know anything about him."

"Haven't you ever heard of the Internet, girl? You know his name. Get on it."

Milo cast one last wistful look at the man of her dreams and finished off the second glass of hot rum over Tekla's protestations.

****

"Done! That's little Cassatt's Christmas stocking off the to-do list." Milo checked the calendar. "And with almost three weeks to spare." She attached the piece—a finely-wrought needlepoint of the three Magi—to a stretcher frame, and admired her work. *I think I've finally mastered the lettering. Isabel will be pleased.* "Now for Mrs. Hirschhorn's pillow." She picked up a sheet of transfer paper on which an intricate pattern of flowers and stems had been roughly sketched out. Mixing some acrylic medium with ink, she traced the lines of the drawing with her artist's pen on a length of 24-count Congress cloth. Then she laid the sketch upside down on the cloth and, taking a preheated iron from its stand, pressed down and counted to ten.

She had pulled out her chalk and begun filling in the colors when Tekla burst through the door. "Sold! Sold!"

Milo put down the chalk. "You sold the cone?"

Tekla paced the room grinning madly, her normally olive complexion a deep rose color, betraying her hot Russian blood. "A man stopped by the studio last week and admired it. Not unusual."

"No," replied Milo drily.

"Anyway, he came back yesterday and asked for my card. He came back today with a check!"

"A check? For one hundred and fifteen thousand dollars?"

"A cashier's check. It's real, Milo. The teller accepted it." She danced about, picking up and letting fall several needlepoint pillows and purses.

Milo snatched one particularly brilliant piece of embroidery out of her hands. "So who is this guy?"

"Dunno. Never saw him before. Here's his card."

Milo took the glossy business card from her friend. " 'Jefferson Doohan. Vice President, More for Less Enterprises.' What's that?"

Tekla took the card back. "No idea. Isn't More for Less one of those big discount chains?"

"Did he say what he planned to do with a bronze cone twenty feet high and ten feet in diameter?"

Her friend shrugged. "I didn't ask. Had to get to the bank. The only thing that would bother me is if he melted it down. Or put it in front of one of those stores."

"That's probably exactly what he plans to do. Oh dear."

"It doesn't matter. One hundred fifteen thousand smackers make it all better. Now I can throw Jacob out. I can afford the whole rent at last!"

Milo hated to sound like her mother, but it couldn't be helped. "You *will* put it in some interest-bearing account, won't you?"

"Yes, yes. Now remember, you promised we'd go for a walk. Are you ready? Sparky's yowling. I can hear him from here."

Tekla gathered her dog while Milo threw on a coat

14

and scarf. They walked out of the Torpedo Factory onto the waterfront. The cold breeze tried to push them back in, but they held firm. A few ice floes added camouflage to the soupy marina water, and the heavy clouds hanging over the Potomac threatened sleet. A pair of American coots bobbed among the usual detritus of a city dock. The two women were alone on the boardwalk except for a couple of waiters hurrying to the Chart House.

"Let's walk up to Oronoco Bay Park," Milo said.

They took the gravel path—empty of other people—through Founders Park, and threaded the alley between the old Robinson terminal and the trucks and railroad cars parked helter-skelter across the road. Skipping across the iron tracks, they came to a sunken roundabout in the middle of a manicured lawn.

"I've always wondered what this was for," mused Tekla.

"The roundabout? The archaeology museum has an exhibit about it. It's one of the few traces left of the nineteenth-century Alexandria and Orange Railroad." Milo pointed back the way they had come. "It originated here and went south down Union Street, then southwest to Orange, Virginia, and eventually to Lynchburg."

Tekla walked the circle of railroad ties. "What happened to it?"

"Let's see...Oh, yes. Union troops and Rebels fought over it all through the Civil War. After the South was defeated it ran into financial difficulties and eventually the Baltimore and Ohio line bought it. What's left is owned by Norfolk Southern now."

"But why isn't this part used anymore?"

"Alexandria grew." Milo nodded at the modern buildings to their left. "Some bits of the A and O remained until the 1980s, when the Old Town Village was built over them." She looked out toward the river and sniffed with disdain. "I don't know why they developed here, unless it was for the exquisite view of the factories and warehouses across the Potomac!"

"I don't care what you say, we're still lucky to live so near the river."

Milo shrugged. "Granted, it's much cleaner than when I was a kid."

"That's right," said a man's voice.

The women spun around. Behind them stood the movie star, also known as Tristram Brodie. He was alone, and apparently being handsome had become a habit with him. His ebony hair ruffled invitingly in the breeze off the river. No longer Armani-clad, he wore jeans, a heavy bottle-green sweatshirt that matched his eyes, and hiking boots. A professional-looking camera hung from his hand.

When the women remained mute, he added, "Thirty years ago you couldn't put a toe in that water. Now people fish in it."

"Really?" Tekla opened her dark Slavic eyes wide. "Where I come from, everything is polluted—sea, land, food, air. Everything seems so pure here."

Milo explained, "Tekla grew up in Russia. She actually stayed with my family when we were kids so she could breathe clean air for six weeks."

He laughed, showing off his perfect teeth. "I see she came back." He turned to Tekla. "I guess six weeks' worth of fresh air wasn't enough, eh?"

Tekla glared at him. "I came here when I lost my

family. The air didn't kill them. The Soviets did."

He stopped laughing. "I'm sorry."

"It was a long time ago," Milo interrupted hastily. *He's going to think we're totally antisocial.* She pointed at the camera. "Are you a photographer?"

He held up the Nikon. "Strictly amateur. Nothing like the photographers at the Factory. Say…" He looked at his watch. "Were you ladies on the way back to work, or may I buy you some coffee?"

Tekla softened but, after a quick glance at Milo, demurred. "I have to get to the bank before it closes," she lied. "You two go on." She picked up Sparky and headed back, leaving behind a grateful best friend.

The remaining two stood uncertainly. Finally Tristram gestured. "This way?" Together they walked up the concrete steps to a large office building. A jauntily beribboned kiosk called Java Jive sold them two cups of muddy coffee, and they continued to walk. They passed a red brick building. "This is where I work."

She looked up at it. The sign said *Law Offices of Zeller, Schwartz, and Katz.* "You're a lawyer?"

He hung his head. "I must confess."

It didn't seem worth it to pursue the line of questioning. Roughly eighty percent of Washingtonians were lawyers.

They reversed their steps and headed back to the Torpedo Factory. As they stood on the boardwalk beside the double doors to the building, Milo murmured, "Well, thanks for the coffee."

"You're welcome."

As she turned to go, he caught her arm, spilling the dregs of his cup on a passing woman, from whom issued a surprisingly colorful curse. When he tried to blot the poor lady's jacket with a large, clumsy hand, she threw him an astonished look and backed away, holding her hands up. He watched her move off and shook his head as if to say, "Women!" He took Milo's arm again. "Listen, may I take you out on a real date? Tonight?"

"Er…" *What about Ursula?*

"Or at least meet me for a drink. Six-thirty, Vermilion's?"

"Okay."

She watched as he loped off, his camera swinging. A drop of icy rain fell on her head, then another. High over the river a scattershot of lightning backlit the boats. She ran inside, found her keys, drove home, and spent the next four hours trying to make herself presentable.

****

The sleet had tapered off and the moon had begun its stroll across the cumulus highway as Milo entered the restaurant. She passed through the dining room to the cozy bar in the back. Tristram sat in one of the overstuffed club chairs. He saw her and waved to the bartender.

"Jack Daniels?"

"Sure."

He ordered drinks and a plate of assorted cheeses.

Three hours, four more rounds, and two more cheese plates later, Milo figured she'd better start asking Tristram some questions. But she didn't really feel like it. She felt like she knew enough already, so she settled for gazing into his deep green eyes and smiling inanely. Which was okay because apparently that's what Tristram had settled for too. Milo realized with a jolt that no one had said anything for at least five minutes. *Come on, Milo. You're too old for crushes.*

"I really must be going. It's been very…"

He reached across the table, put a gentle hand on her neck, and brought her into blissful contact with his lips. "Nice."

She realigned her jaw and her heart and rose a little shakily. "Um."

He jumped up. "I'll walk you to your car."

"I…okay."

They walked stiffly out of the bar, stumbling only once on the threshold. Tristram steadied her. A few minutes later they broke apart to take a breath. The sidewalk had cleared during the evening, and they were alone. He took her back into his arms and kissed her, moving his tongue around the inside of her lips and making slurping noises as though she tasted like a chocolate milkshake.

He pulled away but held onto her hand. "Let's go home."

She let him lead her down King Street to a black Jaguar, and they drove in silence the few blocks to Lee Street. The moon rode high over a little terraced park. They watched it float a minute, then Tristram took her hand and they went inside.

****

"What kind of a ring tone is *that*? And where is it coming from?"

Tristram reached across Milo's naked breasts and punched a button. The drumming stopped. "Dave Brubeck. *Time Further Out*. It's supposed to have aphrodisiac qualities."

Milo blinked to keep the Northern Lights from flashing across her retinas again. "Right now it doesn't." She sat up and gingerly opened one eye. "Where am I?"

A pair of lips closed hers, and a pair of hands testified that she had left her protective gear elsewhere. She decided to take a moment to savor the new sensation before bringing it to a screeching halt.

Tristram sat back. "You have the most amazing eyes, Milo."

The comment surprised her. "Aren't you supposed to say breasts, or body, or…"

"Those too. But your eyes draw me into the rest. It's like floating in red velvet, or in a sea of hot fudge."

"Well, er, thanks." *I'll deal with those images when my head stops hurting.* She looked around. "I don't remember how we got here."

Tristram laughed, threw off the covers, and padded to the bathroom. The tan line hit just above his tight ass. She wondered vaguely where he'd managed to get the tan until what lay below it distracted her. He called over his shoulder, "We were both pretty schnockered, but I remember every detail. If you wish, I'd be happy to enlighten you."

"Oh?" The thought of Ursula reared its ugly face. What if she showed up? *I've got to get out of here.* While he was in the shower she dressed, prepared to make a quick exit. She found the leggings and the wine-colored turtleneck sweater she'd worn the night before—the one that brought out the red flecks in her eyes—as well as one sock, but the bra eluded her. *Damn, that was my Frederick's fifty-dollar push-up.*

"You looking for this?" Tristram came out waving

a wispy bit of black lace, a scarlet ribbon floating from it. She snatched it and stuffed it in her pocket.

"I…um…thanks for a…um…lovely evening, Tristram. I'll see myself out, shall I?"

She plunged down the stairs before he could say anything and found herself in the street shoeless. She saw the black Jaguar parked at the curb, and beyond it a grassy park stretching to the Potomac. To her left, the sign at the crossroad read Wilkes Street. *Thank God— it's only six blocks to the garage.*

"You might be wanting these to get through the puddles." Tristram stood on the doorstep, a towel wrapped around his middle, holding up a pair of boots. She took them and sat down on the stoop. "And this." He handed her the other sock. She couldn't tell if he was laughing at her or he was just one of those insufferable morning persons. Her head still hurt.

"Thanks." She couldn't think of anything else to say. To be honest, she couldn't think at all.

****

It took Milo the whole day and two showers to assuage her guilt. She hadn't even looked at a man since Michael's death, much less…She knew better than to talk to Tekla about it—she wouldn't understand. Even though no one—not even her mother—would agree, it didn't feel right. It was too soon. She still followed the news of the Pacific fleet, mindlessly counting the number of successful F-14 landings as though that would bring him back. *If only…* but Colonel Murray had made it very clear. Neither pilot error nor equipment malfunction caused the crash. The sudden updraft, he explained, caught Michael's wings just as the tailhook latched on. His plane flipped before anyone could move. Michael died instantly.

He wouldn't want me to stagnate. But what if I forget him? What if this Tristram person overwhelms my memories and I lose Michael?

As she washed out the black lace panties and bra in the sink, she could hear her mother—not to mention Tekla—repeating their oft-given advice. "You can't lose Michael, Milo. He's part of your flesh, your fiber. He's the scent of motor oil and Old Spice that still lingers in his empty sock drawer. He's that chunk he carved out of the banister when he lugged your grandfather's bureau up the stairs for you, and the stain on the wall from when he threw a pie at you as a joke but didn't actually have the courage to hit your face. He fills a hundred scrapbooks. He will always be there."

And would he be really pissed at me right now?

The telephone rang. She waited for the answering machine to click on.

"Milo? Tekla gave me your number. She said you were at home. Are you okay? Milo?"

Not yet.

The phone rang again. "Milo? It's me, Tekla. Pick up."

She grabbed the receiver. "Hey."

"Did that guy get hold of you?" Without waiting for a reply she rushed on. "I'm just back from the board meeting. We've got trouble."

"Who's we?"

"The Torpedo Factory. Jefferson Doohan. Remember, I told you he represents that huge box store chain called More for Less? Well, he's made an offer to the City of Alexandria on behalf of the company to buy the Factory and turn it into a superstore."

"*What?*"

"Yup. The only good news is they want to put my cone at the entrance."

"Tekla!"

"Yeah, yeah, I know. Anyway, the city council has scheduled a public hearing for next week. Luisa wants to put together a committee to represent the Artists Cooperative. She's calling Morgana and Esme. Can you come to a meeting at seven in the tower? We'll plan strategy and start drafting talking points. She says the larger the presence, the better chance we have of influencing the decision."

Milo noticed her tired face in the mirror. Six o'clock already. No time for primping. "I'll be there."

She made a sandwich of leftover roast turkey, slathering it with cranberry sauce, and sat staring at the cold fireplace. *First Michael and now my Torpedo Factory? What's next?* She thought of her beautiful studio overlooking the waterfront. The third floor boasted floor-to-ceiling windows, allowing extraordinary light to suffuse the room. The city subsidized her rent, and she knew she would never be able to afford as good a space anywhere else in Old Town.

The phone rang. "Milo? Are you there? I need to talk to you. It's Tristram. Please pick up, Milo."

She unplugged the answering machine, pulled a notebook from her desk drawer, retrieved her coat, and went off to save her piece of the world.

Chapter Two

Milo drew a shaking hand across her brow. "Luisa, I can't work anymore. I'm exhausted."

Her antagonist's lips tightened in that irritating way Milo hated. "Fine, but don't—"

"I won't. I promise."

Tekla broke in, the sibilant Russian syllables calming the testy atmosphere. "It *is* very late, Luisa, and we have three days before the hearing. Let's plan to meet one more time before that. We may know more by then."

"We may have more rivals by then."

"You mean Jacob, don't you?" Tekla's good-humored face darkened. "I told you, he hasn't threatened anything yet. If and when he does, we'll deal with it. The city council is used to his cockamamie proposals—I doubt whether they'll listen seriously to him."

A tiny woman with flaming orange hair and wearing a purple caftan leaned forward. "But Tekla, right now the council is focused on expanding utilization of the building. They're entertaining any and all ideas, even cockamamie ones."

"Morgana's right," interjected the fifth member of the committee, a woman in her sixties with a long, old-fashioned braid and the complexion of a twenty-year-old. "The mayor's been saying 'Use it or lose it' to us for ages. We can't dismiss any alternative proposals out of hand."

Tekla nodded reluctantly. "I hope you're wrong, Esme."

Milo murmured, "Esme may have a point. The mayor actually applauded when Jacob picketed the new adult store that opened on King Street. I think he's developed a soft spot for Jacob."

"Not that Jacob's protest made any difference. Stupid politicians—they were so busy trying to run the dollar store out, they were hoist by their own petard."

"Their what?" The women turned toward Tekla's puzzled face.

Morgana laughed. "How come you know a word like 'cockamamie' but not 'petard'?"

The Russian glowered at her. With the height difference of almost two feet, her chiseled face loomed like a Mount Rushmore head and should have intimidated the little woman, but Morgana stood her ground.

Esme hastily put in, "It just means the city learned the hard way about the law of unintended consequences."

"At any rate," Milo resumed, "if Jacob turns up with a halfway reasonable suggestion, they might listen to him. And we'd have another party to deal with."

All four women rounded on Tekla. She shrugged. "I planned to throw him out this week, but I'll give it a few more days. Maybe he'll confide in me."

At that, they stood up and began to gather their things—with the exception of Luisa, who kept her seat, glaring at them all. Finally she gave up and snapped her briefcase shut.

As she marched out, Tekla called after her, "I'll email you about the next meeting, shall I?"

The fire door slammed behind Luisa's rigid back. The others pushed it open and followed her down the stairs to the third floor.

****

The answering machine blinked red when she came through the door. She clicked Play. "Milo? It's me again. Tristram Brodie. I think I deserve an explanation. Call me." *Click.*

Milo threw her stuff on the armchair and sat down on the sofa. *He's right. I'm not being fair.* It wasn't like he'd forced her to have sex.

A little voice in her ear said, "Make love. You made love. It wasn't just sex."

Well, what's my problem, then? Guilt? Michael died more than a year ago. She had no valid reason not to move on with her life. A broad chest covered with fine black hair, a strong chin, and emerald eyes glowing at her in the dark appeared on her mind screen. *Tristram's awfully handsome. And funny. And sexy.* She smiled to herself, picked up the phone, and dialed.

"Well, hello." He sounded grumpy.

"Did I wake you?" She checked her watch. "Oh my gosh, it's almost midnight. I'm so sorry."

"S'okay. I hadn't gone to bed yet. I've been…thinking. Milo, don't tell me that was a one-night stand."

She laughed. "No, Tristram. I just have…issues to work out. It was very nice."

"Nice? Isn't that sort of like calling my blue-ribbon rhubarb pie 'tasty'? Or saying the girl has a 'nice personality'?"

Oops.

She heard a newspaper rattle. "Look, tomorrow's Saturday. I'm thinking I'd like to go see the Christmas decorations at Mount Vernon. You coming?"

Gulp. "Yes."

"Good. I'll pick you up at five."

****

"Magical."

"Exactly what I was thinking."

On the other side of the river the lights of Fort Washington dotted the water with pinpricks of phosphorescence. Behind the couple on the bench the strings of silver bulbs outlining George Washington's home shone brightly, casting long black shadows across the lawn. Two heads nestled together. Milo purred.

"Are you cold?"

"A little."

"You want to go in?"

"Not yet. I'm too content to move."

She heard the chuckle in his voice. "It's been a...*nice* day, hasn't it?"

She snuggled closer under his arm. "Very."

He kissed the top of her head tentatively. "Do you mind?"

"Uh uh."

He pulled her chin toward him and softly kissed her lips. She was too relaxed, too happy to argue. Tristram peered at her. "I can't see your face. Are you smiling?"

For an answer, she reached up and pulled him to her. A few minutes later he placed a gentle hand on her breast and tickled the nipple through the layers of fabric, making her heart spin.

"Let's go home."

The familiar words brought her back to reality. "What about Ursula?"

"Ursula? What about her?"

"Don't you live together?"

He paused. "No." The unspoken words were clear. No more questions.

On the drive back, her tranquil state gave way to anticipation. Tristram whipped his Jaguar in and out of the sleepy parkway traffic, never overly reckless, but enough to get her heart beating faster. He didn't speak. For some reason, his silence aroused her even more. *What is he thinking? Is he going to make love to me or drop me off like so much used tissue?*

They pulled up in front of Tristram's townhouse on Lee Street. The last time they'd been together, the surroundings had paled before other, more pressing needs. Now, as he handed her out, Milo paused to survey the park that lay between them and the river. The sky opened up here, a change from the tall, impendent row houses and narrow streets of Old Town. Stars flashed in the Milky Way, and the moon grinned at her as she shivered in the chill breeze.

Tristram took her arm. "Do you think we'll have a white Christmas this year?"

The question first hit her as so unromantic, she worried her little dream would dissipate into the night, but then the words took on a cozy kind of comfort, like the chitchat of an old established couple. "I don't know."

He sniffed the air. "Smells like snow. Come on, Milo."

She followed him, stifling both the disappointment

and her desire. *He's going to offer me a drink and send me home. And that's okay. I'll be fine. Oh, but look at that butt and those shoulders. Is he sexier in Armani or L.L. Bean?*

He closed the door behind her, ran his arms around her middle, and kissed the back of her neck. The little hairs rose to meet him. Electricity shot through her like a high-tension power line. He touched the top of her head and slowly spun her around to face him. His eyes burned into hers, and her mouth went dry.

"Milo?"

"Yes, Tristram?"

"Do you know where you are?"

"Um…your house?"

He grinned. "Just checking. You didn't remember much about our last…encounter, and I want to make sure you are conscious during every single minute you spend here."

Yeah, right. Forget the small talk and take me to bed, you big gorgeous lug.

"Okay."

Oh my God, I said that out loud! Shit.

It was too late to take back. He didn't appear to be listening anyway. He dropped her coat on the floor and lifted her, taking the stairs two at a time. Translucent shafts of light from a recessed panel illuminated the California king that took up most of the room.

Tristram lit a tall, white candle on the bureau and touched her shoulder. "May I?" One hand went to the buttons on her blouse, which he undid carefully.

Why did he have to be so polite? Why didn't he just rip her clothes off like he did the last time? *Not that I remember.* She let the blouse fall, her breath coming in short gasps. He reached out and cupped one of her breasts, encased in delicate azure lace. He pulled the lace down with his index finger, allowing the nipple to lift its hungry head. He flicked at it until it stood up hard and ready for something more substantial. Obligingly, he leaned down and licked it. Then he gently unhooked the bra and licked the other nipple. Milo didn't think she could stand much more.

His hand moved to the button of her jeans. She tightened her abdomen as he unzipped them and let his hand reach in and cup the mound. She fought the urge to press against it but gave in when he started to knead.

He pulled the jeans off and knelt before her. His fingers wormed their way under the panties and tickled her yearning lips. Her mind emptied of everything but the aching in her vagina. He rolled the bit of lace off, tossed it in a corner, and began to suck. Slurping and swallowing, he twisted the sensitive flesh and sent his tongue to palpate her clitoris. Milo spread her legs wider, riding his mouth like a rodeo cowgirl. The candle flickered, shimmering on his desire-glazed eyes. She shouldn't have looked at his face—it brought her to instant orgasm. She held a hand to her mouth to stop the scream. He pulled away from her, dribbling wet kisses down the inside of her thighs.

Then her lover moved lightning fast. He tore his clothes off, pushed her onto the bed, and moved up to close with her. His cock, hard and healthy, inserted itself into her. She folded her legs around his back and began the delectable climb to climax. He slid in and out, his penis scratching the itch inside her vagina. *There. Almost there. Almost…arggggh.*

He collapsed on top of her.

****

Something tiptoed across her chest. When she squirmed to escape the tickling, a painful jab told her in no uncertain terms to stay still. "Ouch!"

"Atticus! Scat!"

The orange cat turned half-slit eyes on his master as if to say, "Excuse me?" and coolly retracted his claws. Tristram plopped on the bed, scattering drops of warm water all over Milo. She blinked them away.

"Hey!"

"Come on, m'dear. It's brunch time."

Milo opened one eye. "You go. I'm tired."

"You should be. What an alley cat you are…Pardon me, Atticus."

He pushed the animal to one side and rolled the sheet down, uncovering her breasts. The cold air quickly brought the nipples erect. Lying down beside her, Tristram brushed his teeth across the right one, hardening it, then took the other between his thumb and forefinger and squeezed. The sensation warmed her breasts and went on to ignite all her sexual parts. She grabbed the back of Tristram's neck and brought his mouth to hers, pried his lips open and roamed the tender inner flesh at will. His arms went round her back and down to her buttocks. Desire flashed, and an instant later they were locked together, male to female, rocking back and forth, faster and faster, hoping the pressure would ease the frenzy, working to reach that moment of nirvana when the lust stopped and the love settled down over them.

It came.

When she woke again, the room felt empty. She found a note on the bedside table. "Urgent call from boss. Had to go to meeting. Make yourself at home. Atticus will show you around."

She took note of her heaped clothes. *Make myself at home? Yeah, like I'm going to start moving furniture and picking out wallpaper.* She gathered the assorted garments and attached them to the appropriate appendages. *Time to go home.* She tiptoed down the stairs, retrieved her coat and purse, and left. Feeling rather like a bedraggled field mouse, she trudged the mile and a half to her apartment. The sleet resumed its attack, aided by a freezing wind. Not until she reached home did it occur to her she hadn't even looked around his townhouse, much less noted the address. Oh well, that only confirmed the temporary nature of this relationship..

****

Just a little touchup to the stems and she'd be done. Milo mixed a tube of Liquitex chromium oxide green with some textile medium and carefully painted a thread intersection. *And voilà.* She studied the canvas. Stems and leaves coiled in intricate patterns around an explosion of purple violets and canary yellow primroses. The pillow would make a dramatic focus for Mrs. Hirschhorn's stark white drawing room. She pursed her lips. If only she knew for sure that her client—who had never finished a project as far as Milo knew—would actually complete the embroidery. She'd better take one more stab at offering to do it for her.

Milo taped the edges, slipped it into a marked plastic bag along with the Persian yarns she'd already selected, and picked up the canvas she'd been working on for Mrs. Carrollton. She stared in dreary anticipation at the image. "Why do they always want the same dumb unicorn scene from the Bayeux tapestry?"

An older woman in a cloth coat trimmed with what looked like antique muskrat peeked around the door to the studio. Milo waved graciously at her.

"It's all right. The studios here are open to the public. We encourage visitors to watch us work."

The woman ventured in. "Really? That's wonderful. So many of the galleries I've been to won't allow that." She approached the counter on which Milo had displayed several vividly colored Bargello clutches. Holding five of them up, she said shyly, "I saw these yesterday. I can't resist them."

Milo warmed to the woman. She'd enjoyed designing the little bags—the long Bargello stitches made it easy to whip up a few in her spare time, and the technique's geometric style allowed her to play with yarn colors and patterns.

"Aren't they precious? Which one would you like?"

"All five, please." The woman checked around the studio as though making sure they were alone and whispered, "I went home and counted up my nieces and grandchildren to justify it."

"You sure you didn't leave anyone out?"

The woman shot a quick glance at Milo and relaxed when she saw the twinkle in her eye. "Nope." She tittered. "Not even me." Milo's little joke seemed to break the ice, and the woman chattered on. "I heard about these from some people down at the gift shop. They should make wonderful gifts. This one's my favorite." She pointed at a small egg-shaped purse. "Its surface feels like liquid gold."

"Yes, I've been experimenting with different

fibers. You can achieve such a variety of textures."

"Have you…have you thought of making some eyeglass cases or makeup bags? I'd buy as many as you make."

"Thank you. I'll think about it." *As if I had the time…*

As Milo wrapped the package, Tekla bounded in. "Milo? Did you forget the meeting?"

"There's another one? This is getting ridiculous, Tekla."

"Luisa thinks we should rehearse. She's petrified that our presentation won't be impressive enough. She wants to blow the council out of the water."

Milo rolled her eyes. "We don't want to terrorize them. Besides, she forgets that we not only have tradition and public opinion on our side, but we have friends in high places. Morgana's on the waterfront advisory commission, and Esme's husband has a lot of clout in this town."

Tekla shook her head, hurling her wild black locks out in all directions. "He can't help us. He says it would be a conflict of interest. God, these Americans and their principles…"

"Now, dear, I can't believe the More for Less folks have a chance of convincing the council that a huge, ugly box store in the center of Old Town is a good idea."

Tekla drew in a long breath and relaxed. "At least it would have a dynamite entrance."

"If you persuade the council to reject the box store, I guarantee the Artists Cooperative will vote to install your cone anywhere you want!"

"Yeah, yeah. Come on."

****

The council hearing room filled up quickly. Milo, Tekla, and Morgana found three seats on one side while Luisa and Esme made their way to the front rows that were reserved for scheduled speakers. The hubbub grew as the clock ticked closer to seven. The mayor arrived, and a few minutes later the six council members drifted in.

Someone behind Milo whispered to his neighbor. "Looks like a full contingent this time. Last couple of hearings, only two or three showed up."

"Yeah," muttered his companion. "It's only the Republican members who think coming to public hearings is part of their job."

"Ha ha. That's just for face time—it's not like they have any influence either here or in the city."

"Ha ha."

The cynicism of the two depressed Milo. Her own home town had always enjoyed a vigorous dialogue between the different parties, and she was used to political opponents respecting each other and searching for common ground. Finding a conservative in Alexandria was harder than finding one in Hollywood, and the long-entrenched Democrats were rarely required to justify their positions. It certainly made for boring debates. Still, she couldn't believe these die-hard liberals would countenance a box store, especially after the King Street zoning fiasco. A dollar store mid-block had wanted to expand, but the city considered it too low-brow for such a prestigious neighborhood and denied the permit. In retaliation, the store owner sold the space to a well-known purveyor of sex toys. A few months later La Volupté moved in, and the city had no choice but to accept it. The local Brahmins huffed and puffed and wrote fevered editorials in the local paper to no avail.

The mayor raised his hand for quiet and gaveled the meeting to order. He recognized the council members and the city manager. "Let the record show that council members Worthy, Dundicut, Ennis, Hilgartner, Beyer, and Stevens are present, as well as our city manager Bill Paterson. Mr. Paterson will make his report, and then we shall hear from our scheduled speakers. Ladies and gentlemen—"

As he launched into his opening remarks, his rich bass tones gracing the room just as they did the choir at Emmaus Baptist Church, a door banged open in the back of the hall. A thin, reedy voice shouted, "You can't keep me out. I know my rights!"

Tekla hunkered down in her seat. "It's Jacob. I knew it. I couldn't wheedle anything out of him all week. Every time I'd ask a question, he'd do that thing he does and I'd be distracted."

"Distracted? How?"

Tekla blushed. "I told you. He's the most…imaginative lover I've ever had." Her eyes went dreamy. "So ingenious…"

Morgana—a devourer of bodice rippers despite being happily married and the mother of two faultless children—leaned forward eagerly. "What sorts of…activities does he think up?"

Milo put a restraining hand on her. "Not now, dear. Why do you think he's here, Tekla?"

"I suspect he plans to stage a disruption."

"What for?"

"Oh…" Tears welled up in her eyes, allowing

streaks of dark blue kohl to trickle down her cheeks. "He's come up with some crazy idea for the Factory. He wouldn't go into detail, but he told me if they don't accept it, he's going to chain himself to something."

Milo snickered despite her apprehension. "Surely not your cone!"

Tekla shot her a dirty look. "That's not funny."

Morgana interrupted. "Enter capitalist running dogs, stage right."

"You mean the More for Less contingent?" Tekla craned her neck.

Milo looked up in time to see the last person she expected. Lithe and handsome in his impeccably-tailored pinstripe suit, Tristram trailed a bear of a man upholstered in a regrettable fringed leather jacket. They and their entourage took up three rows on the right. Tristram pulled out a file and began to whisper urgently to the big man. Milo ducked down behind the seat in front of her, hoping he hadn't seen her. *What the hell is he doing here?*

Morgana tapped Milo's elbow. "Who's the fat man in front?"

"Not a clue."

"Doesn't exactly fit in, does he?"

Tekla grunted. "He looks like Wild Bill Hickok only in dreadful physical shape. Wait a minute. Isn't Chuck Doyle supposed to be from Oklahoma or something?"

"Doyle? The chairman of More for Less?"

At that moment Tekla's boyfriend Jacob went racing past them, two security guards in hot pursuit. He reached the podium and flung himself on the step. "Mayor Carstairs, I demand asylum!"

The room fell silent. The mayor, a chubby fellow with rosy cheeks and a permanently cheerful expression, rose uncertainly. "This isn't a church, young fellow. What exactly do you need sanctuary for? Or from?" He cast a look of confusion at his colleagues.

Jacob waved a dirty hand at the guards. "From the pigs, the coppers, the fuzz! Can't you see they're trying to suppress my right to free speech?" In the commotion his bright orange stocking cap branded with *Greenpeace* had fallen off, revealing the remains of a mouse-colored comb-over. He pulled a dingy handkerchief out of his pocket and wiped his nose. His watery blue eyes rose in appeal to the stricken council members.

A staffer moved behind the mayor and whispered something to him. His Honor nodded. "This is a public hearing, sir. We have scheduled speakers, but if you care to wait till they have concluded their presentations, we shall allow a short period to entertain comments from the floor. Mister…Stickler, isn't it? Why don't you have a seat?"

Tekla giggled. "These guys are a hoot. They all know Jacob—he's been at every public hearing for the last two years."

Milo tried to follow the proceedings but found herself consumed by the horrible revelation that Tristram worked for the biggest retail merchant in the country, a company known for its merciless takeovers of mom-and-pop stores and wholesale destruction of villages—the poster-child for sterile building design and drably homogenous product lines. *A lobbyist. One who wants to eviscerate the Torpedo Factory. Nasty, vile, rotten stinker.*

Tekla patted her shoulder. "Isn't that your fellow up there? The guy we met with the camera? It looks as though he's with the More for Less gang. You don't think—"

"Tristram Brodie sure as hell isn't *my* fellow."

Her friend blinked. "If I didn't know better, I'd venture a guess that you slept with him. Indifference doesn't breed that level of hostility." She cocked her head. "What's the matter? Was he…inadequate?"

"*Tekla.*" Milo knew that any further display of emotion would only solidify her friend's suspicions, but she soldiered on. "He never mentioned the fact that he's a sell-out."

"Now don't go off half-cocked," Tekla said soothingly, although Milo detected a muffled snigger in her voice. "We don't know anything yet. Oh, look, they're about to start."

The city manager came up to the podium. "Mr. Mayor, Council Members. Two weeks ago you asked me to issue a public announcement requesting ideas on how to attract more visitors to the Torpedo Factory and the waterfront. We've received more than seventy-five proposals since then and have scheduled a series of hearings to review them. On today's agenda, we have Luisa Miller of the Torpedo Factory Artists Cooperative and Mr. Remington Doyle, chairman of More for Less Industries."

Tristram stood. Milo's angry thoughts paused to allow a short break for admiration. *God, he's handsome. Why does he have to be such a prick?*

He introduced the fellow in the fringe jacket as Remington Doyle—"Chuck to his friends."

I bet that *nickname doesn't get much use.*

Tristram then proceeded to give an extremely professional PowerPoint presentation. Milo had to admit he covered all the bases and made a persuasive case for the economic merits of a large store in such a strategic location.

"However, we want to make it clear that this would not be your usual More for Less. Our blueprint reconfigures the space so that, while shoppers can easily find the automotive supplies and electronics and groceries they expect from any More for Less superstore, they'll also have access to the works of local artisans which are not often available to More for Less patrons. In order to ensure a successful mixed use, the upper stories will be opened up to allow more efficient access to the merchandise. We plan to convert the main floor foyer into a showplace for local art and handicrafts. Mr. Doyle sees this as a great opportunity to bring art to the community—good business for the artists and for us. Not to mention hefty tax revenues for the city."

The three women behind her watched Luisa's back stiffen. They knew no way on God's green earth would she accept such a cataclysmic transformation.

Morgana leaned over. "Interesting."

Tekla grinned. "I *like* it."

Milo wasn't ready to accede. "There's a catch. Gotta be. There won't be room for all of us artists. They'll charge us an outrageous rent. They'll dictate what we can sell."

The mayor had asked a question. Tristram answered. "Yes, sir. We think we'll be able to accommodate all the current studio owners. To that end, we intend to work out a Memorandum of

Understanding to spell out their rights and privileges. Our architects believe there is a large amount of wasted space in the building that could be used more efficiently."

Tekla turned a quizzical eye on Milo. She had no chance to reply before Luisa stood.

"*Mister Mayor...*Your Honor, I believe it's the Cooperative's turn to present?"

Mayor Carstairs, clearly enthused by Tristram's proposal, halted in mid-question. "Oh...er...yes. Ms. Miller? You have the floor." He nodded at Tristram and Doyle. "Thank you, gentlemen."

Luisa made an impassioned plea for the status quo that annoyed everyone in the room. Before she could finish, however, Jacob started shouting.

"It's eight o'clock! Scheduled speech time is over. Said so on the agenda. My turn! My turn!"

The council seemed almost relieved to turn the dais over to Jacob. Luisa sat down, her angry snort so loud even the janitor sweeping the hall heard it. Paterson beckoned Jacob to the podium, and the young man gaped at him.

Tekla whispered, "I bet he never really expected to be allowed to speak."

"Uh." Jacob stumped up to the microphone. He pulled off his backpack, bent down, and rooted around in it, finally extracting a sheaf of dog-eared papers. Waving them with a spasmodic hand, he cried, "Here it is! Here's the plan." He drew a bent pair of glasses from his back pocket and tried unsuccessfully to level them on his nose, glanced over the papers—dropping several—and peered myopically at his listeners.

"Why do I feel like I'm watching a hapless

Christian surrounded by hungry lions?" whispered Morgana.

The audience held its breath.

Jacob licked his lips. "First thing, we throw out all the artists."

Milo put a restraining hand on Tekla.

"Then we clear the building of all the symbols of the glorification of war and imperialism."

"Excuse me?" One of the council members, the newly elected Republican, Rachel Worthy, leaned forward. "What are you talking about?"

Jacob turned a sneer on the questioner. "I don't expect a *Republican* to understand."

Councilman Stevens patted his colleague's arm indulgently and said, "He means the torpedoes, Rachel."

"The torpedoes? But aren't they museum pieces? To illustrate the original purpose of the building? It's not like they work or anything."

"Young man," the mayor interrupted. "You're not suggesting we destroy historical artifacts, are you?"

"Of course I am." The bit of spittle on his lip detracted only a little from his wild eyes. "We don't need history. We need to live in the present, just like our animal friends do. We must move on toward a utopian paradise where there is no war and everyone is provided with what they need."

"I see." The Republican member sat back, a tiny smile on her face. Milo could tell she was thinking this fellow hardly needed help to hang himself.

Jacob must have assumed he'd won his point, for he riffled through his notes, pulled out a stained napkin, and flattened it on the dais. Clearing his throat, he announced, "Third, we turn it into a showpiece for green energy. We'll put wind turbines on the roof and solar panels on all the windows."

The other female council member, Dottie Dundicut, pulled the microphone closer. "Will that generate enough power to light the studios? Artists need a lot of light, Mr. Stickler."

"Not to mention cutting *off* the light with those stupid panels," muttered Morgana indignantly.

Jacob shook his head vigorously, finally dislodging the bit of spittle. "The new generation of artists we'll select won't need the light. Or the studios. We shall allow only performance artists, who will be approved on a rotating basis, one at a time. Once a piece is finished, it will be dismantled. The Torpedo Factory will remain undefiled by human refuse. It'll be like..." He stuck his head deep into the backpack and pulled out another ragged sheet of paper. Holding it out before him, he intoned, "Like 'a wilderness, where the earth and its community of life are untrammeled by man, where man himself is a visitor who does not remain.' " He flung the paper down in triumph.

Both Tristram and Doyle stared open-mouthed at Jacob. Tristram started to whisper something, but Doyle interrupted in a voice audible to the entire assembly. "I know that language. It's from the damned Wilderness Act, for Christ's sake. It's about keeping *pristine land* in its natural state. What kind of a lamebrain is this guy?"

Snickers rolled through the audience. The mayor waved feebly, and the city manager stood up and called for quiet.

Stevens pulled his microphone over. "Mister..."

He looked at his notes. "Mister Stickler. If I understand you correctly, you would only have one artist occupy the Factory at any given time, and that artist would have to remove his art and vacate the premises at the conclusion of his or her...performance? Wouldn't that be kind of a waste of the space?"

"Yes, yes!" Ms. Worthy chirped. "And just how much revenue would that kind of art generate? I mean, if the artists didn't have to rent space, and there's nothing for people to buy?" The rest of the council nodded vigorously. Milo grinned. *Nothing like the word "revenue" to bring normally opposing viewpoints together.*

Another councilman chimed in. "Why, that would turn the Torpedo Factory into a giant money-sucking hole!"

As if sensing the mob turning against him, Jacob frowned. "I suppose we could allow a few artists to maintain studios—but only if they use recycled materials."

"I see. Well." The mayor peered at his watch. "Mr. Stickler, you've got an interesting idea there. Why don't you put together a formal proposal, and we'll take a look at it at a future hearing?" He pounded the gavel. "Meeting is adjourned."

Within thirty seconds, most of the room had cleared, leaving Jacob with his jaw slack, Luisa whispering furiously to a city staffer, and Milo pretending to look on the floor for her keys. When she figured Tristram and his party had had enough time to decamp, she started to rise, only to be confronted with a mirror image of her face staring out from a pair of brilliant black wingtips.

"Hello, Milo."

She expected to be embarrassed, but the anger came to her rescue. "You."

Evidently she'd packed enough venom into the word that he stepped back, eyes wide. She took the opportunity to grab her purse, whip around him, and march out of the room, taking care to listen for his call.

None came.

****

"Well, I did it. I threw Jacob out."

Milo pushed a needle back through her stitches and snipped the thread off close to the canvas. "How did he take it?"

"As expected. He shouted at me, called me all sorts of names—none of which I understood—and then tried to seduce me. It almost worked."

"I don't want to hear." The vision of Tekla's grubby ex-boyfriend making lewd suggestions did not titillate her. "Where's he going to live? Did he say?"

"No. And I didn't ask."

Milo picked up a skein of turquoise Persian wool and laid it next to the teal she'd already chosen for her latest project.

Tekla looked at the little case with interest. "I'm glad you've branched out into eyeglass cases. Clutches are pretty much out of fashion nowadays. You should be able to sell a lot of these." She picked up a coin purse with a vivid red and orange zigzag pattern. "What's this kind of needlework called?"

"Bargello. Named after a collection of chairs in a Florentine museum. It makes a nice thick mat—good for heavy use items. Of course, the technique limits you to geometric designs. I still prefer needlepoint for pillows."

"You don't do crewel anymore?"

Milo pointed at a glass counter. "Just a few things—special orders. It's too time-consuming and fragile. I'm thinking I might concentrate on hand-painting the canvases and selling them as kits."

"I dunno. I prefer to work with something harder and bigger than I am."

Milo laughed. "That's an interesting way to describe your work." She opened up the skein and began to separate the yarn into three plies. "So what was the last straw? With Jacob, I mean?"

Sparky gave an expressive yip. Tekla patted his head and went to the little refrigerator in the rear of the studio. She pulled a bottle of water out and tipped some into a bowl for the schnauzer, tossing the rest down her throat. "He chained himself to the Burke & Herbert branch office down on Jamieson Avenue, near the new government center. Claims they're laundering money for the oil companies. I had to bail him out again. It's getting so the sheriff's deputy pulls the paperwork out when he sees me walk in the door. I'd be embarrassed, but that uniform's kind of cute. I wonder if he's married…" Tekla lapsed into a reverie.

"Hello? You haven't told me why you threw Jacob out."

Tekla started. "I'm getting to that. When they released him from jail, he came home without a word. You know something? I don't think his heart was in that latest protest. He gave up after only eight hours."

"Really? *Hmm.*"

"I know. Milo, I'm beginning to suspect that he's losing his marbles. He always felt so strongly about his environmental causes—the whales, nuclear power, overpopulation, the whole gamut, but lately he's been completely fixated on the Torpedo Factory and this bizarre idea of restricting it to performance art. When I try to talk to him, he goes all unhinged on me, raving about how I'm part of the problem—how I hate the earth and want to rape her for her ore to create my sculptures. He says all artists exploit nature—"

"Except the recyclers. I know."

"Well, calling *me*—Tekla Anastasia Spirikova—a despoiler of the earth. It was too much. I—who escaped Russia, where they systematically poisoned entire seas and polluted the atmosphere of a whole continent. I don't think I exploit—what does he call it? Gaia? Do you?"

"No, Tekla."

She pulled Sparky's ears absently. "At least now that he doesn't have me as his punching bag he'll focus on the council. He's been hanging around City Hall ever since that hearing. I think he buttonholes every staffer he can find."

Milo scratched a bump on her elbow, a bad habit she had when she needed distraction. She couldn't go on with her work until she'd let some blood. She eyed Tekla's wild black tresses and ruby red mouth. *I wonder if there are Russian vampires.*

Her friend jumped up, her hand to her mouth. "Oh, damn. I forgot! Marshall's is delivering my sheet metal at five. I'd better run down to the loading dock." Over her shoulder she yelled, "Luisa said she left some files for you in the tower."

"Files?"

Tekla's voice floated back. "Factory history. She

says you're to put them in chronological order by tomorrow."

"What? No! I..." But Tekla was long gone. Milo sighed and went back to her yarn. *I'll take the files home with me. It'll give me something to do.* One advantage of Jacob's expulsion would be that Tekla could spend more time with her. *I need to get out, do things, stop dwelling on...him.*

She hadn't heard from Tristram since the hearing. Meanwhile, the city council continued its deliberations. The day before, they had requested more details from the various factions. She'd learned from Luisa that Tristram was the point man on the project for Doyle. *So he's probably very busy. Not that I'd talk to him. Prick.* He'd deliberately kept his business a secret from her. He knew she was a member of the Artists Cooperative. He knew she worked on the committee to save the Torpedo Factory. She ignored the little voice that tut-tutted in her ear that she'd never actually told him any of that. Never mind. He had to know how she would feel about a box store taking over her beautiful art center. He just didn't care.

Milo continued to mutter and grumble as she worked until the building manager came by to tell her he was closing up.

"Is it that late already, Archie?" She checked her watch. Ten o'clock—his usual time to do the rounds of the building and shut off lights before locking the main doors to the center.

"Yup. You can leave by the side door if you want to stay."

"No, no, I'm coming. I'm starving! I'll follow you out, Archie."

Archie Chisholm, a fixture for thirty years at the Torpedo Factory, nodded silently. His face and body were simultaneously ageless and nondescript. He'd kept his gray hair in a crew cut for as long as Milo could remember, and he wore the same khaki chinos and flannel shirt every day, season in, season out. Gray eyes set deep were usually hooded, cloaking his expression. Several of the artists insisted he never actually left the building. Some claimed he was born in it. As it stood, he knew every nook and cranny of the place, every artist who had ever had a studio there, every event, public or private, that occurred there. He treated the Torpedo Factory like a baby, nursing it along through crisis after crisis in its checkered history, defending it against all enemies. Milo felt privileged that he would even suggest leaving it in her hands.

She looked up to see him patiently waiting in the corridor. *Of course, he wouldn't. He's making sure I'm cleanly out of here.* She packed her stuff, locked the studio, and followed him down the stairs. They walked through the cavernous main hall of the former munitions plant. Walkways on each of three floors followed the contours of the building. Studios lined the walks and snaked in and out of corridors in a maze of cubbyholes. She caught herself thinking Tristram might be right—the rooms could easily be remodeled to be more accessible and provide more exhibit space. *Why, that back stairway to the Friends' office could...Oh shit.*

"Archie, you go on. Luisa left something for me up in the tower. I'd better get it tonight or there will be hell to pay."

Archie waved and walked on without turning

around. Milo took the stairs two at a time to the third floor. The serpentine halls and studios were unlit, and she shook off the sensation of menace smoldering in the gloom. *For heaven's sake, Milo, don't be a sissy. Everyone's gone home.* She opened the door that led up to the tower office used by the Friends of the Torpedo Factory. Wide windows opened onto the waterfront from the stairwell. As she watched, the lamps on the boardwalk dimmed, leaving only the tiny lights twinkling along the ornate iron railings of the sternwheeler named the *Cherry Blossom.* The cabin cruisers and launches in the marina bobbed at their moorings, lifeless except for an open powerboat at the far end. A lantern danced in its stern, flickering on and off like a tiny buoy. No light shone from the rest of the buildings, not even the Chart House. *That's right, it closes early on Monday.*

She reached the fire door and pulled out her key. The little room, only about ten by ten, lay in darkness. Usually the city lights let a bit of illumination into the room, but someone had pulled the blinds across the bay windows that looked south and north. She tripped over some stacked chairs and bumped into the worktable that filled the middle of the room. Backing up, she fumbled for the switch, flipped it, and screamed.

Chapter Three

"Hello! Hello? 911?"

"Please state the nature of your emergency."

"A body. There's a b…b…body." The word came out as a gurgle.

"Yes, ma'am. Now tell me where you are."

Milo looked wildly around the darkened corridor. "Second floor. No lights."

"Ma'am? Second floor of what?"

"Oh, er, the Torpedo Factory. I ran downstairs. I…"

"The Torpedo Factory? You mean the building at 105 North Union Street?"

Milo almost snapped, "How many torpedo factories do you know?" but thought better of it. "Yes."

"All right, ma'am. Now, you say you've found a body? Is it dead?"

"Don't be ridiculous. Of course it's dead. Dead. A dead body. In the office."

"The office?"

"The tower. Look, can you send the police? I'm all alone in the building. Except for the body, of course. I mean, it's pitch black in here. Please?" She knew she sounded less than rational, but weren't 911 operators trained to weed out the gibberish and cut to the chase?

"I've already sent out a call. The police should be arriving any minute. Now, will they be able to enter the building?"

"Oh! Er. I don't know. Archie's already locked up."

"Archie?"

"The super. He's long gone, though."

"Can you get to a door to let them in?"

Milo's shoes must have found bubble gum on the floor all by themselves, since they appeared to be stuck. "I…uh…I can't get to the doors." Nothing but silence on the other end. *She must think I'm lazy. Or a coward. I'll bet she knows how to wait people out, to force them to do her bidding.* "I'm *not* lazy, miss. I'm just…I'm wondering. What if the murderer is hiding somewhere, still in the building?"

"Murderer? You think the victim was murdered?"

Every *CSI* show she'd ever watched, plus a couple of *X Files*, fast-forwarded through her brain. Somewhere in the reruns she found the answer. "I don't know. That's for the experts to decide." *Thank you, Gil Grissom.*

"Okay, ma'am. Listen to me carefully. If the building is locked, the police will have to break the door down, but first they'll have to go to a judge and get a search warrant. So you see, the quickest way they can help you is if you let them in. Now, do you think you can go down the stairs to the door?"

Milo drew in a long, ragged breath, holding it until her head began to spin. As she let it out, she managed, "Yes. I'm on the landing. Can you stay on the line with me in case I'm attacked?"

"I sure will."

Milo felt her way with one hand toward the middle stairwell. "I'm on the stairs now. Now I'm walking down the stairs."

"Yes, ma'am."

The central staircase of the factory only had a single metal railing and thus was exposed to the entire main hall. If anyone still lurked in the building he could easily see (and hear) her. She stopped halfway down and looked across the main lobby to the front entrance, a set of doublewide, glass-paned sliding doors. "There are flashing lights and sirens coming from Union Street."

"Yes, ma'am. That would be the police."

Well, duh. Milo had the uncomfortable feeling that the dispatcher was reluctantly stifling assorted rude remarks. She reached the ground floor and waved at a policeman who stood facing her outside the portal. He waved back. She realized he expected her to open it, but she had no idea how. She knew Archie flipped some kind of switch somewhere to activate it, but she'd never actually seen him do it. She searched frantically around in the gloom. The revolving light from the police cars only made it harder to see. Milo gave up and, pointing to her left, ran down the main hall to a small vestibule. For the benefit of artists who worked late, Archie usually left the alarm off at one unmarked exit that emptied onto Union Street. She pushed open the heavy steel door.

Two burly Alexandria cops shouldered their way in. Behind them, a short, chubby fellow in a raincoat tipped a cowboy hat.

"Ma'am? We have a report of a corpse?"

"Yes, yes, in the office…I mean the tower. Fourth floor."

Cowboy hat nodded at the policemen, who headed

toward the main stairs. The detective pulled out a notebook. "My name is Webley, Lieutenant Webley, Alexandria Police Criminal Investigations. Could I get your name please? Your occupation? And your reason for being in the Factory after hours? On whose authority are you here?"

Milo ignored the detective's staccato questions and sprinted after the policemen, who had dashed up the main stairs. She caught up with them on the third floor landing, where they milled around with puzzled looks.

The detective brought up the rear, puffing even harder than Milo. She started to take the lead, but he put a warning hand on her arm. "Miss? Could you answer my questions first?"

"Milo Everhart. I have a studio here. I was working late."

"In the tower?"

"The tower? Why would I—? No, in my studio."

"May I ask why you went up to the tower?"

"The Artists Cooperative keeps records there. I went to fetch a couple of files before I went home. Could we maybe get a move on?"

"Sure." His tone made it clear that he did not consider accommodating her a top priority at the moment.

Since Milo still grappled with the issue of a dead body in her building, she couldn't spare the time to worry about some gumshoe's disapproval. "This way, gentlemen."

She led them around the curving corridor to a small door marked "Friends of the Torpedo Factory" and pulled it open. "The tower door is kept locked. The key is over the lintel. I'll just—" The detective was gazing over her shoulder. She followed his gaze to the top of the narrow stairs. The fire door stood slightly ajar. "Oh. Uh. I must have left it open when I ran down the stairs."

She stepped back to let the men go ahead of her. One of the policemen pulled a convenient cinder block out to wedge the door wider. Fluorescent light shone out onto the landing. By the time Milo reached the little room, the first policeman was calling for an ambulance while the other one ran yellow tape around the room.

The detective stood at the door, blocking her view. He flipped open his phone. "We have a one-eighty-seven. Male. Caucasian. Fully clothed."

Milo stepped back, hand to heart. *He didn't really think...*

"Looks like his head's been smashed in...With a what? A blunt instrument?...Ha ha, Joey, real funny...No, I can't tell yet—he's lying on his back. Get the CSI team over stat."

He hung up and stepped aside, giving Milo a view of the room. She stared down at the thing that lay between the table and the far door as if for the first time.

"Ms. Everhart, looks like we'll be spending some quality time with each other. Now, do you want to tell me everything you heard and saw?"

Milo continued to stare at the body. She gulped for air and managed a faint mumble. "I don't think I can tell you much."

"That's all right, ma'am, just the facts." He grinned. "Tell us how you found it."

"That's the problem, Mr. Webley. I can't. This isn't my body."

Silence pervaded the tiny room. She thought she

heard a snuffle from one of the cops but couldn't be sure.

Finally the detective spoke. "Not…er…*your* body?"

"I mean, it's not the body I saw. This is a different body. Someone else's body."

"I see." He clearly didn't. "So…what do you think happened to your body?"

That was definitely a snigger. Sheesh. How could these guys laugh at a time like this? "How would I know, Detective? It was right here when I left."

To Milo's relief, Webley refrained from asking why she couldn't keep track of her corpses. He did say, "Well, it didn't just get up and walk away. Are you sure it was dead?"

Reminded unpleasantly of the 911 operator, Milo responded stiffly, "There's no call to be sarcastic, Officer. Something must have happened to it." *Is it just me or is this whole conversation heading into the twilight zone?*

Webley must have agreed, for he answered in a carefully neutral tone, "We'll take a look around when we're finished here. Do you by any chance know *this* man?"

Milo studied it, frowning. "I'm afraid not, although he seems vaguely familiar. He could have been a visitor to the Factory or someone I saw on the street." She shook her head. "Sorry, I can't help you."

The noise of heavily shod feet came from the stairwell. Three people tried to squeeze through the fire door into the crowded room. A fellow in a crisp white shirt and black windbreaker emblazoned with CACSI, wearing what Milo guessed was a habitual grin, set a briefcase on the table.

"Lieutenant Jasper, Crime Scene Investigations. You fellows want to move out so we can do our job?"

Webley took Milo's arm. "Let's go down to that little table on the third floor and discuss this." He turned to the technicians. "After you finish with this one, you might want to check around for another body. Apparently we have two."

The three men, intently pulling on vinyl gloves, didn't laugh. Milo wondered how often they had heard similar statements.

She sat down at the round wooden table by Fred Leonard's studio. Ranged along the floor-to-ceiling windows, the artist's famous monumental panels of stained glass hung cheek by jowl like so many slabs of beef. The pale light of the moon hit them, letting loose a cacophony of colors that jiggled and throbbed. Milo shielded her eyes. At that instant the building flooded with light.

Webley laid his flashlight on the table. "That's better. Okay, tell me exactly what you did and saw from the time you left your studio."

Milo recounted her movements as precisely as she could. Halfway through, she took a peek at her watch. Almost midnight. *Time flies.*

The detective must have noticed. "I know it's late, Ms. Everhart. We'll try to get this over quickly. The whole process would have gone a lot faster if we hadn't hit this minor snag."

"You mean a second victim?"

"That too."

"That too? That too?" Panic-fueled bile rose in her throat. *He doesn't think I...No!* She coughed. "What are you talking about?"

"Calm down, miss." Webley tried to smile reassuringly, an operation clearly unfamiliar to his features. "I mean, a *missing* victim. That's all."

"Oh." She sucked in air, feeling the acid burn.

"Look. Are you absolutely sure you didn't see or hear anyone else in the building?"

Milo closed her eyes. She tried to go back in her mind to that quiet climb. "I'd said good night to Archie and then remembered I needed the files from the tower."

"Did you see him leave?"

"Not exactly. He was almost at the end of the hall. He told me he was going home."

"*Hmm.*"

Milo's loyalty kicked in. "Look here. The Torpedo Factory is Archie's life. He's a good man. He'd never do anything to harm it."

"Maybe he was defending it."

"I hadn't thought of that." The idea had a dismayingly authentic ring to it. *Would Archie do that? Could he kill a man to save the Factory?*

"We'll question him when we're through here. By the way, did you recognize the first victim?"

Her eyes opened wide. "As a matter of fact, I didn't."

"Can you describe him? You did say it was a man, didn't you?"

Milo closed her eyes again. The instant the tower light flashed on, her brain had taken a snapshot of the scene before terror took over and she fled. "A white male. Slim. Medium height. He had a heavy dark coat and hat on."

"Could you see his face?"

"No. He lay face down. His hat hadn't come off."

"Strange. How did you know he was white?"

"His hands were flung out to either side as though he'd tried to break his fall. They were white."

Webley jotted something down. "I guess we'll have to presume the rest of him matched the hands." Milo almost giggled but stopped when it threatened to turn into hysterics. "Did you notice anything else?"

"N...no. I turned and ran out of the room. I'm sorry—I should have looked around more, but—"

"But you were terrified. Like any normal person would be."

"Thanks." *Why am I thanking him?* "Er, actually, there was something I *didn't* see." The detective cocked his head and waited. "I...I...didn't see any blood."

"If he was killed from the front, his body may have covered the blood. How did you know he was dead?"

Milo regarded him, her eyes puzzled. "I just knew. Don't you always?"

They were interrupted by loud tramping. One of the forensics people flung open the steel door "Lieutenant, we found something interesting. Wanna come up?"

Webley rose, and Milo trailed behind him. They paused to let the EMT team maneuver a covered stretcher around the half landing.

The genial Jasper greeted them and pointed to a dark stain on the carpet. "This blood doesn't belong to the victim."

"How do you know?"

A hint of exasperation seeped into the CSI man's hearty voice. "It's my job, Webley. The victim died of a blow to the head. He lay here, facing up. See?" He indicated a small wet blotch. "The other blood pooled under his legs. Either it's someone else's blood, or the murderer cut him off at the knees. Your choice."

Webley didn't smile at the joke. "No evidence of other wounds?"

"Not visibly. The stains on his trousers looked superficial. In other words, they didn't spread from the body outward. The coroner will be able to tell us after the PM."

"Does the doctor think he died instantly?"

"Most likely. We found no evidence that he crawled anywhere. Perp carried him in here. Found blood droplets on the stairs."

"Have your people see where they lead. And let me know which blood matches the vic's." Jasper nodded, and Webley turned to Milo. "I guess your story checks out. There must have been a second corpse."

Milo's anger boiled over. "Of course it does! Why would I lie about it?"

Webley started at the sound of banging from the other side of the room. "What does that door lead to?"

"To the roof."

The fingerprint man said, "You can let them in. We're finished dusting."

Milo pulled the door open to let in one of Webley's men. He blew on his hands and stamped his feet. "Freezing out there."

"Did you find anything?"

"Nope. Combed the roof. Nothing. Even looked over the edge. No bodies on the sidewalk."

Webley rolled his eyes. "I think we'd have heard by now if a body came hurtling down into the street."

The CSI man looked from Milo to the policeman to the detective. "Well, if there was a second body, where'd it go then?"

Milo collapsed on a chair, and Webley patted her awkwardly. "Look, Ms. Everhart, why don't you go home? I've got your address and phone number. I'll get in touch tomorrow once we've finished the preliminary investigation."

She kept her eyes open long enough to assure him she'd heard, and he gestured at one of the policemen. "Buckler, would you escort Ms. Everhart home?"

The sergeant took her arm and led her to the front door. Lights still flashed from an ambulance and three cars marked "City of Alexandria Police." A cluster of onlookers had gathered despite the late hour, and Milo heard a gasp from the crowd as Buckler handed her into the squad car.

She couldn't repress a grin. "There goes my reputation, Officer!"

He chuckled. "By the way, before we head out you might want to take a gander at those folks—anyone look suspicious?"

Milo scanned the eager audience and stopped. Archie stood there frozen, his mouth open. When he saw her face, he turned and melted back into the crowd.

****

The pounding woke her. "Milo! Open the door!"

Tristram. *Great. Just what I need.* She pulled on the ivory silk peignoir that matched her negligee and hobbled out of the bedroom. The clock in the living room chimed twelve. Noon. She must have slept ten hours. She caught a glimpse of her face in the hall mirror.

"Hang on a minute!" She popped into the powder room, splashed water on her face, and ran her fingers through the thick, dark blonde curls, thanking God and the patron saint for good hair that hers actually looked better messy. "Coming!"

She opened the door and caught her breath. It had only been a week, but she'd forgotten how he made her heart pound. He'd roughed up his hair, making it stand out all over his head, and he looked as though he'd slept a lot less than she had.

He strode in. "Milo, what the hell is going on?"

She kept her face still, hoping to veil her pleasure at seeing him. "Whatever do you mean? And how did you know where I live?"

"Torpedo Factory website."

"I see. And how did you get up to my apartment?"

"Hassan let me in. Don't worry, I explained." He didn't wait for the obvious question, but hurried on. "There's a police car out front. Not to mention a News 8 truck down the block pointing their odious thingies toward your building. This wouldn't have anything to do with the body they found in the Torpedo Factory last night, would it?"

I'm not going to let him make me feel guilty. She spun around and walked stiffly to the kitchen. He followed her, dropping outer gear along the way.

"Milo…"

"I'll tell you when the coffee's ready." She set the coffee to brew, pulled out a bag of pumpernickel bagels, some smoked salmon and cream cheese, grapefruit juice, two plates, two mugs, and two napkins.

"What are you doing?"

"What does it look like?"

He sat down on a ladder-back chair and ruffled his hair again, his fingers unconsciously sculpting a perfect bird's nest. He peered around at her tiny kitchen. "I like the red tiles. Different. Cheery."

She nodded. "I hate those bland blue or beige kitchens. When I bought here, I insisted they let me redo the kitchen. The fire-engine red never gets old, and it makes me feel like cooking." She set a bowl of ripe Anjou pears on the table and split the bagels in half.

Tristram poured two cups of coffee and let Milo take a hefty slug of juice before he spoke. "Now, are you going to confess?"

"Confess? I didn't kill them!"

"*Kill*? I just meant that you missed me."

"Oh." *Typical male. All he thinks about is himself.* "No. I've been…busy."

"I see." His green eyes glinted, setting off a chain of physical reactions in her body that started with her toes, moved in waves across the sensitive parts, and ended in a warm flush around her ears. "By the way, did I mention they found a dead body in the Torpedo Factory last night?"

"I know. I found it. Well, at least the first one."

"The first one?" He put down his fork. "Wait a minute. You said 'kill *them*,' didn't you?"

Milo took a sip of coffee to give herself time to think. *How much should I tell him? More specifically, how much can I tell him legally?* She carefully spread cream cheese on her bagel then laid pieces of smoked salmon in a crosshatch design on top. *That might make a lovely needlepoint—something for the kitchen. I'd better take a photo—*

"Milo? Are you going to explain yourself? What

did you mean by 'them'?"

"Huh? Oh yes." She gazed at his face. His strong nose sat at a perfect right angle to his mouth, now shut in a frustrated grimace. The verdant eyes glared at her from the thicket of black locks like seedlings breaking through rich loam. *I can't help it. I trust him. Even though he lied to me.* "All right." She related the events of the evening before.

He listened quietly, squeezing her hand once when she described finding the corpse. When she had finished, he drank his juice in one gulp.

"They didn't find your victim? I mean...er..."

"It's okay. No. Not unless it was after I'd gone. Detective Webley sent me home about one o'clock."

"The news this morning only mentioned one body. It's been identified."

"Really? Who is it?"

"Guy by the name of Randall Galt. Chief of staff to Dottie Dundicut."

"The city councilwoman?"

"Yup."

"I thought he looked familiar. I must have seen him at the hearing. The hearing for..." She put her cup down and shot him a furious glance.

"Now, Milo..."

As she stood, her robe opened, revealing the nearly transparent silk negligee beneath it—not to mention her breasts and dark-shadowed mound. He gazed hungrily at her willowy curves beneath the ivory folds until, with obvious reluctance, he lifted his eyes as she raised her voice.

"You lied to me. You didn't tell me you wanted to destroy my beautiful Torpedo Factory. That you were helping some filthy entrepreneur ravage it!"

Tristram shook his head, but she didn't know if it was to deny her assertion or to clear it of lascivious thoughts. "I didn't lie to you. You never asked me what I did or who my clients were."

"You told me you were a Marine!"

"A *retired* Marine. I also told you I'm a lawyer. Remember? After all, I have to do something with my time. At least when I'm not bedding the most beautiful woman in the world."

His attempted leer made her laugh despite her anger. The sight of those pearly teeth and the upturned lips that made him look so much like a Scottish elf distracted her. He must have sensed her confusion, for he stood and took her hand. "Let me explain all this somewhere more comfortable, okay?"

Milo tried to keep the anger flowing, but the urge to kiss him filled her like a hot air balloon and pressed against her heart, blocking any emotion but desire. Two minutes later, they were upstairs, her negligee lying in shreds on the floor under a pile of male accessories.

Tristram had a tender hold on one of her nipples while his hands explored the skin between her thighs. He let the nipple go long enough to whisper, "It's been way too long, Milo. I've been thinking about the back of your neck…oh, and that little knob on your left earlobe…for a week."

Milo left her head on the pillow and raised her belly to grind against him. She wanted to push herself all the way inside him, to be part of his body, to meld with him like a Vulcan queen. He ground back once, letting her know that his penis was ready any time to please her. Then he sat up.

"What? Tristram! Come back here."

"Not yet, m'dear. I've been pondering during this unnecessary hiatus how the skin inside your elbow tasted."

He kissed her fingers, then, holding the arm out, planted kisses up her forearm. When he reached his goal, he nipped it. She grabbed for him, but he'd relocated to her toes. He lifted her leg and kissed up the calf to the back of her knee. Pulling a tiny fold of skin between his lips, he sucked on it. The sensation was amazing and arousing and unbearable all at once. She lifted her thighs higher and circled his back. He had no choice but to dip into the fountain. He licked her vaginal lips gently, then blew on each fold. Milo stifled a yelp as her orgasm ripped through her, and she bucked uncontrollably against his mouth. Just as she reached the peak, she drew him to her. His penis found its proper place and drove home.

"Oh my God, Milo. Oh...my...God."

He stiffened, and warm liquid filled her. She held him tightly, ignoring the tears.

He drew himself up on his elbows and peered at her. With a wondering finger, he touched her face. "You're crying. Did I hurt you?"

"No, Tristram. I'm just...happy." She tried to take a breath, but the weight of his body crushed her sternum. "Would you mind?"

"Oh, sorry." He rolled off her.

She lay rigid, her brain reeling with chaotic thoughts of guilt, worry, joy, and grief. *I did it again. I let my guard down. I let him in. What was I thinking? Of Michael? Not of Michael, that's for sure. Am I that fickle? And with Tristram—a suit, a lobbyist, a...a capitalist. What would my hippie mother think? Just what she thought when I brought a Marine pilot home.* Her mother had come to terms with that, but not until after many a tumultuous argument. And how had Milo won her over? *Oh, yes. I told her I loved him and it didn't matter what he did—it only mattered who he was.* She drifted into memories of her late husband.

They'd had one idyllic year together once her mother finally gave her blessing. After six months planning an elaborate wedding, Michael came to her a week before the big day waving a letter. He'd been ordered to report to Corpus Christi, Texas, for flight training. It took less than a minute to decide to elope.

"No St. Maarten honeymoon I'm afraid, love. But we'll have little ones every time I come home on leave—how's that?"

She'd laughed and asked if he meant babies or honeymoons. She begged to be on base with him, but he disagreed. "It's too far from Virginia. You have your business—I know, I know, your artwork. Anyway, I'm only there for six months. If I'm assigned to fly the Hornet, they could send me anywhere—California, South Carolina, who knows—but I won't stay anywhere very long. Eventually I'm bound to be deployed to the Middle East. Keep your apartment. I'll be back."

She'd given in and didn't regret the decision. He'd been assigned to three bases in nine months. Whenever he had a few days' leave, she flew out to be with him. Then in November, at the naval air station in Kingsville, Texas, he told her his orders had come through.

"I'll be based on the carrier USS Ronald Reagan,

flying missions over the Pacific. Very safe. No wars to speak of. Only thing you'll have to worry about is a stray geisha." He kissed her and waved her off at the airport. "I'll be home next week—they're giving me a couple of days off." A month later, Lieutenant Colonel Murray stood at her door.

She must have sighed because Tristram leaned over and kissed her lips. "Everything okay?"

How she longed to confess, to tell him about Michael, to tell him how mixed-up she felt. *It's not yet time for that. I'm not ready.* "I'm fine. But I'd better get dressed. Detective Webley said he'd call me today."

"*Hmm*, yes. Look, I have a teleconference I can't get out of, or I'd go with you to the station. How about if I pick you up for dinner? Will you be at the Factory?"

The afternoon loomed ahead, and it didn't look good. "I don't know, Tristram. You'd better go."

He got out of bed and picked up his clothes. Giving her a sheepish look, he mumbled, "Are we...are we...?"

"What, Tristram?" The impatience came out of nowhere. *I don't have time for this. I've got a murder on my hands and two canvases to finish before Christmas. Not to mention the planned guilt trip.* "Look, I'm probably going to be busy today. Perhaps lunch tomorrow? Why don't I call you?"

His face would have broken her heart if he'd given it time, but his expression quickly turned from dismay to resentment. He took the bundle and stalked naked into the living room. He must have tripped over something, for he let out a singularly imaginative oath. A few minutes later the door slammed.

Instead of distress, she felt a wave of relief wash

over her. Too many things to deal with. She turned the taps on and stepped into the steam.

Chapter Four

Milo punched the answer button just before the call went to voicemail. "Hello?"

"Oh, Ms. Everhart. Lieutenant Webley here. I thought you'd gone out. We have some news. Can you come down to the police station?"

Milo thought ruefully of her unfinished orders. Only a week until Christmas and three more kits to put together. "I'll be there. Um, where is it, and is there parking?"

Webley laughed. "I'm rather relieved you don't know where we are! It's on Wheeler Avenue, off Mill Road. Tell you what. I'll have a squad car come pick you up."

"Oh no! I mean, no thank you. If I can park there, I'll drive. I have to get back to work as soon as possible."

"I see. An artist's work is never done, huh?"

"No, it isn't."

"Yeah. Well. Tell the desk sergeant to send you along to my office when you arrive."

Good, her frigid tone had hit the mark. It still amazed her that people didn't see art as a real job. She spent more time training, studying, practicing, and creating than any bureaucrat did. Maybe they figured it didn't count because no one made her do it. *If you enjoy it, it must not be work.*

****

"We've identified the body."

"The second one?"

"The only one we have." Webley's tone was dry. "It's Randall Galt, Chief of Staff to Councilwoman Dottie Dundicut."

"I know."

"You do? Oh, hell. It's been in the papers already?"

Milo thought of the innumerable press reports she'd seen yesterday in the *Alexandria Times*, on Channel 8, even the *Washington Post*. "Don't you pay attention to the news?"

Webley spit out his coffee. As he mopped it up with a wad of tissues, he muttered, "Like I have time to sit around and browse the local rags."

"Well, I'm sorry." *Sheesh, it's not my fault.* "How much have you made public so far?"

"The sheriff held a news conference yesterday. I didn't go."

"Well, evidently he named me as well as Galt. There's been a television van parked at my building for two days. Does the sheriff know about the body I found?"

"Only the alleged existence of it. I haven't had a chance to fully brief him." She could tell the detective was indulging in all kinds of unacceptable language in his head. "I'll give him a call when we're through. The lab did find two different blood types at the scene, so I can definitively say there were two people in the room. Whether or not there were three is anybody's guess at this point. I sent another team to the Torpedo Factory this morning to examine every stairwell and exit for blood spatters."

Milo accepted a cracked mug with suspicious stains and set it down on the cracked and stained table, still damp from Webley's spill. "I've been thinking. Archie usually locks all the doors except the one in the south corner, the one you came in. He went out that way Monday night, so he'd have noticed a stranger. Therefore the murderer must have still been in the building when I discovered the...the man." She squeezed her hands together to hide the tremor.

"Yes, I figured that. How else would it have disappeared after you left unless the killer moved it?"

Milo felt a chill. The hot coffee only helped a little. "Then, he might even have been in the room with me?"

Webley shook his head. "It's a tiny room, and the fluorescent light is long enough to illuminate the whole interior. I feel sure you would have noticed a blood-soaked brute hovering over you with murder on his breath. No, either the killer ran back up the stairs after you went down them to call 911 and moved the body, or he was hiding on the roof when you came in."

Milo took a minute to relocate Webley's graphic description of the perpetrator to a mental cubbyhole inaccessible to her conscious mind before she returned to his theory. "But how did he get my body out before the second victim appeared? And who left the second one? And where did *he* go?" Milo's head began to swim.

"Dunno, but I bet we only have one killer, even if we have two bodies. Way too complicated otherwise. I just have to discover what the connection is between them."

"Don't you have to actually have the first victim in

hand before you can do that?"

Before he could answer, the detective's cell phone rang. Milo could hear a raspy voice talk rapid-fire into his ear before he flipped it closed. "The councilwoman—Dundicut—is holding a press conference. Sorry, Ms. Everhart, I'd better go to this one. I'll let you know if we need you again."

Milo found herself on the sidewalk. When she walked into the Factory, Archie sat at his usual spot in the gift shop.

"I hear I missed some excitement the other night."

Milo thought of his face in the crowd. What had he been doing there? "What have you heard?"

"It was all over the news yesterday. You found a dead guy in the tower. Some city council staffer apparently." He stopped and peered at her from under his bristly gray eyebrows. "Must've been after we said good night. I didn't see anything."

Milo couldn't help it. "You went straight home?"

Archie's face closed down. "I told you I was going home. Don't you remember?"

But I didn't actually see you leave. "Did you notice anyone besides me on your way out?"

He shook his head. "The police already asked me. Not a soul." A large group of tourists approached the counter, and Archie stood up to help them. "Keep me in the loop, will you? Once the news gets out, we'll probably be inundated with nosy Parkers."

Milo took the elevator to her studio. The place seemed curiously quiet after the commotion below. She pulled out a canvas, snapped it into a frame, mixed some acrylics with a bit of medium, and started to outline a pine forest, carefully painting each stitch intersection. The sun beamed cheerfully through the huge windows, and soon she'd forgotten everything but the need to get the trees and the foreground in proper perspective.

An hour later, she stared at her work, dissatisfied. The weather had taken a turn for the worse as well. *I hate landscapes. Now why did I accept this order again? Oh, yes, for the money.* She took the canvas to the window, passing Mrs. Hirschhorn's half-finished picture of violets and primroses. *Give me a still life any day. Much more appropriate for needlepoint.*

She thought about one customer, a former congresswoman, who kept after her to do a likeness of her grandchildren. "It would be *such* a conversation piece!" Milo didn't like the implication that her embroidery was little more than coffee table material. She also thought a needlepoint portrait would be a disaster.

"Didn't we have a luncheon date?"

She swung around to find Tristram standing at the door. "Oh, sorry, I'd forgotten all about it."

He didn't take it the wrong way. *Maybe it's all that ego working overtime.* "S'okay. I didn't want you to think I still held a grudge from yesterday morning. I only dropped in to tell you I have to beg off."

"Oh?"

He gave her a lopsided grimace. "It's Ursula. Have to escort her on a shopping spree. One of my favorite activities."

Milo hoped the green paint on her fingers was the only green that showed. Jealousy surged through her like undigested chili. "I see. Well, you'd better get along then." She turned back to the easel. A finger touched the nape of her neck and traced the fine hairs around to her chin.

"Milo, it's business. You remember Chuck Doyle—my client? When he first zeroed in on this area for potential development, he bought a house over on Cameron Street. Now, in anticipation of the city council's accepting his new outlet with all due fanfare, he wants to make the house a showpiece of fine furniture and collectibles. And with his usual lack of patience, he wants it done in days, not weeks. He asked around for the best interior designer in Alexandria, and Ursula's name popped up—or rather, dropped from the eager lips of several hundred of the Old Town aristocracy. Since I'm already acquainted with the dear little thing, I've been designated the official go-between, even though I know next to nothing about antiques."

Yeah, right. Deep breath, girl. "So, she's an interior decorator?"

"The top tier. Her clients range from the rich to the superrich. That's how she can afford all those pretty clothes. Not to mention the plastic surgery."

Milo couldn't help it. She giggled. "Meow."

"Don't tell me you weren't thinking the same thing." He chucked her under the chin and kissed her nose. "At any rate, I must go forth to battle. See you later?"

Wouldn't that be wonderful? "I don't think so, Tristram. I have several orders to finish before Christmas. Besides, the police may need me again."

His mouth set in the thin line she was beginning to recognize. *He's annoyed with me.*

He spun on his heel and left. Milo tried to go back

to the painting but sat instead, chin in hand, staring out at the Potomac. Both water and sky shared the same gray tones, with here and there a splash of white gull. The water taxi chugged toward the Wilson Bridge and National Harbor. A line of people waited to board the *Admiral Tilp*, shivering in their down parkas and stamping their feet. She watched a crew stringing colored lights on the city Christmas tree.

Ursula.

She picked up a coin purse she'd been working on and put it down. *Ursula.* Blocking the path between Milo and romance lurched the buxom Amazon in a silk Dior suit, crimson lipstick matching her Prada heels, barely concealed contempt suffusing her face. *She's not very nice, is she?* On the other hand, she might just be jealous. *Like me.*

On an impulse, she went to the computer and searched on the name Ursula Baines. A website featuring an array of expensive-looking tschochkes and a shot of Ursula draped over a Steinway listed several impressive clients along with their glowing recommendations. "Ursula found the most adorable eighteenth-century Staffordshire puppies for my Pomeranian's bedroom!" and "I never in my wildest dreams thought Ursula could find the perfect Kang-xi Famille Verte vase to match my new Ralph Lauren sofa! She's a gem."

Milo closed the laptop before she threw up on the keyboard. She grabbed her purse and went out for a walk.

Despite the cold, the waterfront was packed with pedestrians. A few snowflakes drifted down, spackling the bevy of ruddy ducks that milled around the marina—their perky little tails pointing straight up. The white-helmeted sky promised more snow. She pulled her thin, quilted jacket closer and decided to limit the walk to the few blocks surrounding the Torpedo Factory. She turned right toward the Old Dominion Boat Club, still proudly derelict despite all the city's efforts to take over the prime piece of property. Passing the Alexandria history store, she turned onto King. The antique store on the corner seemed to be closed. Someone had taped a sign to the door:

Legerdemain Fine Furnishings
Closed Indefinitely

It struck Milo as odd. After all, with so many tourists and shoppers in town for Christmas, business usually boomed around this time. Still, shops came and went quickly in Old Town. Taxes were exorbitant, and the elitist community decidedly, albeit hypocritically, anti-business. She laughed, remembering the brouhaha over the adult store that had opened on King Street.

Milo passed the offending store, a discreet sign identifying it as La Volupté with a red heart in lieu of the "o." She peered through the shop windows, inhabited by Barbie-esque models in skimpy Santa suits. After all the hysteria, one hardly noticed the store. A couple of men came out, clutching unmarked shopping bags, anticipatory smirks on their faces. *It's apparently successful too.* She thought of Chuck Doyle and his box store. Had the city fathers learned their lesson yet?

By the time Milo got back to the studio, the snow was falling steadily. She turned on WMAL to check the weather and went to the window. Meteorologist Ken gave his prognosis: four to five inches. The radio host intoned gravely, "You heard it here. Snow predicted. The city will shut down immediately. Abandon your cars now." She tittered. *How true.* Washington was notorious for panicking at the sight of even a heavy dew. By the first snowflake the citizens would be huddled in their dens, peering like frightened voles out at the cold, cruel world.

Milo watched the gulls sailing gracefully in and out of the snow-laden clouds. A flock of big black birds landed on the waterfront, squawking and screeching. She took a closer look. Vultures. *There must be something dead in the water.*

She clapped a hand to her mouth. "Oh my God, maybe that's where the first body is—in the marina!"

A young couple pushing a stroller paused outside her door and stared in at her. Milo gave them a minute to pass, then quietly closed the door.

But wait. Don't bodies rise to the surface after three days? It had been ages since the murder. She counted back on her fingers. *No, just two. Day before yesterday. How strange.* Her eyes swept the murky water one more time. The snow thickened, obscuring the view. A patch of ice floated near the gangplank. She wondered idly whether cold temperatures accelerated or inhibited decomposition.

Just as she began to think she should call Webley to discuss her latest notion, the vultures rose in a great black swath of feathers and fearsome cries and flew up past her window. *It's my imagination running away with me, that's all.* She picked up her paintbrush.

"Milo? You hungry?"

Milo raised distracted eyes, searching for the source of the question.

Tekla stomped in. "It's two o'clock. Have you had lunch yet?"

A gurgle emanated from her lower regions. "No. I forgot."

"I need a break. I've been wrangling with a big sheet of aluminum, and it's not cooperating. Let's go over to the Wharf and see what's biting."

"Good idea."

Milo grabbed her purse and followed Tekla out. The snow had tapered off, but the air remained damp and chilly. A rush of toasty air enticed them into the restaurant. They found a booth and greeted the waitress as an old friend.

"Glass of anything, ladies?"

Tekla perused the wine list. "Lemme have a glass of the Barboursville Octagon, Roxie. It's 2004? Good. I need something to warm me up."

Milo started to order tea but changed her mind. *If I'd had lunch with Tristram, I'd have had a cocktail.* "How about this Fox Meadow 2008 Renard Rouge? I heard it won a medal."

"Oh, yeah, that one. It's a blend of cabernet franc and merlot. Spicy nose and good tannin. I'd recommend it on a cold day."

"Fine."

When Roxie returned with the wine, Tekla, with the haughty look she claimed turned chefs to jelly, threw down her menu. "The crab cake. Can you certify that it's authentic Chesapeake Bay blue or is it that insipid white stuff from Indonesia? *Hmm*?"

Roxie looked daggers at her. "You know better than to ask that here, Tekla."

"Now, now, ladies." Milo checked the specials.

"How's the rockfish?"

The waitress swiveled to Milo, ignoring Tekla's snort. "Came in an hour ago."

"I'll have that."

As Roxie trundled off, they settled back on the leather seats. Tekla took an appreciative sip of her wine. "Um. Cinnamony. Perfect. At least something is going right."

"You mean the aluminum? What are you trying to do with it?"

"Didn't I tell you? I won the bid for a piece to hang in the new Metro station that's opening in the spring. I'm thinking a large gourd. Pear-shaped. Something reminiscent of a fertility goddess. Maybe with spikes all over it."

How to respond? Milo decided to move on. "That's it? That's what's bothering you?"

Tekla shook her head. Pushing the glass to one side, she leaned over the table and spoke in a confidential whisper. "It's Jacob."

"Is he back?"

"No, and it's worrying me."

"But I thought you threw him out!"

Tekla accepted the platter from Roxie and squeezed lemon over two medallions of broiled crab, scented with Old Bay seasoning. The waitress set a whole crispy, browned fish before Milo. Its eye stared up at her with reproach, as if to say, "Only a few hours ago I was swimming freely with my schoolmates, and then..." Breaking the spell, Roxie plopped a plate of roasted Brussels sprouts, shiny with glazed butter, on the table between them.

Tekla waited for the waitress to leave. "I did throw

him out. For the fourth time. The thing about Jacob is, he always turns back up, but I haven't heard a squeak out of him for three days."

"And this makes you unhappy?"

"No, not unhappy, just perplexed. He's been acting so weird lately—" Milo almost spit out her wine. Tekla pouted. "All right, weird-*er*. He's obsessed with this idea of turning the art center into a performance art venue. He badgered the council so much they banned him from City Hall. The only one left who'd even take a call from him was some staffer in Dottie Dundicut's office."

"Really? Did he mention which one?"

"Yes, now let me see…" Tekla's dropped her fork and lifted a shocked face up to her companion. "I think…yes…Milo, it was the man they just found murdered!"

"Randall Galt?"

"That's the one. Oh, poor Jacob. Now his only friend is gone."

"I doubt that Dundicut's chief of staff could be called a friend—more likely he chose the short straw. Anyway, Tekla, how can you feel sorry for Jacob? He's a wacko, and not even a nice one."

"When you spend three years with someone, it's hard not to have some feelings for him. He's such a pathetic creature, Milo."

"Yeah." Milo gave her a sly look. "And the fact that he's dynamite in bed has nothing to do with it."

Tekla's mouth twitched. "Well, there are *some* things I miss about him."

Lunch over, the two artists slogged through the melting slush back to their studios, hopping over the deeper puddles in the uneven cobblestone sidewalks. Since the inch or so of sleet had been enough to flood the bottom of King Street, they had to walk down Union Street and go through the alley to the back entrance of the Factory. As they turned the corner, the flock of vultures flushed, shrieking with anger.

Tekla jumped back. "Vultures! How horrible! What on earth are they doing here?"

Milo watched them settle on the tower roof. "I noticed them earlier today. Maybe they're seeking shelter."

"Not them. They're looking for food." Tekla spat in a distinctly foreign gesture. "They give me the willies."

Milo regarded her with amusement. "Of course they're disgusting. They're carrion eaters. Why do they bother *you* so much?"

Tekla closed her eyes. "I remember driving through a deserted village in the Ukraine once. The only living things we saw were mobs of vultures leering at us hungrily."

"The Ukraine? That's a long way from Yaroslavl. What were you doing there?"

"I don't remember—I think my father had business in Kiev and decided to take the family along."

"What made the people abandon the village?"

"You know how in the final years of the Soviet Union the economy deteriorated and the pollution worsened? Ukrainians by the thousands left their farms and villages to seek work in the big cities. Then after the Chernobyl disaster, many more ran away to escape the radiation. The people of the village had left their animals and pets behind when they fled. I'll never forget the sight of whole skeletons of cows and dogs, picked clean. Huge black birds roosted on every chimney." She shuddered, her ebony eyes flashing. "A harbinger of death, vultures. This is a bad omen."

They pushed open the doors to the main hall and walked past the gift shop. The building manager hunched over his computer behind the books and souvenirs, a scarf wound around his neck. The two women shivered.

"Archie?" Milo approached the counter. "Why's it so cold in here?"

Without looking up he muttered, "Hello, ladies. The heat's on the fritz. Not sure what's wrong. I called the service company. They should be here soon." He shook his head. "We're lucky they were willing to come—six inches of snow predicted for tonight."

Tekla headed off to her studio. Students flocked down the stairs from the classrooms on the second floor, shooed from behind by a petite brunette in an apron splattered with colorful handprints.

Milo waved at her. "Ginger? Where's your class going?"

"Home. They closed the Art League for the day. I'm relieved—it would have been a nightmare trying to drive across the bridge a couple of hours from now."

Milo passed several other artists locking up their studios. "Morgana, are you leaving early too? You only live a block away!"

Her friend zipped up a fur-trimmed parka that dwarfed her tiny five-foot frame, leaving only her pumpkin-colored bangs showing. "*Brrrr*. Too cold for a hot-blooded wench like me."

Milo walked into her studio to be greeted by a blast

of icy air. The window stood open. As she pulled the casement in, a whiff of something nauseating hit her nostrils. "Whew! What a stench!" She looked out at the dark, scummy water swirling in the harbor. *Must be dead fish.* She settled down at her workbench, but before long, the creeping chill began to insinuate itself. When she couldn't feel her fingers anymore, she stood up. *I might as well go home too.* She picked up a small needlepoint case she'd been working on and got her coat.

Outside, the soft, wet flakes drizzled down, clinging to her eyelashes and melting on her nose. She found a rare parking spot in the covered lot of her building, for a brief moment allaying the sense of impending doom. That is, until Pinkie greeted her at the door with a snarl.

****

The insistent ringing woke her up. She felt for the cell phone on the side table, dropping a book on the floor and almost tipping the water glass over. The alarm clock chirped the time in bright red colors: 7:00. The gray light of a December dawn filtered through the curtains. She pulled the phone from her purse with fumbling fingers and pressed the redial button.

"Milo? Are you all right?"

"Tristram?"

"Yes. I just got to the office. I can see the Torpedo Factory from here. Did I mention that?"

One of the perks of having the richest man in the country for a client, I guess. "No, you didn't. Which floor are you on?"

Tristram's voice came, clipped and impatient. "Never mind that. Something is going on at the Factory.

People are swarming all over the roof. You don't know what's happening?"

"The heat went out in the building yesterday. It's probably just the repairmen. The furnace and air conditioning are on the roof."

"Oh. Good. I was worried. Trouble seems to spontaneously reproduce in that place." He paused. "Milo? Are you...er...busy tonight?"

She could hear the longing even over the phone. The thought of another session of lovemaking sent glowing tendrils snaking through her loins. Her heart thumped at the memory of the last time. *No, Milo. You're not ready for a daily grind. At least not emotionally.* Before she could reply, the annoying buzz that signaled an incoming call intruded.

"I've got to go. I've got another call." She clicked the answer button.

"Ms. Everhart? Webley here. We need you again."

Lucky me. "Right now?"

"Afraid so. Can you come down to the Factory? I'll send a squad car so you don't have to negotiate the snow."

"The Torpedo Factory! Why?"

"I think we've found your body. Unless there's a third one hanging around."

A noise from her window drew her attention. A dove roosted on the sill, trying to get out of the wind. Milo could hear the soft coo through the glass, and sudden inspiration struck. *I'll bet I know where they found it.* "I'll be right there."

Half an hour later, she stood next to Webley, the scene distressingly reminiscent of one only a few days earlier. *So this is what death smells like.*

The detective handed Milo a disposable facemask. She took it gratefully.

"Do you recognize him?"

"No. I told you, I only saw his back."

"I understand, but do you know who the man is?"

Milo studied him. "I don't think so. Didn't he have any identification on him?"

He looked at the body on the stretcher. "We're lucky he had any clothes left at all. Once he started decomposing, the vultures homed in on the nicest little all-you-can-eat buffet in Old Town. Al fresco—just the way they like it. If he hadn't been dumped face down, we'd have no way of identifying him other than dental charts."

The paramedics picked up the stretcher and took it down the stairs. Webley and Milo walked out onto the flat roof. Here and there, huge air conditioning units reared up like Celtic standing stones. The pale morning light seeped through the clouds, pinging off the blanket of snow that hid the layer of rough pebbles covering the surface.

When the wind hit her, Milo staggered. "So you found the body on the roof?"

"Yup."

"Why didn't you see it the other night then?"

He pointed up. "By roof, I mean the roof of the tower itself. When the repairmen came out here to fix the HVAC, they didn't see anything, but the smell and the vultures were enough to make them call us. We found a ladder over there—" He pointed toward a low wall. "The murderer must have used it to lift the body up and throw it over the parapet. If it weren't for the snow, we might have found the body sooner."

"Because?"

"It kept it cold and slowed decomposition. You can thank the repairmen—and the vultures—that we discovered him at all."

"I don't know about that. You couldn't miss the smell. I noticed it from my studio."

"But would you have reported it?"

"N…no. I guess not." Milo bit her lip. *So it wasn't dead fish after all.* "So where do you think the murderer hid then? Was he here when I came in?"

"We think so. Probably hiding outside. After you left he came in, picked up the body, and lugged it back outside."

"Leaving the other one?"

"He likely only had time to get rid of one."

"But how could he have gotten away? It didn't take you that long to get here."

Webley's face showed his frustration. "He probably hid up there, skulking on the tower roof, the whole time we were searching the crime scene. He'd knocked the ladder away from the wall, or we might've connected the dots. After we left, he snuck out."

"But your investigation went on for hours. He would have frozen to death!"

"Better than getting caught I suppose."

Milo thought of something. "Didn't you post policemen at the exits? How could he have gotten past them?"

"We only put men at the main entrances, I'm afraid. At that point we'd searched the building, and it seemed more likely that the killer would try to return to the scene than escape from it. I left a couple of exit-only doors unmanned."

"So the murderer just walked out later that night."

They pulled open the heavy steel door to the tower, and the detective led her downstairs. "You can go on home if you want. I only called you in in case you could identify the deceased."

"What will you do now?"

"I guess we'll have to go the missing persons route."

They descended the main stairs, to be greeted by mobs of curious tourists flocking in the main hall, drawn by the prospect of a thrilling brush with homicide. Archie waved his arms like a demented octopus, trying to shoo them out the front doors. Webley doffed his hat and walked to a waiting police car. Milo checked her watch. Only an hour had passed. She went back up to her studio, determined to put all the grisly events out of her mind and get some work done.

Three hours later, she gave it up as a bad job and went home. For the last hour all she'd thought about was calling Tristram. She wanted to hear his rich baritone flow through her ears to her heart. Instead, she pulled out a cast iron skillet, poured a dollop of olive oil into it, chopped onions, garlic, and some Italian frying peppers, and dropped them into the smoking oil. As she shook the pan, she mused. *It's true. I like him. Yes, I want him. And maybe I* am *ready to move on from Michael. But what about his work?* He wanted to destroy what made Old Town such a delightful place to live and work. *He wants to turn the historic city we've worked so hard to preserve into a...a...suburb. What'll come next? Strip malls? McDonald's?* She sighed and added slices of sweet Italian sausage to the simmering pan and dropped in a tablespoonful of spicy sriracha sauce. The aromas of chilis, fennel, and sage filled the room.

The telephone rang. "Milo? What happened today? You didn't call back."

Milo took a moment to savor his voice before replying. "They found my body."

"Your body?"

"I mean the one I discovered."

"Ah, the first victim. And they wanted you to identify it?"

"Yes. But I couldn't. I'd never seen him before. At least I don't think so."

"I see." Quiet comfort flowed through the receiver. "Probably just as well. I'm sure they can take it from here." He paused. "Do you want company?"

Milo looked at the mess of sausages and peppers. "Sure."

He didn't bother to say goodbye. The phone clicked. *Lessee.* He lived a grand total of eighteen blocks from her. That left her ten minutes.

Eleven minutes later—*not bad for a female*—a beautiful woman in the prime of her life, with glowing honey-blonde curls and wearing a short, dark russet dress that matched her eyes, casually strolled out of her bedroom. Mahogany-colored tights and matching flats set off her shapely legs to perfection. The hall mirror gave as good as it got. *Lookin' fine, girl. But I wonder—should I have bought that teensy Santa suit in La Volupté's window?*

She looked up to find Tristram standing on the threshold. In the corridor behind him, a gray-haired woman carrying a grocery bag stopped to stare at them.

"Your door was unlocked, Milo, and…" He ended his sentence with a gulp.

Milo fought for breath as well. Tristram wore a soft navy cashmere blazer over a pink oxford shirt and jeans. His swimmer's build—broad shoulders and narrow waist—worked so well on her libido she began to hiccup. She reached around him. "Sorry, Mrs. Peale." The old lady gave her a rueful smile as the door closed.

Milo faced Tristram. "By the way, have you…have you ever been in that adult store on King? La Volupté?"

"Me? No. Have you?"

"No. No. Of course not." *Yet.* She pointed toward the kitchen. "I made sausage and peppers if you're hungry."

He held up a bottle of wine and grinned. "Then a Barolo should go nicely."

Milo checked the label: Famiglia Anselma Barolo. "Sounds homey."

"It had better not be. It's one of the best Barolos of the 2000 vintage."

While he opened it, Milo sliced some dark rye bread she'd picked up at a bakery in Fairlington. Everything felt so comfortable…just like…Her mood suddenly crashed. *What am I doing?* She looked at Tristram. *That's not Michael.* What right did she have to be contentedly slicing bread and sipping wine with this man? *What a slut you are, Milo.* She put the glass down.

He must have sensed the change in atmosphere. "Everything all right?"

How the hell do I get him out of here? "Er…I just remembered. I have a phone call to make." How lame could she get?

"I see." He stood, his face transmuting into that of a stranger. She watched anger, frustration, and exasperation crisscross his features. "It's because of the More for Less deal, isn't it? You can't forgive me for it."

She saw her opening. Any excuse would be preferable to confessing her dread that the memory of her late husband would slip away. "I'm sorry. But if you succeed, my livelihood, my life, the Torpedo Factory—it will all disappear."

His fist flashed, and she heard a crack as it hit the table. "You know that's not true, Milo. You were there at the hearing. You heard our proposal. We wouldn't displace any of the artists. In fact, it would result in more and better space allocation for you and attract a whole new set of customers. Isn't that what you want? Or does your elitist bigotry recoil at the thought of the great unwashed fingering your precious art?"

He paused, sucking in air, unaware he had plenty of time to catch his breath while Milo recovered from the onslaught. His words had the sting of truth, but she wasn't prepared to surrender just yet.

Just as she collected her wits to form the retort, he resumed his tirade. "And what does your snotty artist community want to do? Keep the building as is—a cold, noisy, unwelcoming warren of dark little rooms where every bead-stringer and silk-screener can cater to his own personal niche market."

The images of Digby Kramer huddled over his macramé like an old hag and of Luisa with her fussy, overly precise collages, rose uninvited. She rallied. "Oh yeah?" *Ooh, that's impressive. You've got him on the ropes now.* "Well, you…you're the worst kind of snob, Tristram, a bourgeois one. You disdain anything that's refined and beautiful and…yes, precious. You praise sticky fingers and cheap merchandise and consider them superior to taste and delicate workmanship. You don't appreciate—"

The staccato notes of Beethoven's *Rage over a Lost Penny* pealed from her pocket. She pulled out her cell phone, thanking her lucky stars that something had stopped her before she really screwed up the relationship, not to mention the argument. "Hello?" She peeked at Tristram, who stood snorting and fuming like a great ox fresh from hauling a ten-ton load of bricks.

"Ms. Everhart? I thought you'd like to know. We've identified your corpse."

Chapter Five

Milo gestured toward the wine. Tristram handed her her glass and sat back, arms crossed. His narrowed eyes told her he hadn't finished yet. She ignored him and spoke clearly. "You know who the first victim is, Lieutenant Webley?" She noted with satisfaction that her adversary started at the words.

"It's a man by the name of—I'm not kidding—Eustice von der Dieb. He owned the antique store on the corner of Union and King called Legerdemain."

"Legerdemain? That's funny. Just the other day I noticed the store had a 'Closed' sign taped to the door."

"Really? What day was that? It could help us pinpoint the time of death. The physical remains are too far gone to give us an accurate window."

Milo tried to recall the date. *Did I see it before or after I found the body?* "I'm not sure. I'd taken a walk. It was snowing." She shut her eyes, the better to recollect. "I'll have to think. I'm sorry."

"Okay, well, I'm sure we can find other locals who noticed the sign. I've got a forensics team going over the premises for any signs of struggle. We haven't definitively established the tower as the primary scene of the crime."

"You mean he may not have been killed there?"

"We have to take every scenario into consideration."

"Yes, but…"

"Look, Ms. Everhart, we appreciate your insights. We really do, but I've got to get over to the investigation. I just thought you'd like to be informed of our progress." He hung up.

The phone rang again. "Milo? It's Tekla. The city council has scheduled a business meeting. Luisa thinks they may be ready to take a vote on the Factory's fate."

Milo turned to Tristram to give him the news, but he had his own phone to his ear. "Okay, when? Any ideas on what their decision is? Yeah, I'm on my way." He drained his wine and stood stiffly. "I guess we'll soon see which plan for the Torpedo Factory is more *precious* to the city."

She let him go without a word, poured another glass, and stared at her untouched plate. *It's what I wanted, isn't it?* Now she wouldn't have to wallow in guilt every time she found herself slavering over Tristram. She could get on with her life—*well, my work at least*. She slumped down on the chair and began to cry.

****

Luisa shuffled papers officiously as the mayor strutted in, waving a hand as though he expected Hail to the Chief to accompany his entrance. One by one the other council members arrived. Dottie Dundicut's face drooped with fatigue, her eyes red-rimmed. With all the succeeding shocks, Milo had almost forgotten that the first victim—or at least the first one they found—was Randall Galt, her chief of staff. For once Milo found herself feeling sorry for Ms. Dundicut, though the woman had always come across as arrogant and condescending—the epitome of the nanny state mentality.

Dundicut had been in the vanguard of the bridge-playing biddies pressing to run the dollar store out of town, only to find her fabricated ordinances working in the adult store's favor. She'd lobbied to prohibit smoking in private homes and busied herself removing sodas from vending machines and taking candy from babies. Despite periodic outcries over her predations, the citizens of Old Town reelected her term after term. *I guess when you're not accountable, you have the right to think you're infallible.* Yet even the great and powerful councilwoman couldn't protect her chief of staff. Ms. Dundicut wiped away a tear. An assistant jumped to her aid, but she waved him away. Her face clearly showed her thought. *You're not Randall.*

As the room filled, Milo mulled over what she knew of Galt. Very little. He'd been with Dundicut for five years, which implied either that he agreed with her politics or that power agreed with him. The night of his death, he ended up in the tower, dead or alive. *But why there? What on earth was he doing there? Who would want to kill him?*

The council settled down, aides rushing back and forth in a plucky if fruitless attempt to prove their indispensability. *Could Galt's murder have anything to do with the city's plans for the Torpedo Factory?* The council had only held its first hearing a few days before. No one had any idea then—and still didn't—what their decision would be.

Tekla leaned over. "It's about to start. Tristram just came in with Doyle and the rest of the capitalist mafia."

Milo absently mumbled her standard reply—"Remember, dear, it's okay to like capitalism now that you're an American"—and went back to her ruminations. Thankfully, they distracted her from her erstwhile beau. *Perhaps someone was trying to bribe Galt before the council made a choice, and the scheme went wrong. But who?* She raised her eyes and looked straight into Tristram's stormy ones. He glowered at her before swiveling to help Doyle to his seat. His stiff back spoke volumes. Good thing she never wanted to see him again, since it looked like she wouldn't. She straightened and stared at the tall figure. *Wait a minute...Tristram?*

The horrible thought that her lover could be capable of bribery, let alone murder, buzzed around like a vicious fairy in Milo's brain. Tekla broke into her trance with a sharp elbow to the ribs.

"Ouch! What is it?"

"They're about to begin. Do you notice anything unusual?"

Other than a potential killer in the room? "No. What are you talking about?"

"Anyone missing?"

Milo took a perfunctory sweep of the room. This time Luisa, Esme, and Morgana sat in the front row to the right, Tristram, Doyle, and their retinue to the left. Most of the other chairs were unoccupied. She shook her head.

"Jacob!" Tekla hissed. "Jacob's not here. They're going to vote on his proposal today. There's something wrong." Her brow creased and her worried eyes darted here and there.

"Maybe he knows there's no chance the council will go for an empty building on their waterfront."

"Since when has reality ever trespassed on my

Jacob's twisted universe?"

"Good point." Milo set a hand on her friend's shoulder, hoping to reassure her. "There's nothing we can do right now." Tekla nodded reluctantly but began to rock back and forth on her folding chair, hands clasped tightly together. Since the chairs were hooked together, Milo found herself rocking as well.

"Tekla! Stop it!"

Her friend's lower lip trembled. "I know he's a pig and a nut, but I'm all he has. I'm going out to look for him."

Tekla's Russian soul at full strength could overpower even an armor-plated Arnold Schwarzenegger. Milo acknowledged the inevitable. "Go." With a sweep of silk brocade and a jingle of beads, her friend left. Milo turned back to the proceedings.

Mayor Carstairs rapped his gavel. "The council has now conducted four hearings on the question of the enhanced exploitation of the Torpedo Factory Art Center space. We've heard from fifteen different groups and many concerned citizens. While the news coverage has not always been fair—"

A titter tiptoed around the room. The audience knew he referred to a less than flattering segment on the WMAL morning radio program. Carstairs could not complain that the talk show host hadn't offered a balanced presentation—he'd given airtime to every faction with a dog in the fight. By all accounts, of them all, only the mayor's interview did not go swimmingly. Pundits used words like "mercenary" and "paranoid" to describe his responses.

"—the Council and I feel that we have done

everything possible to ensure all proposals and points of view have been taken into consideration. I now call on the members for any opening statements, after which Mr. Paterson will present his budget report and his recommendations for the Torpedo Factory revitalization project."

One by one, the council members took the microphone. *How can they make this so achingly boring and yet stressfully suspenseful at the same time? Must be a gift.* Milo tuned out while the voices droned on, until a subtle new pressure coming from her lower region intruded on her consciousness. *I forgot to pee before I left home, didn't I?* She tried to listen to the speeches, but their logorrhea failed to hold back the tide of her physical discomfort. She snuck a look at Tristram. He was murmuring to Doyle. The older man seemed upset about something. At one point he grabbed Tristram's lapel—*don't you dare stretch that gorgeous merino wool!*—and whispered in an agitated way. Milo hoped it meant he knew he'd lost, but she didn't count on it. She could see Esme and Morgana watching the argument as well, although Luisa kept her eyes riveted on the current speaker, Councilwoman Worthy.

"We have to weigh the merits of full utilization of the building with the desire to maintain the ambience that is Old Town. I think we're all agreed"—she paused to scan her fellow council members—"that whatever is installed in such a pivotal location should be welcoming to all segments of our community, not just a privileged few. An improved real estate assessment would sure come in handy as well." Nods all around. "With that, I look forward to hearing Mr. Paterson's recommendations."

The manager stood and dropped a large binder on the lectern. Milo wanted to pay attention, but the pressure in her bladder had reached undeniable proportions. She tried squirming, which only made it worse. Paterson began to talk about the latest school budget. She checked the agenda. The Torpedo Factory Revitalization Study was listed as Roman numeral four.

The manager pulled out a folder, opened it, and said, "Item Two. I shall briefly summarize the reports numbered one through fourteen, before moving to Report number fifteen. They can be found in the file marked Document Ten-oh-five. If you'll please open to page forty-three…"

That's it. I'm going for it. She slipped out the rear door. The first two bathrooms she found were locked. By now, one of her organs threatened to eclipse all other functions, so she took the exit stairs and hurried across Market Square to the public restrooms.

Ten minutes later, she made her way back to City Hall. As she neared the great doors, Tristram and Doyle came out. Doyle was shouting, his face purple and his arms pumping like a marathoner. He walked ahead of Tristram, chucking word spears over his shoulder at his unfortunate counsel.

"I can't *believe* these morons. This town is as short-sighted, close-minded, backward-thinking as Georgetown. Now I understand why Washington has the highest cost-of-living and the worst traffic congestion in the country. No one wants to do anything sensible. I'm out a-here."

Tristram caught sight of Milo and flashed her a look that mixed animosity and gloom in equal parts. Milo didn't know whether to be elated or depressed.

Luisa, Morgana, and Esme rushed out, talking over each other in ever-higher voices. "There you are, Milo. We won! We won!"

Morgana waved her fan. "The Factory is staying as is for now. They rejected the box store. Isn't it delightful?"

"What about Jacob Stickler's plan?"

The three women stared at her. Luisa shrugged. "No one took that seriously except Jacob."

Esme chuckled. "Maybe not even Jacob. He wasn't here to defend it, was he?"

"Go find Tekla, will you?" put in Morgana. "We're going to celebrate. Meet you at Murphy's?"

"Okay." Milo watched them walk up King Street and pulled out her phone. She punched in Tekla's number. No answer. *I hope she found Jacob. He'll need a friend.* Her phone rang in her hand. "Tekla? Where are you?"

"I couldn't find Jacob anywhere, so I came back to the studio. What happened at the hearing?"

Milo heard again Doyle's angry words and saw the mournful look on Tristram's face. *He could be fired.* Somehow the thought didn't cheer her the way it should. "We won. At least, Luisa won. They turned down the More for Less."

"That's wonderful! Oh…I guess that isn't such good news for your boyfriend though."

Milo gritted her teeth. "He's *not* my boyfriend, Tekla."

"Yeah, right." Tekla sighed. "I guess we're both sans lovers for now."

"Oh, for heaven's sake, we'll manage. I'm coming back to the Factory. The others went to Murphy's if you

100

want to join them. Esme's buying." She heard a click and the dial tone. Tekla never missed an opportunity for a free drink.

As she turned the corner onto Union Street, a policeman stood before the sliding doors. A group of elderly tourists huddled on the sidewalk, their guide gesticulating and yelling in what sounded like Italian. Two squad cars took up the space in front, their lights flashing. Milo had always hated the feeling of déjà vu.

She recognized the policeman. "Sergeant Buckler? What's going on?"

"Oh, Ms. Everhart. Lieutenant Webley is looking for you. He wants you to come to the station with us."

"Has anything happened?"

"We're—"

The doors opened to reveal two more officers. Between them, held up by the long arms of the law, sagged Archie. His face was bright red, and a vein in his neck beat furiously. He saw Milo and cried out, his voice a high-pitched squeak. "Milo! Help! They're arresting me!"

Fighting to hold in the scream, she grabbed the sergeant's wrist. "No! You're making a mistake!"

Webley appeared behind Archie. "Ms. Everhart, why don't you come along in my car? We'll need a statement from you."

"Why on earth are you arresting Archie? This is crazy!"

"All in good time, Ms. Everhart. This way."

Milo sat in the back seat and fumed all the way to the police station. She and Webley came through the entrance in time to catch sight of a handcuffed Archie, his eyes shut tight and his face blotchy with fear. Milo watched in misery as an officer led him away. Webley took her into a small room. A thin little man in a frayed tweed suit sat on a wooden chair behind the desk. He had a notebook open and waited expectantly, clicking a ballpoint pen. Webley held the other chair out for Milo and leaned against the wall.

"Milo, I want you tell me again what happened in the Torpedo Factory on the night of December 16. Mr. Beasley here will take your words down verbatim. We'll have you sign the statement when we're done." He didn't have to tell her that fudging the truth to protect Archie was not an option.

Milo took a deep breath. The memory of her friend's bowed shoulders and hesitating steps gave her courage. "First you have to tell me why you're arresting him. Archie Chisholm's been known to carry beetles out of the building rather than squash them. He could hardly murder a human being in cold blood."

Webley looked at his partner. "Ms. Everhart, we must have your statement first, if you please."

Milo described the events in question once again, with only a twinge of guilt at omitting her sighting of Archie in the crowd. When she'd finished, the second man rose and left. The detective said, "Mr. Beasley will be back in a minute for your signature. Thanks for your help."

"Okay, now that you know I saw Archie leave, you're going to have to explain how you think he nipped back in, passed me on the stairs, murdered a man, nipped back down and home without my seeing or hearing anything?"

"Simple. Mr. Chisholm had already killed von der Dieb. He came to tell you he was going home in order to set up an alibi. He walked ahead so you would believe he'd left. When you turned back, he ran up the back stairs. He heard you scream and run down to the main hall. At that point, he heaved the body onto the roof and snuck out a side door while you were still downstairs with the police."

"But how did he know I would have to go up to the tower? I'd forgotten until that moment."

"He didn't. When you called after him, he realized you'd find the body. He probably planned to dispose of it after you left."

The scenario makes too much sense. But...Archie? "What about a motive? I can see Archie threatening Jacob Stickler, or Mr. Doyle—*or Tristram*—but why an antique store owner? He has nothing to do with the Torpedo Factory."

"We're still working on that. Von der Dieb's store sits on the same block. There's probably a connection we haven't found yet."

Another thought sideswiped her already teeming brain. "What about the second victim? Mr....Galt? Are you charging Archie with his murder too?"

"We have a working hypothesis for that. See, after you ran down to call the police, Chisholm went back to hide the body, but when he got there, he found Mr. Galt in the tower along with the corpse. Nothing for it but to kill the witness."

"But then why didn't we find both bodies?"

"Because," Webley said, an I'm-trying-to-be-patient look painted on his face, "Chisholm only had time to hide the first one. By that time, he could hear the police sirens and knew he had to get out of there. Probably counted on the fact that nothing linked him to

Galt."

"Except the city council's intentions for the building." The minute she said the words, Milo saw the trap.

"*Hmm*. Yeah. Could be worth looking into." A light gleamed in the detective's eyes. "We may have been looking at this backwards. Chisholm's original victim could have been Galt, and von der Dieb was in the wrong place at the wrong time. That would explain the drops of Galt's blood on the stairs." He grinned happily. "Endless possibilities, eh?"

****

The celebrants had departed by the time Milo reached Murphy's. She found a small table by the fire, ordered a Jameson's, and sat brooding. Tommy Makem and the Clancy Brothers crooned softly in the background, and twinkly colored lights enlivened the tiny tree on the bar. Soon the comfort of an Irish pub at Christmastime began to soothe her roiling thoughts. The place filled up as the work day shut down. People came in stamping their feet, pulling off outerwear and shouting for pints. Milo ordered a bowl of Scotch broth. The pot came with a side of soda bread bursting with dark raisins, and a bowl of fresh butter on ice. She took the cover off and inhaled the aromas of lamb and cabbage. *Perhaps life isn't so bad.* She wished she didn't have to go back to the Factory. If only she had something to work on at home.

Two men in suits took the table next to hers, bringing with them frothing pints of Guinness. "*Mmm*," said one of them, wiping foam off his lips. "I deserve this."

"Oh, you think so? It's not like you did the

yeoman's work on Paterson's report, Carey."

"I did the hard part. I talked Dundicut into dropping that insane idea of hers about performance art."

"Where'd she come up with that, anyway? I missed some of the hearings."

"Oh, that jackass Stickler—you know, the enviro-nazi?—he proposed it at the first hearing. When it got the derision it deserved, he went on to pester her twenty-four-seven about it."

"What did he want to do?"

Carey took a deep pull at his mug. "Basically he wanted to leave the whole building empty most of the time. Sometimes I swear Dundicut doesn't understand the city is in this for the money."

The other fellow, a large man whose bulging waist and florid cheeks augured a short but jolly life, finished his stout and signaled to the waitress for another. "She's a dinosaur. Still thinks of Alexandria as a fiefdom of the Old Town aristocracy. *Noblesse oblige,* that sort of thing. The Torpedo Factory has been their playground since the seventies. She doesn't see it as the cash cow it could be."

"Yeah, that it should be an asset for the whole community, not just for 'the ladies who lunch.' " Carey unbuttoned his jacket, revealing a belly that could hold its own against his friend's in a shoving match. "Order me another Guinness, will you, Martin? I'm gonna take a whizz." He knocked into Milo's table as he weaved a path to the men's room. Mere seconds later—*how do men do that?*—he returned and picked up the refilled mug. "Thanks. Yeah, I'm glad I could talk her Honorableness out of the Stickler plan."

"It probably didn't hurt to have Randall Galt out of the way, eh?"

"Randy? Yeah, he was the main advocate of Stickler's idea. Really pushed it hard. Boy, will he be pissed to hear they didn't even discuss it when he gets back."

"Back?" Martin put his mug down, jiggling the wobbly table and splashing stout onto Milo's shoe. "What do you mean? You didn't hear? He's dead."

Carey's jaw dropped. "Randy Galt? I thought he was on vacation!"

"Nope. They found his body at the Factory last week. Murdered."

"Oh, my God." Carey caught the waitress's eye and raised his mug. "I'm going to have to start watching the local news again. No wonder I could persuade Dottie so easily. Without Randy, Stickler had no allies."

The two men fell silent, no doubt considering their next meal and not the late, apparently unlamented Randy Galt. Milo had forgotten her soup while she eavesdropped shamelessly on her neighbors' conversation. She took a sip. Cold. She put her credit card on the bill and waved it at the bartender.

As she walked to her car, picking her way through the puddles, she considered what she'd overheard. *So Galt did actually want Jacob's plan to be adopted. I'd better tell Tekla. It might console her.* She dialed her friend's number. A tearful voice answered.

"Tekla? Have you heard from Jacob?"

"No. I've checked all his usual haunts—the recycling center, Greenpeace's offices, that new PETA restaurant. You know, the one that won't even serve root vegetables because they scream when you pull them from the ground? I think the menu only lists water and berries. He hasn't been seen anywhere. I'm really worried, Milo."

"He didn't answer his phone?"

Tekla laughed wistfully. "You should know better than that. He doesn't own a telephone. He thinks cans on a string constitute degradation of the environment. No, I'll just have to wait till he contacts me." She paused. "You don't think I should go to the police, do you?"

Oh dear. "No. He's a grown man—of sorts. He'll turn up." Milo had reached her car. "Tekla, do you remember Randall Galt? Dottie Dundicut's chief of staff?"

"The murder victim? Of course I do. Jacob said Galt was on board with his idea." Tekla sighed. "Jacob's plan might have had a chance if he were still alive."

Doubtful. Milo kept the thought to herself. No sense in adding to her friend's woes. "Oh, by the way, did I remember to tell you we won?"

"Yes, you did, and the ladies gave me all the particulars. The city council voted to keep the Torpedo Factory as is. No box store." Her voice dropped, "Maybe that's why Jacob has disappeared. He must be so disappointed. You don't think…"

Milo held her breath. "What?"

"That he killed himself? Do you?"

Chapter Six

Milo found one last unadorned spot on a lower branch and hung a bulb on it. She stood back to admire the effect. Not as overdone as in the days when Michael did the decorating. *Oh well.* The timer went off and she pulled her mincemeat pie out of the oven. The spicy sweet scent filled the house. *I think that's it, except for the champagne.* She checked her day planner. *Oh good, I don't have to be at Isabel's until one o'clock tomorrow.* Milo opened the sliding door to her balcony an inch and gulped in the cold, fresh air. A light dusting of snow had fallen overnight and the sky matched the earth, with just a ribbon of dark gray river winding through it.

She set the bags of gifts by the front door so she wouldn't forget them like she had the year before. Little Emerson had been so upset. She wondered how her nephew was dealing with his new sister on her first Christmas. *Thank God Isabel let him put up baby Cassatt's stocking—that helped. I can't believe I finished it on time what with all the commotion.*

It had taken all her concentration to complete the needlepoint canvases for her clients over the last week. She hadn't seen or heard from Tristram, but she didn't expect to. Her feelings were so muddled at this point, she wouldn't know what to say to him. With the box store a moot point now, the specter of Michael was all that stood between them. Only Tristram didn't know that. *Anyway, considering the furious expression on his face the last time I saw him, losing his case hadn't dulled his anger.*

The waning light of late afternoon dribbled into her thoughts. Winter's near-continuous twilight always depressed her. The doctor had explained she suffered from a syndrome—seasonal light disorder or something like that—but knowing the cause didn't alleviate the symptoms. She turned on all the lights in the apartment and checked the kitchen clock. Only four. A walk into Old Town before the Christmas party might help. There were times when she wished the tenants in her building, Harbor Towers, weren't quite so sociable. Parties every weekend—bridge clubs, bowling leagues, barbecues by the pool in the summer, celebrations of every holiday of every ethnic group represented—which turned out to be twenty-four. *Thanks a lot, Washington.* If this were Des Moines, maybe she'd have a weekend off once in awhile.

She drew on her goose-down parka, found her hat and gloves, and went down to the lobby. A chubby woman with a cascade of tight, artificially blonde curls waddled toward her. "Milo! Where are you going? You're not skipping out on our soiree, are you?" Her squeaky little voice hardly matched the hefty bosom fighting for release. Conspicuous bulges above and below her chest hinted at an investment in the hyperbolically named Fab-U-Lous "Extra Slimming Body Shaper." *Maybe that's why she squeaks.* She wore jingle bell earrings.

"Oh, hi, Tammy. I'm just taking a walk. I'll be back in good time."

The other woman picked up the little white dog that tugged at her shoe, its pompadour beribboned and belled in painful imitation of her mistress. "You do that. Mickie and I expect all our people here for our Christmas Eve party, don't we, Mickie'ums?" She nuzzled the bichon. "Your mommy wuvs you, doesn't she?"

Milo forced a smile and went through the revolving door. She knew poor Tammy had little else to dote on, but it still seemed weird and a bit repulsive for her to refer to her dog as her child. Milo nodded at a tall, rangy woman of about seventy passing through the other door herding three tiny black pugs. She barely noticed Milo, focusing intently on the dogs and whispering sweet nothings at them. *Then again, Tammy's not alone.*

She drove a few blocks and parked across from Founders' Park. The city hadn't yet cleared the sidewalks of the leftover black snow from the week before, forcing her to climb up and down endless miniature mountains, slipping and cursing. In the last few days, the temperatures had hit the forties before dropping precipitously the night before, and the inch or so of new ice made her progress even trickier. Those who'd been hoping for a blanket of white on Christmas walked around sullenly, kicking at slush and muttering. Milo shivered and pulled her pink cashmere scarf closer.

A couple passed her, arguing. "I tell you, Sanford, weather-dot-com claims we're going down to the twenties tonight. We'll have more snow tomorrow, mark my words."

Her companion shrugged. "For one thing, Harriet,

it has to be warmer than that to get any real snow. For another, why should I care about a white Christmas? I'm Jewish." Luckily they had moved too far away for Milo to hear Harriet's response, but the tone of her voice did not convey approval.

By the time she reached St. Asaph's Street, her thighs were complaining bitterly, but she forced herself to go another block to Washington Street, the main thoroughfare through Old Town. To her south rose the spires of Christ Church. Built in 1773, the beautiful ivy-covered brick enclosure had been the young town's first house of worship. She checked her watch. Five o'clock. *Might as well take a peek inside.* As she approached, bells began to peal. *Oh shoot, of course! They must be holding Christmas Eve services.* She wasn't dressed for the tony crowd that would attend the venerable old Episcopal church, so she turned right instead, planning to circle around and take Oronoco Street back to the car.

Halfway down the block, she tripped on a cobblestone and stopped to catch her breath. She noticed a small group gathered across the street on the front steps of the Lee-Fendall House. Every time the door opened, she heard piano music and laughter and the chink of glasses. The historic marker reminded her that Lighthorse Harry Lee often attended parties at the graceful eighteenth-century mansion. *Guess it's still the hot spot for the smart set.* The festive sounds drew her. She began to cross the road but jumped back when a black Jaguar roared past and pulled into a parking space in front of the house. As she watched, a familiar form unfolded his long legs from the sports car. Tristram went round to the other side to hand out...*Ursula?*

What's he doing with her? I thought...I thought...well, I didn't think, did I? Milo backed off slowly, turned, and sprinted as fast as she could down Orinoco to her car.

When she reached Harbor Towers, Tammy stood at the door with a box of tinsel in her hand. "Oh good, here you are. You're so artistic, dear. Help me toss this around the room so it looks unaffected. You know, as though it doesn't care." Without waiting for an answer, she handed Milo a carton and skipped off to annex her next victim.

For once, the woman's zeal came as welcome relief, and Milo spent the next hour mechanically tossing silver strands everywhere and setting out covered dishes, her mind kept deliberately blank. She spent another two hours listening to dog stories, suppressing the impulse to launch into a lengthy paean to her cat. Tammy graciously allowed her to beg off at nine.

Not until the elevator doors opened on the eleventh floor and Milo sought her own bed did the jealousy hit with all the pent-up vengeance of a horny banshee. She gave up after an hour, rose, and, throwing a heavy sweater over her flannel pajamas, padded into the kitchen. *The bastard. How dare he go out with that...that devil in Prada? Or was it Kate Spade? And by what right then is he angry with me?* She popped the cork on a bottle of Moët champagne she kept in the refrigerator for emergencies and filled a glass.

A blast of cold air hit her when she stepped onto the balcony, but the moon shone clear in the dark sky. A flock of Canada geese honked lustily as they followed the river south. She sat shivering and sipping her wine and fuming. When that didn't work, she forced herself to take stock. *So why am I jealous?* I'm *the one who put* him *off. I'm the one who couldn't deal with my attraction to someone other than my husband. Yeah, but he's the one who tried to destroy everything I care for that's still alive.* A little voice reminded her, "But he didn't succeed, did he?" She finished the champagne and started back inside. *What would Doyle do now that his proposal had been turned down? Would he fire Tristram? Could he?*

The image of Tristram, coatless and homeless, weeping as the repo men towed away his Jaguar, improved her mood considerably. She licked the last drop of wine from the rim and went inside to take a hot shower.

****

"Oh, Milo, how beautiful! Thank you so much!" Her sister Isabel danced around the room holding up the embroidered vest. "However did you find the time? I can never get anything done now that Cassatt's crawling." She gazed fondly at the toddler, instantly forgetting her husband and son, not to mention her sister. "Cassatt! What are you doing? Don't touch Auntie M's purse. Oh...now look what you've done." She dropped the vest on the floor, missing the puddle of milk but not the half-chewed cookie. "Hal, dear, will you get that? Thanks. And could you...?"

She held Cassatt out to her affable husband, who carried the baby out of the room, leaving a whiff of what he was about to find in her diaper in his wake. Their older child Emerson tagged after him, his high piercing voice repeating for the hundredth time that he, Emerson, could use the potty now. All by himself.

Isabel sat down and took a swig from her punch

cup. She made a face and looked around for the brandy. "Don't look so disapproving, Milo. I'm not nursing anymore." She poured a healthy tot of Courvoisier into her eggnog and snuggled up next to her sister. "So, did you have a good Christmas?"

Milo toyed with the idea of bringing up her recent encounters with corpses, but it didn't seem worth it. Isabel—like most young mothers—could manage perhaps ninety seconds of adult conversation before her attention returned to the spawn. And from the way little Cassatt behaved at the golden age of one, Isabel would have to focus like a laser on her for the next fifteen years if the child were to survive.

"Yes, dear, very nice. Thanks for hosting. Did you like the pie?"

"Well, I'm not much of a mincemeat person…but it smelled good!"

Milo checked her watch. "Oh my, I'd better be getting back."

"Why?" Since she was already glancing toward the nursery, Milo knew her sister's curiosity sprang from courtesy rather than any real interest. "Whatever could you have to do today?"

Think. "I'm…um…expecting a long-distance call."

"From?"

"Oh, a fellow I met. He lives in…Hawaii." *Wait…No! Take it back. Damn.*

Isabel pivoted in a heartbeat and charged. "A fellow? Is he nice? Is he cute? How long have you known him? Are you dating again? Hey, Hal, guess what? Milo's finally dating someone! So, how…" Isabel's voice faded as Milo grabbed her coat and the remains of the pie and hightailed it out the door.

The streets were empty as the late afternoon sun glinted feebly through the cold clouds. Milo drove down Prince Street and turned left on St. Asaph's. Instead of going home, she took a right on Cameron and followed it to the Union Street garage. Parking the car, she walked north through Founder's Park and along the river. A cheerless mist floated just above the ground. Logs and trash and dirty foam lined the shore. A couple of mallards poked around in the slop with dispirited zeal. She found a bench and dropped on it with a sigh. The tears welled up without warning. Ever since Michael's death, she'd find herself suddenly crying without cause or purpose. This time, though, she wasn't thinking about Michael at all. *I miss him. I miss Tristram.* The revelation stung. *I don't need this. And anyway, I can't have him.* He hadn't called since the council meeting. And now she knew he'd gone back to Ursula. She'd blown it.

She wiped her eyes and nose and stood up. *Take your presents and go home, Milo.*

As she turned back to the path, a mellifluous baritone floated out of the mist. "Milo?"

Where the hell did my voice go? Okay, breathe. One, two, in, out. Now turn slowly. "Tristram?"

He stood on the path behind her, holding a heavy scarf around his throat with one hand and a miniature, wild-haired dog furiously barking at Milo with the other. He let the dog down and took a couple of steps toward her. The terrier stopped barking, cocked his head, and scrutinized the two humans with a keen air.

"Are you…I mean, do you…?"

Milo could only nod, hoping he would understand and do the proper thing. He did. He took her in his arms and kissed her gently. It was a good thing he held her so tightly, since she'd lost all feeling in her toes. When he let her go, she stumbled back to the bench. He sat beside her, an expectant smile on his lips. She searched for something to say that didn't involve apologies.

"Is…is that your dog? I don't remember you having a dog? Don't you have a cat?"

Tristram leaned down and attached a leash to the little fellow. "I do. Atticus, the alley cat. You remembered." He scratched the dog's head. "This is Yum-yum. He belongs to Ursula."

One. Two. Three. Four. "Oh?" He seemed oblivious. *Men.*

"I'm babysitting while she's off antique buying in Brazil. He's really not a bad little guy." He scratched the little Yorkie's ear.

Milo stood up. "Well, I'd best be getting home."

Tristram took her hand. "Why? Can't we walk a little? Wait—you're not thinking…No. Milo!" He kissed her nose and grinned. "You're jealous!"

It was precisely the wrong thing to say. *But of course—again—he's a man.* She shook him off and strode rapidly toward the parking garage. She had made it halfway when a large gloved hand grabbed her from behind.

"You're not disappearing on me again, young lady. Come with me." He escorted her firmly across an empty Union Street to Princess, only stopping to allow Yum-yum to catch up, and tossed her unceremoniously into the Jaguar.

It wasn't until they reached Wilkes Street and parked that she discovered he'd locked the car doors. He came around and pulled her out and half carried her

116

into his house. The minute he put her down, she tried to make a break for it, but the dog blocked her egress, jumping up and down to make himself look taller.

"Good dog, Yum-yum. You get a treat." After locking the front door, Tristram took her coat, led her to the sofa, and handed her a glass of whiskey. "Take your shoes off. You're staying awhile."

Milo was speechless. No one had ever treated her this way. *Is he going to be violent?*

Tristram stood before her, hands in his pockets, annoyingly composed. "I want you to listen carefully to me, Milo. Ursula Baines means nothing to me. Never has. I have had to wine and dine her at Doyle's request, for which she's repaid me by misinterpreting my motives. Despite my repeatedly explaining the nature of our relationship, she continues to tell her cronies that we're a couple and to ask little favors of me." He gestured at Yum-yum, who sat up expectantly. "Exhibit A. Fortunately, it won't be much longer. Doyle's decided to sell the house on Cameron Street, so he won't be requiring her services anymore. He hasn't yet said if he will need mine in light of the council's decision."

Milo decided to save the discussion about Doyle for later and scratch the first itch. She put down her glass and faced Tristram. Taking hold of his shirtfront, she pulled him toward her, giving him a wet, smacking kiss. His eyes opened wide. He started to say something, then snapped his mouth shut, picked her up without a word, and climbed the stairs. The pitter-patter of tiny paws followed them.

She was down to her lace balconette and bikini by the time they reached the bedroom. Tristram's shirt hung buttonless and his belt lay like a black snake on the stairs. Their lips met and stuck while they finished the rest of the shedding process. Tristram pushed Milo down onto the bed and set one arm on each side of her, gazing at her hungrily. She didn't want to wait—she took hold of his nipples and pulled him down on top of her.

"Next time we'll take it slow," she whispered.

His mouth went down on hers. She writhed under him as he sucked on her lips then moved down to her neck. Flames licked her skin, sending warm tongues of desire to her breasts and belly. He followed them with his own. When it touched the heated flesh of her sex with a tentative lick, then thrust inside, she came in a paroxysm of joy, bucking against him until the itch dissolved. "Oh, Tristram. More."

He rolled on his back, his erection perpendicular and pulsing. She curled her body over him, and touched the tip of his penis with her tongue. He let out a sigh. She cupped his balls and began stroking the shaft with her fingers. "Your mouth, love. Please." She obliged, opening her lips and sliding them up and down, relishing the rough skin, the rigidity of the muscle. His back lifted off the bed as he pressed down her throat, moaning. Suddenly he stiffened, and a warm trickle seeped out of her mouth. "Oh, Milo. More."

She lay back, and he covered her, kissing each nipple, spearing her belly button with his tongue. They rubbed their bodies together like animals, reveling in the lust. A minute later, he lifted her hips, pulled her thighs around his back, and entered her. The pounding increased, rolling over her like a train, until she rose to meet him. They stopped in mid-air for a breathless second and fell together onto the soft quilt.

I'll close my eyes in a second. I want to memorize his face first.

****

Something distracted her. *A down feather from the quilt? Dust bunny? What is that?* She curled her toes to get away from the soft fluttering thing. In response, a low growl came from the end of the bed. "Yum-yum! Get off!"

The little Yorkie gave her a dirty look and jumped off the bed. Tristram walked in. He had an apron over his T-shirt and jeans and held a spatula in one hand. A slow grin passed over his mouth. "Aptly named creature. Yum."

Milo pulled the quilt up to her chin. "What happened to Atticus?"

"Oh, he's around. Been making himself scarce while the canine's in residence."

"Poor thing."

"Believe me, he can take care of himself. He showed up before Thanksgiving and has been eating me out of house and home ever since."

"Someone may have lost him. You can't just take him in without making an effort to find his mistress." That had happened once to Milo, and she still remembered the loss vividly. "Did you advertise?"

"Mistress?" His eyebrows went up. "How do you know?"

"Never mind. Well, did you?"

"Advertise? Yes, of course I did." His voice snapped with impatience. "For two solid weeks. No one came forward. The puss is most assuredly a feral cat. I finally sprang for shots, which cost me an arm and a leg. Atticus is legally mine." He picked up Yum-yum. "I'm beginning to bond with this little guy, too. I wonder if Ursula will want him back?" He cocked an eyebrow at Milo, waiting for her reaction.

She threw a pillow at him. "Ursula can go f—"

"Now, now. I explained all that. Do you want breakfast? I made pancakes in honor of Boxing Day."

"Boxing Day? Oh, I forgot! Today is Boxing Day!" She paused. "Why is it called that, anyway? For the Boxer Rebellion in China?"

Tristram roared with delight. "You have an impressive grasp of history, m'dear, but no. In England, it's traditionally the day people give gifts to the tradesmen and service people they've dealt with during the year. The name came about because churches distributed the money from their alms boxes to the poor on the day after Christmas."

"Interesting. But what does that have to do with pancakes? Aren't you supposed to serve those on Shrove Tuesday—on Mardi Gras?"

"So they say, but I forgot to do it then. Actually, I didn't have anyone to make them for. I've been waiting half a year to find the right woman to flip for."

She laughed and threw off the covers. Enjoying the intake of breath from across the room, she tossed her head and did a little twirl. "Bathroom's this way, right?"

A luxurious shower later, she dressed and followed the aroma of maple syrup and melted butter down the stairs. Tristram had coffee and juice ready and plopped two large pancakes on her plate. She savored a few quiet, cozy minutes before the silence grew slightly uncomfortable. Milo knew Tristram expected an explanation for her erratic behavior. She tried a couple of different openings in her head but nothing sounded right.

"Tristram?"

"Yes, love?"

"The other night when you left in a huff?"

"Y...es." He opened his mouth and closed it. She knew he struggled with the desire to correct her and loved him for not indulging it.

"It had nothing to do with the box store or Doyle or the Factory. I...I let you think that."

"I see." He took a sip of coffee. "Then what is it?"

"I...um...I think I may have mentioned I'm a widow?"

Milo had never seen a jaw drop quite that dramatically. "A *widow*? No. In fact, you haven't told me anything about your past."

"I...guess it didn't come up." She gazed pleadingly at him. "Michael—my husband—died a year ago. He was a Marine..." Tristram blinked. "A Marine pilot. Assigned to an aircraft carrier. On a routine training flight, his...his plane flipped on landing. He...died instantly."

Tristram said nothing but pulled a can of dog food out and began to fill a dish. Facing away from her he mumbled, "I'm sorry, Milo."

She moved to him and put a hand on his arm. "It's okay. I'm sorry I didn't tell you sooner. It hasn't been an easy year. It...it...seemed too soon for another relationship. I thought...my feelings were...wicked." When he swung around, Milo saw with surprise that his eyes were wet with unspilled tears. "What is it?"

"You should have told me. I feel like a heel. I

shouldn't have pressed you. It's just—"

"Just what?"

He pushed his plate aside, sat down, and put his head in his hands. His voice came low and muffled. "Milo, I wanted you from the first moment I saw you. You are the most beautiful creature I've ever seen, and I couldn't wait to make love to you. You were right, you know—I purposely didn't mention my client because I knew you'd hate me for it. And I didn't ask you any questions because I didn't want to hear anything that would keep us from being together. If I could pretend you were unattached—implausible though it seemed for a woman as perfect as you—I could pursue you without guilt. I couldn't bear the idea that you were unavailable. Not after I'd been alone so long."

Most of his words filled her with comfort, as though she'd heard them before in a dream. *He is my savior.* But before she could draw him into her arms, his last sentence penetrated and she stopped.

"What do you mean, alone so long?"

He raised his eyes to hers, his face sheathed in sadness. "I lost my wife five years ago. We'd only been married three months. She was a Foreign Service specialist based in Saõ Paulo. I'd just been posted to the Marine Corps liaison office in the Senate, and she'd wangled a transfer to Washington, but had to return to Brazil for some final paperwork. Her plane crashed on the way there. A hundred and eighty-seven people died."

The homey little kitchen scene collapsed like a flimsy stage set. She knew it was irrational, but instead of feeling sympathy for his pain, his story rekindled all her grief over Michael. Her eyes blurred as she went back in time to the day she'd kissed him goodbye for the last time. They'd laughed through the tears, promising each other special gifts and favors when he came back on leave. She'd waved him off wearing nothing but a crimson bow in her hair, Michael grinning in that lopsided, endearing way he had. When she went back upstairs, a Hershey kiss lay on the night table, a token of his love. She'd scarfed it down, thinking she had no reason to save it. *He'll give me many more.* After Colonel Murray left that awful day, she had walked in a trance to the candy store on Fairfax Street, where she bought a five-pound box of Hershey kisses. She put them in a crystal bowl on his side of the four-poster, and there they lay still.

Too many deaths. Too many lost loves. She backed out into the living room, grabbed her purse and coat, and made a run for it. She heard him call but knew he wouldn't come after her. *We both need to sort this out. Alone.*

She made it home without incident. The desk clerk called to her as she passed, but she waved him off. *What I need is a long bath. And a hot cry.*

****

"Hey, Milo, where's Archie?" Tekla dropped Sparky long enough to catch the tail end of the topaz-colored woolen scarf Isabel had given Milo for Christmas. "I heard they let him out on bail."

"I haven't seen him. Did you ask Luisa?"

"Haven't seen her either. Gee, I hope Archie isn't ashamed to show his face here. This whole thing is absurd—Archie's no murderer."

"Much less a double murderer." Morgana stuck her

123

head between the two. "Milo, you've been up to your ears in this. What's going on? Why can't they find the real killer?"

"I have no idea. I haven't talked to Lieutenant Webley since before Christmas. They did identify both bodies. Say, Morgana, did you know the second victim, Eustice von der Dieb? He owned the antique store on the corner."

"Did you say von der Dieb?" Morgana's orange hair bobbed with suppressed laughter. "Poor thing."

"What's so funny, Morgana?"

"You don't know what the name means?" She tittered again. "It's German for—" She had to stop to catch her breath, "Thief!"

"Thief? That makes sense," said Tekla. "His prices amounted to highway robbery. But that's Old Town for you."

Milo persisted. "So, did you know him?"

Morgana sobered. "No. Esme may, though. His store catered to very wealthy clients and usually worked with decorators rather than sell to people off the street. I wonder what will happen to his inventory."

Tekla squealed. "Ooh, maybe they'll hold an auction. I adore that Azeri carpet he's had in the window for the past decade."

"And that Queen Anne highboy too—what a sublime piece. Did you know he wanted three thousand dollars for that? Ridiculous. Probably why it's been there as long as the carpet." Morgana sniffed in parsimonious disdain.

Esme came up behind them. "Ladies, ladies. He's hardly cold. Give it a rest."

"Esme, Morgana says you may have known the

dead man. Eustice von der Dieb. Did you?"

Her untidy gray braid presenting a winsome contrast to her beautifully tailored Chanel suit and rope of perfect pearls, Esme shook her head. "Not well. Homer and I ran into him at parties now and then. I never bought anything in his shop, although Homer did. The atmosphere smelled...er...unwholesome. Not sure why. I remember he had a wife—a voluptuous brunette in high heels who towered over him. Funny about that. I could have sworn he was gay."

"*Hmm.*" Milo felt betrayed by Webley. Why hadn't he told her any of this? *Oh yeah—because it's none of my business.* Nevertheless, she resolved to give him a call to see what she could find out. *It'll distract me from my...post-Christmas blues.*

Morgana spoke up, bursting with juicier gossip. "Hey, did you hear the other news? Remington Doyle—the More for Less magnate? He's bought land next to National Harbor. It took him all of a week to get a permit from Prince Georges County to build a store."

The four women grinned at each other. "The nail in the coffin," said Tekla with satisfaction.

"We've definitely won," crowed Esme.

Milo kept silent—she remembered Tristram's words about losing his job after the council's decision. *Doyle is only one client of many, I hope...*

"Furthermore," Morgana remarked, "I heard he's selling that house he bought on Cameron Street."

"Why do that? If he's going to have a store at National Harbor, it's still as convenient."

"Dunno." Tekla snickered. "Maybe it's a slap at the city for not giving him what he wanted."

"Sounds like something he'd do." Morgana had a

knack for dismissive hauteur.

"Really? What's he like? That ridiculous fringed jacket he wore to the hearing seemed so 'country.' " Tekla drew two imaginary quotation marks in the air.

"A nod to his Oklahoma roots, that's all. Didn't you see that article in the *Alexandria Times*? They said he's not someone you want to cross. Divorced three times. None of 'em got a penny. And merciless in business dealings as well."

Esme took a handful of pearls and clinked them together. "I remember that article. It also mentioned he's a known connoisseur. Homer and I went to Genevieve Pickens's party last week—that one in the Morrison House? I love their chef. Anyway, Genevieve claimed Doyle had been filling the Cameron Street place with all kinds of fabulous stuff, especially porcelains. Say, if he's moving, I wonder if he'll sell it all."

"Wow. His stuff, plus Legerdemain. This could be a bonanza for antique collectors." Tekla's eyes lit up. "Can you find out for us, Esme?"

"I could get in touch with that decorator of his I suppose."

Something tickled the back of Milo's mind. *Ursula.* "Who is it? Do you know?"

"Of course. Ursula Baines. She's the top decorator in Old Town—no one's more high-end than she is. Wait a minute—I just remembered something. She was the Amazon. Eustice von der Dieb's wife. Small world, isn't it!"

Chapter Seven

"What do you mean, he's not coming back? That's ridiculous."

"What are we going to do without him on First Night?"

"There will be hundreds of people here on New Year's Eve expecting lights and music and games and...and...Archie's always been in charge of those things!"

Luisa shrugged. It reminded Milo that she'd never liked the woman. Even on her best behavior, she rubbed people the wrong way, and she tended to be overbearing and rude with the other artists in the cooperative. Archie, of course, was beneath her notice entirely.

"We'll have to hire someone. It's not like Archie's indispensable."

"Oh really? Do you even *know* what he does around here?"

"Yes, yes, I know how you all feel about him." Luisa produced the martyred sigh she had perfected after many years of family reunions. "He said he's taking some vacation days. Lord knows he's never been away from the Factory for more than an hour, but I still don't know where he gets off thinking he gets paid vacation."

Tekla asked mildly, "Did he ask for money?"

"No, but I'm sure he expects it." Luisa rolled her eyes. "I suppose I'll have to ask the board for some kind of compensation for him."

This was too much for Milo. "Look, *Luisa*, Archie's given his heart and soul to this place and now he's in trouble. No one—not even you—thinks he committed those murders. He needs our help and our sympathy right now."

"And maybe donations." They hadn't noticed Esme arrive. "I don't know where he got the bail money. Come to think of it, I don't know what he lives on. Does anybody?"

Luisa snorted. "He gets a salary from the cooperative. You vote on it every year, Esme."

"Oh. That's good." Esme was known to be exceedingly generous but, without ever having to worry about finances herself, completely clueless when it came to budgets.

Milo kissed her softly wrinkled cheek. "You're a sweetie, Esme. Homer paid the bail—didn't you know?"

The older woman blushed. "The dear. I'll have to find a way to thank him. Do any of you girls know where the nearest Victoria's Secret is?" At Luisa's shocked expression, she winked at her. "Oh, I nearly forgot to tell you. That Doyle fellow is auctioning off the contents of his house after all. I hear the house itself sold for two million, but the buyers want it unfurnished."

"Do you know who's running the auction?"

"Haven't heard."

"When is it?"

"Oh, not for a while, I should think. He has to have

all the stuff independently appraised first." Esme shook her head. "My friend Amy Branson's a real estate agent, and she gave me a quick tour yesterday. It boggles the mind how he managed to accumulate so much so fast."

"Valuable things?"

"*Very* valuable things."

Luisa elbowed Milo aside. "Like what?"

"Oh, I saw some gorgeous Chinese ceramics and what looked to me like a Bernard Leach pot—very rare in the U.S. I don't know much about furniture, but it all appeared quite fine."

Tekla picked Sparky up and started down the hall. "Well, keep us informed, will you? I'm definitely interested."

Milo climbed the stairs to her studio. She hadn't heard from Tristram since she ran out of his house. She had calmed down quickly, but shame kept her from calling him. Her mind still whirled with his revelation and her reaction to it. She turned on all the lights to cheer herself up. It had snowed again, the temperature dropping over the last two days to a numbing twenty degrees. She pulled out a sketchpad. It always took awhile to get enthused about a new project after she'd finished one, and since she'd completed three canvases plus Cassatt's stocking before Christmas, she needed to mellow out a bit before taking the plunge into something else. She stared at the paper. Without thinking, she picked up a colored pencil and began to draw.

As she worked, she thought about Archie. *I know he didn't kill either of those fellows, but he was the only one besides me in the Factory at the time of their deaths. And seeing him in the middle of those rubberneckers on the street...* She hated the tiny knot of suspicion that twisted her gut every time she remembered his expression that night—not worried or curious or even alarmed. More like...angry. It didn't make any sense.

But if not Archie, who? Who would have a reason to kill the two men? What was the connection between them? *Better review.* First victim, Eustice von der Dieb, antique dealer. According to Esme, he was Ursula's husband...*Wait a minute, if she's already married, where does she get off dating Tristram?* Didn't he say she'd been telling her friends they were a couple? Open marriage? *But that's neither here nor there.* Not to mention moot since hubby currently slept with the fishes. Milo pressed her lips together to help her think. Maybe the relationship, if any, between the two victims wasn't the key. Maybe she should be looking for their ties to the Factory. Von der Dieb's antique store, Legerdemain, lay on the same city block, albeit in the next building. Could von der Dieb have been secretly negotiating with Doyle to sell his lot to More for Less? Maybe he and Doyle had a falling out. *And Doyle...*

Okay, consider the other victim. Randall Galt, Chief of Staff to Councilwoman Dottie Dundicut, principal, and possibly only, backer of Jacob Stickler's proposal. The fellow in Murphy's claimed Galt had convinced his boss to support it. The decision by the city council had to be unanimous, so if Dundicut voted for Jacob's plan, any deal with Doyle would fall apart. *If Doyle thought he had everyone on board and then discovered one wobbly member, what would he do?*

Doyle's reputation as a ruthless businessman came

to mind. The *Alexandria Times* article on him appeared the week he announced his plan to transform the Torpedo Factory into a redneck shopper's paradise. The introduction described how a young Remington "Chuck" Doyle from the tiny town of Bartlesville had raced up through the ranks of the Dollar Express organization like wildfire, ultimately acquiring a majority share in the company. A year later, he sold it to a South Korean firm that immediately closed down operations in the U.S. and fired 25,000 employees. Rumor had it Doyle knew it would happen and didn't care. He took the cash and started his own company, More for Less, in Oklahoma City. Within a year, it had locked up eighty percent of the American discount retail market. No one except his shareholders had a good word to say about him. What had Tekla called him? Merciless?

So...if Doyle found out Dundicut was wavering and believed only Randall Galt and Eustice von der Dieb stood between his latest dream and reality, would he...Oh my God, he may have killed them both! Milo put down her pencil. *I should call Lieutenant Webley. Now where did I put the phone?* She started to clear the worktable of clutter—and caught sight of the picture she'd been doodling. Tristram.

She stared at the image. *It's him—the heavy black lashes over those deep green eyes. That one stray curl that always falls across his forehead. The regal nose, the strong chin, the...mouth.* She'd drawn his lips tightly closed, the way she'd last seen them. In pain? Or disappointment? She had the phone in her hand. Instead of calling the police station, she clicked on her message history, found Tristram's number, and dialed it.

He answered on the first ring. "Yes?"

She almost lost her nerve. "Tristram? It's me."

Did she hear a sigh? She waited. Finally he spoke, his voice low and taut. "Hello, Milo."

She had to wait for the knocking in her chest to diminish before she could talk. "Tristram? I...I'm sorry." She couldn't think of anything more effective.

Another pause. "Fine."

He's going to hang up. "Wait!"

"What is it?"

"I need to talk to you." Inspiration flicked her sluggish brain into gear. "I have an idea about the murders. I'd like to bounce it off you before I go to the police with it. Can we...can we get together tonight?" *Please don't let him hear the desperation.*

"All right. Meet me at La Tasca. The one on King. Six o'clock." She heard a click.

I guess that went well. She looked out the window. Clouds hung just above her, menacing snow, darkening the noon sky to dusk. In fact, they seemed to be leaking flurries. A cormorant huddled on the pilings. Bundled up in matching down jackets, a family of four stood at the railing. Ranged according to height, they reminded Milo of the Russian nesting dolls Tekla had given her for Christmas.

The next day Old Town would celebrate First Night, a festival of non-alcoholic events intended for families. There would be music and food and art activities at the Factory. Milo would not attend. She planned to be home with Pinkie, curled up before the fire, quaffing something with a kick.

****

Six-thirty. She sat on her stool shaking the ice in

her Jack Daniels. What did this scene remind her of? *Oh. Yeah. O'Connell's.* Rain. Shiny shoes and a face to stop a heart.

The bartender leaned over the counter. "Another JD, Miss? Might as well."

She nodded. *What could be keeping him?* She'd spent the entire afternoon showering, washing, blow-drying, making up, and eliminating fourteen different outfits. She'd finally settled on a light wool sheath, sage green with a mandarin collar and a deep vee neck. She wore her grandmother's heavy gold necklace and gold knot earrings. Her tawny curls were swept back with a pair of ivory combs, framing her heart-shaped face. The thin stockings meant her legs were freezing, but since— at thirty-five—they were by far her best feature, she bore the discomfort. She kicked her high heels against the stool. Six-forty-five.

"Hello, Milo." Tristram sat down on the next stool but kept his eyes on the bartender. "Manuel, let me have a glass of your best red wine."

The bartender rooted around below the bar. "This I keep for myself." He uncorked a bottle and poured wine the color of heliotrope into a balloon glass. "Artadi Viña el Pisón 2004. Tinto reserva, ninety-nine percent Tempranillo grapes."

Tristram sipped. "Excellent. Tell me about it."

Manuel beamed. "It's from a bodega owned by a cousin of mine, Juan Carlos Lopez de la Calle, in Alavesa. The vineyard is part of a former monastery, a walled close planted by his grandfather in 1947, but the vines are older." He tapped his chest to indicate his kinship with the vintner. "Juan Carlos is a genius—his reds are far richer and more aromatic than most Rioja wines."

Tristram took another taste and let the wine sit on his tongue a minute before swallowing. "It has layers and layers of fruit—very complex. Thank you."

Milo had been tapping her shoes on the brass railing during the conversation. Finally she interrupted. "So nice of you to join me for a drink, *Tristram.*" Manuel took the hint and moved off.

Tristram swung on her, his manner abrupt, bordering on hostile. "You had an idea you wanted to tell me about."

Milo sat back. *Where did all that anger come from?* "Er, yes. Would you…would you like to order a couple of tapas first?"

"No."

He won't even look at me. Have I blown it completely? A sheen of terror dampened the nape of her neck. She felt a drop of perspiration make its unpleasant way down her back. *I've lost him. I've lost him.* She finished her whiskey and took a deep breath. Okay, she'd just pretend everything was perfectly normal. That way she could at least hear his voice one more time before he walked out on her.

"Um…er…I've been thinking about the murders. It seems to me the only person with a motive to do away with both victims is…Mr. Doyle."

That got his attention. Tristram stared at her. "Excuse me?"

"Yes. I'm not sure about the opportunity—"

"Not to mention that he's incapable of such behavior."

"But, see, both victims were involved in the future of the Torpedo Factory. Von der Dieb owned part of the building lot that would be affected, and Galt was gaining headway in persuading the council to go with Jacob's—Mr. Stickler's—performance art proposal. Doyle has a reputation as a pitiless, soulless businessman. If they stood in the way of his plans…"

Tristram stood up. "This is ridiculous, Milo. I'm leaving."

A bubble of hysteria filled her throat. Her mind vaulted from one jittery thought to another, none of which answered the question—*how do I keep him here?* She knew instinctively that if he walked out the door she'd never see him again. She grabbed blindly for his elbow. "Wait."

He paused, exuding suppressed energy, like a horse longing to break free of the reins and gallop away across the fields. His jaw worked, grinding his teeth together with a cracking sound even she could hear. Suddenly, she knew she had to let him go, to give him his head.

"I'm sorry, Tristram. For everything. I won't keep you."

That did it. He wheeled and put his arms around her. When her tears began to fall, he drew her into a dark corner away from the bar. He settled her in the booth and signaled to Manuel for a drink. After it came, he sat down next to her. By then Milo's tears had slowed, but she couldn't breathe and gulped for air.

"It's all right, Milo. I forgive you."

Somehow the words didn't make her feel better. Implicit in them lay what one radio talk show host called a "But monkey." She decided to go on offense. "But?"

"Look." He handed her the wine. "You know how I

feel about you, but you're obviously not ready to be with another man. Everything comes back to…Michael, is it? He colors your every move, your every thought. I can see it in your eyes. Not when we make love, but all the rest of the time. He's still too big a part of you, Milo. I can't compete with that, and I don't want to."

She whispered, "I don't want to lose him, Tristram. I feel so guilty when I forget him, even for a minute. What happens if I turn around and he's gone forever?"

He took her hand and squeezed it. "You know that will never happen. Olivia, my wife, is still part of me. We'd known each other since childhood, and I loved her with all my heart. Try as I might—and believe me, I have—I'll never rid myself of her memory. Or of that irritating way she had of being right."

Milo blew her nose on a cocktail napkin. "What do you mean?"

He chuckled. "She left me a note the day she flew to Brazil—the same note she left every time. Olivia hated to travel—I know, I know, she admitted she'd chosen the wrong profession. Flying terrified her. She kept saying, 'This is my last trip, Brodie. I want to be home with you. I want to cook and garden and putter.' After she died, I dreamed every night for weeks that she stood outside the window waving a pot and a trowel at me."

"And the note?"

"Oh, yes." He closed his eyes and recited, " 'Dearest Brodie, be good while I'm gone. When I come back, I'll know by your eyes whether you have. If I don't come back, I'll know by your soul. And if God wants me more than you do, promise to open your heart to someone else. I'll nag you till you do.' And she has, the witch."

"Nagged you?"

"Yup."

Despite the twinge of jealousy, Milo laughed.

Tristram watched her, an enigmatic smile on his face. He pulled out some bills and laid them on the table. "I'll take you home."

She knew enough not to argue.

When they reached the entrance to Harbor Towers, he stopped the car but stayed at the wheel when she got out. "Good night, Milo."

The panic returned for a horrible second. "Tristram…"

He reached through the passenger window and touched her cheek. "I'll be around when you need me. You'll recognize me—I'll have that henpecked look."

She turned before he could see the agony on her face. A thought struck her, and she spun around as he put the Jaguar into gear. "What about Doyle?"

"Put it out of your head. Ridiculous idea. For one thing, if he wanted a person dead, he'd have someone else do it."

He left Milo with her mouth hanging open.

****

She slept deeply for eight hours that night and awoke strangely calm. Knowing where she stood with Tristram comforted her. *He's giving me time for all my feelings to sift into place.* Of course, he might not hang around for as long as it took to get her act together, but she had no choice. She wouldn't be able to fool him into believing she was ready when she wasn't. Somehow he knew her—understood her heart, like no one ever had before—not even Michael. She could sense his affection, his tenderness even now. His silent support allowed her to relax and enjoy life again. She dressed and walked to the Factory, ready to work.

"You look cold, Milo. Where's your car?"

"I left it in the garage last night. Tristram took me home."

Tekla grinned lasciviously. "Really? Was he good?"

"He *was* good, yes, Tekla. He left me at my door, thank you."

Her friend's disappointment seemed more rancid than usual. "Damn, I hoped at least *you* were getting a little action. Someone should."

"No word from Jacob yet?"

"None. I'm going to file a missing persons report."

Milo looked up at the second floor, where Barbara Dimity leaned precariously over the railing to hang festoons of ribbons. "You may have to wait till Thursday. Tomorrow's New Year's Day you know. Offices are probably closed."

"Even the police station?"

"Well, I don't know. You could try, but with so much going on—First Night and all the parties—you may not get an immediate response."

"Well, a few more days won't matter. I'll be gone until the weekend anyway—did I mention my cousin Leonid is getting his U.S. citizenship? I'm going to the ceremony." Tekla shook her long black hair, her large silver hoop earrings glimmering in the Christmas lights. "I feel in my bones that Jacob is all right. But where *is* he?"

Milo kissed her friend's cheek, inhaling the haunting aroma of wet dog. Sparky barked at her.

"Think of it this way, Tekla. This is your golden opportunity to get over him, branch out, maybe find someone…sane."

The sculptress's normally somber Russian face descended deeper into a tragic mask. "I miss him, though. Where will I ever find another lover who can use honey so creatively? Not to mention rubber gloves?"

"That is so definitely on a need-to-know basis, Tekla. And I don't. Need to know."

Milo opened the studio and pulled the curtains aside. Sickly sun poured in through the great bay window. She set her easel up, attached a large piece of Zweigart mono canvas to it with clips, and began to blend her paints. The sketch of Tristram caught her eye. *It's not bad, actually. I've never done a portrait before. I wonder…*

Instead, she started tracing the outlines of a pot of geraniums. Work soon drew her in.

"You'd better get out of here before the hordes arrive, Milo."

She jumped at Morgana's voice in her ear. "What time is it?"

"Six o'clock. The festivities are about to begin."

Milo put away her paints, rolled up the canvas and put it in its cubby, then pulled her coat off the hook. "What are you doing for New Year's, Morgana?"

"The usual. Stewie is grilling steaks, and the girls will demand to be allowed to watch the ball come down. I will let them just so I have some company after Stewie drops off. Plus they give me an excuse to salivate over Ryan Seacrest."

"Sounds very domestic."

"And you?"

Milo waved a thick volume before stuffing it in her bag. "Jane Austen, Pinkie, and I will spend a cozy evening by the fire."

"No champagne?"

"Of course, but only for me. Pinkie gets Fancy Feast, and Jane gets my undivided attention."

She waved goodbye to assorted artists on the way out. It had been a productive day, and she felt quite tranquil. No dead bodies, no police sirens, no foreclosures on the building. As she stepped off the curb, something exploded over her head. *Please make that be a firecracker.* She looked up to see a golden shower of sparks. Another explosion came, this time accompanied by red and purple stars wiggling like tadpoles down to the roofs. *A perfect ending to a satisfying day.* She was halfway across the street when a bicyclist almost sideswiped her. As she spun around to yell at him, an angular, hunched figure hurried past the Torpedo Factory, eyes on the sidewalk. *Jacob.*

"Jacob? Jacob!" The figure bent lower and began to run. She watched him out of sight, wondering whether she should tell Tekla. *Not yet. She deserves a break. But at least I know he's alive.* She drove home.

****

"Milo, you did agree to be on the Archives Committee, you know."

Milo hoped her resentment didn't show too much. Luisa was always at her most officious when she'd just been reelected president of the Artists Cooperative. "And?"

"Well, the city council wants to have a look at the last ten years of our finances. I need you to go up into the tower and pull them together."

"Why do they want to see them?"

Luisa lowered her voice. "I've heard they're thinking about establishing some kind of oversight over the Factory."

"I thought they'd decided we could keep running it!"

"For now. They're still looking to increase revenues from the building. We have to show it's efficiently run, or they may decide to take over the management themselves."

So after all they'd been through, they could lose control anyway. "All right, I'll go up today and take a look."

"Good girl."

Excuse me? You're five years younger than me, Luisa. I may not look my age, but I think I act it. "Yes, Luisa."

Just to annoy her, Milo sat down to finish the latest edition of the *Alexandria Times* before obeying orders. According to reporter Jesse Joplin, the appraisal of Doyle's furnishings would be complete by the following week. Ms. Joplin gushed over the significant collection of artisan and medieval Chinese pottery Doyle had accumulated, items that would likely be on the auction block as soon as Sotheby's could schedule it.

Half an hour later, she trudged up the back stairs to the tower. She hadn't been there since the night of the murders, and she hesitated a second before pushing the heavy door open. With some relief, she found the room clean and the chairs stacked in one corner. She drew the blinds and looked out over the river toward the Wilson

Bridge. The landscape of chimneys and industrial machinery in a sea of snow-covered rooftops made a bleak picture. She turned back into the room. "Suck it up, Milo. Let's get to work."

She opened one of the wall cabinets. Stacked inside were four boxes marked "Documents." Starting with the first, she began to sift and weed. An hour later, she had a large plastic bag full of trash by the door and the papers down to one small pile. She opened the next cabinet. More boxes. She pulled them out and weeded them as well. The third cabinet was locked. *What the—?*

Luckily she knew where Archie hid his extra keys. She ran down to the gift shop and felt around under the counter until she found the magnetic box. Pulling out a set of tiny round keys, she took them back up to the tower. The cabinet opened on the second try. Inside she found two metal boxes. She hefted one with difficulty—it seemed to be some kind of safe. Dragging them to the table, she fiddled with the handle of the first. Locked. The second opened easily, revealing several file folders. She emptied them onto the worktable and picked up one marked "Kangxi— Jackson." It held forms detailing the import and authentication of several Chinese vases, plus invoices from an E. Jackson, Chemists Lane, Manchester, England. A file labeled "Leach—Milestone" listed appraisals of pots by the famous English ceramicist Bernard Leach, with canceled checks to a B. Milestone in Utah. *Jackson and Milestone must be the appraisers.* She sucked in her breath at the size of the checks. *The work is sure lucrative.*

She thumbed through several more folders. They

all held documents relating to valuable antiques. For the life of her, Milo couldn't figure out what they had to do with the mostly avant garde but, at any rate, contemporary work of the Artists Cooperative. She decided to take a couple of the files downstairs and see if any of the older members knew anything about them.

When she reached her studio, a milling band of tourists in boiled wool coats, sweat coursing down their foreheads, stood at her door. A very large woman in a severe black pantsuit and what looked suspiciously like a wig marched toward her.

"Ms. Everhart? We were told downstairs you'd be open." Her aggressive tone revealed more about the impatience of her clients than her own. Milo knew her vaguely. She ran a travel agency on Pitt Street and had a reputation for both successfully handling difficult customers and having an irrepressibly upbeat nature.

"Ms. Burnside, I do apologize. I'll be happy to open up for you. Right this way."

The large woman smiled and whispered as Milo passed her. "Sorry. Have to keep up appearances, you know."

The tour group, all female and all grand examples of robust Scandinavian physiology, straggled in after her. Ms. Burnside introduced them as the Lutheran Women's Circle of Lake Wannabegone, Minnesota. Milo dropped the files on her desk and proceeded with amiable grace to answer questions and demonstrate her art. Three hours and several dozen visitors later she sprawled wearily in her chair.

Esme peeked in. "Busiest time of the year, I swear. Everyone's buying the stuff they didn't get for Christmas."

"Too right. I sold seven canvases, Esme!"

Her friend looked at the empty display cases. "And all the Bargello purses? Wow. Uncle Sam will love you."

"Not if I hide it first." Milo laughed at Esme's shocked expression. "Kidding. I promise to share my hard-earned dollars with the overweening state."

Esme checked her watch. "Luisa's closing the building in a half an hour. They're predicting a heavy snowfall over night."

"How is she managing without Archie?"

"Oh, it's amazing how much she won't confess. She finally asked the board for money to hire a temporary manager. Archie is proving remarkably indispensable after all. By the way, when is his trial?"

Milo had done some research and called Lieutenant Webley, so she had the answer ready. "He has a preliminary hearing coming up next week. At that point the prosecutors will probably ask for a grand jury."

"That sounds good."

"Not really. According to my sources, the grand jury is not exactly blind justice. There's no judge, and only the prosecution can present evidence and witnesses. The defense can't even be in the room, much less ask questions, so the jury only hears one side of the story. Most of the time the prosecuting attorney easily walks away with an indictment."

"I guess that's why my Homer says a good prosecutor can get a grand jury to indict a ham sandwich."

"Yes. And since they've found no other suspects, Archie is looking at a full-blown murder trial."

Esme wiped a tear away. "At least Homer found

him the top lawyer in Virginia. Aloysius Tupper is our best chance at clearing poor Archie's name." She sniffed. "I do love my husband."

"Don't we all, Esme. Don't we all." Especially since Homer Leventhal, Esme's husband and richer even than Chuck Doyle, was picking up the tab for the inestimable Tupper.

When Milo got home, she poured herself a drink and turned on the evening news. *Oh goody, another dyed-blonde, carmine-lipsticked, anchor broad.* This one breathlessly informed "our viewers" of breaking news in "the quaint historic town of Alexandria, Virginia." Milo turned up the volume.

"Mr. Remington Doyle, multimillionaire founder of the More for Less chain, is about to make a statement. Let's go live to his house on Cameron Street. Martin?"

A man in a Brooks Brothers camelhair coat jumped and peered into the camera. "Rebecca?"

"Martin?"

Do they even know how this works?

"Oh...er..." The man smoothed his glistening hair and brought a microphone to his full lips. "This is Martin Craven, reporting from Old Town Alexandria. The press conference should start any minute now. All we know so far is that a burglary has taken place at Remington Doyle's house on Cameron Street. The house sold last week for a cool two million dollars, and Doyle had vacated it, but...Okay, here they come."

The camera swung away from Martin to a narrow brick townhouse typical of eighteenth-century Federal-style architecture. A large Palladian window centered under the pitched roof overlooked a fanlighted porch.

Christmas decorations lent a festive air to the houses on either side, but only squad cars and camera lights illumined Doyle's house. Police swarmed everywhere, reminding Milo unpleasantly of recent events.

Martin's producer trained his lens on a red-faced Doyle striding up to a bank of microphones. Next to him stood the chief of police and Mayor Carstairs, both looking extremely uncomfortable. Doyle yelled something about shysters and crooks. When he started throwing around the word "corruption," the mayor put a hand under his elbow and gently moved him away from the cameras, then coughed and flicked a mike.

"Chief Jones and I are deeply concerned about this crime and intend to put all our resources on the case. A robbery of this size and scope cannot remain unsolved for long. We want to assure the public and Mr. Doyle that the valuable collection of antiques he purchased right here in our fair city will be recovered."

The scene faded, and the anchor babe chirped, "We'll have more on what's being called the heist of the century—the disappearance of half of the antiques in Remington Doyle's mansion in Alexandria—after these messages."

Milo sat back, spilling her drink in her lap. *Oh my God.*

Chapter Eight

Coverage of the sensational robbery engulfed the next few news cycles. While her friends feasted on the gossip about Doyle's threatened lawsuit against the city, Milo focused on one tidbit of news tucked away in a *Washington Post* article. Doyle had summarily dismissed Tristram's firm Zeller, Schwartz, and Katz, singling Tristram out for a special dose of invective. Evidently, in addition to his other faults, Doyle liked to find scapegoats for his failures. He went on both the *O'Reilly Factor* and Jon Stewart's *Daily Show* and raged about his former counsel's incompetence and inability to execute even the simplest requests. When Stewart pointed out that the city council, not Mr. Brodie, had made the decision to reject the box store, Doyle stormed out of the studio. He didn't spare the mayor or the police either, disgorging vilification at innumerable press conferences. Luckily, the attendance at those briefings dwindled when it became clear Doyle had nothing newsworthy to offer.

Two days after the robbery, an anonymous tip led detectives to a warehouse in La Plata, where they discovered a portion of the stolen merchandise. In a letter to the mayor, published in the *Post*, Doyle appended a less than gracious thank-you to an imperious directive to find the rest. When he tried to pick up the recovered antiques, however, the authorities refused, claiming they needed to hold them as evidence. A brief legal duel ensued, which Doyle lost, exacerbating his foul mood.

"I don't see why he's fussing. After all, he had to have them appraised before he sold them anyway," said Esme, folding the paper. "Homer says the city is required to appraise the stuff, so they'll pick up the tab. He should be pleased."

"I don't know about that, Esme," said Tekla. "I'll bet he had his own guy, one who would have put a higher price tag on the stuff. This way, the true value will be advertised, and he won't be able to rake in as much."

"But he only just bought most of it," Milo pointed out. "Wouldn't the selling price still be available?"

"Would it?" Morgana appealed to Esme. "Even if he bought them through a decorator?"

Esme shook her head. "You know that bronze horse of mine? As I recall, when Homer went behind my back and bought it from Ursula Baines, she made him sign something about confidentiality."

Milo pursed her lips. "That doesn't sound kosher. There are so many scams and fake antiques out there. Why would anyone buy something unless they had unimpeachable proof of its authenticity?"

"I don't think that's why she does it. I had the impression she wanted to protect her suppliers. Homer saw the horse in Legerdemain and knew I'd love it, but Eustice wouldn't sell it to him directly—said it belonged to Baines and he was holding it for her. Well, you know how Homer is when he wants something, so he eventually got the woman to sell it to him. Paid a hefty price for it."

"I know you forgave him, Esme," laughed Morgana. "That little horse has pride of place in your foyer. It's a lovely piece."

"I know. I hate to admit it, but Homer's got a good eye for art."

"Of course he does, dear. He's built up one of the finest collections of Esme Leventhal oils in the country."

Esme blushed. "Gawn. Anyway, I'm off to lunch. My friend Amy Branson—remember her? The Realtor? She claims she has all kinds of inside information about the Cameron Street burglary. I'll let you ladies know if I hear anything interesting."

The others scattered to their studios, leaving Milo to meditate. She hadn't gone to Lieutenant Webley with her suspicions about Doyle yet. With all the subsequent events, the murders had faded from the public screen. Besides, Tristram had made it clear he considered her idea hogwash. How had he put it? "If Doyle wanted to kill someone, he's have an underling do it." Or something like that. From what she'd seen lately of Doyle's modus operandi, that made sense. *And then he'd finger the lackey.*

She worried about Tristram. Even though his firm was well-established and he a junior partner, the bad publicity could jeopardize his career. What would he do if Zeller, Schwartz, and Katz canned him? Where would he go? Back to the Marines? She couldn't see him shedding the Armani suits and Gucci shoes for an itchy uniform. Home town, then? It occurred to her that she did not, in fact, know where he came from. *Left home at seventeen, he said. Joined the Marines to avoid juvie, he said.* Sounded like a bit of a checkered career.

Of course the Marines straightened him out. How many of Michael's friends had told her the military literally saved them? Not Michael, of course. He'd always wanted to be a pilot. Actually, he'd always wanted to be an astronaut. He chose the Marines because the program was smaller than that of the Air Force, and he figured he'd have a better shot at getting into the space program. *So maybe that didn't work out, but at least he got to do what he loved—fly high and fast.*

Her stomach rumbled. *Time for lunch.* She stood up to find her foot had fallen asleep. As she hopped around the studio, shaking her leg and trying to reconnect with her toes, she knocked the computer mouse off the desk. Tekla's suggestion of so long ago echoed. *That's it!* A couple of clicks later, she had what she wanted. From his law firm's website and the Marine Corps directory, she learned that Tristram Brodie came originally from a village called Red Hook on the Hudson River in upstate New York. The town newspaper archives mentioned him as the most promising son of Red Hook in decades. He'd been at the top of his high school class, student council president, and star lacrosse player. At that point the stories broke off abruptly, except for a mention in the crime ledger of one T. Brodie, charged with breaking and entering, arraigned in Dutchess County Criminal Court on June 26, 1989. *He said juvie.* If he's forty, he'd have to have been just shy of eighteen. A plea bargain to join the Marines, perhaps?

She thought of Tristram's spit-shined shoes. He must have done well. *Didn't he say he inspected embassy security guards?* She pulled what she knew of the Marine Corps out of her memory banks. Michael had gone to OCS, Basic, and then flight training. He was already a college graduate, but one of his friends had reenlisted so the Marines would pay for his schooling. *That's right. Tristram said they sent him to college.* His wife Olivia died five years ago. Would that have given him enough time to retire from the Marines, go to law school, and make junior partner? Her loyalty kicked in. *For someone as brilliant as Tristram, sure it did.*

Her stomach growled again. She found her jacket and boots and trudged over to the Union Street Public House. Her favorite booth, an octagon in the corner that afforded a panoramic view of the bar, beckoned. A Duck Rabbit brown ale and an oyster po'boy later, she came out to be greeted by a decidedly chillier day. She zipped up her jacket and leaned into the wind. Ice sprinkles scratched her face. A short sharp gust blew her scarf off. She ran into the street to retrieve it, and when she turned around, a familiar figure stood on the corner. *Jacob.* "Jacob!" The figure jumped at her voice, then took off down the street.

"Jacob! Don't run away!" She tried to catch him, but he increased his speed, turned left at the corner and disappeared. Milo gave up and walked on down Union Street to the Factory. Tekla stood at the information booth talking to the temporary manager. Sparky struggled under her arm.

"Tekla! I just saw Jacob again!"

"What? Where?"

"He ran up King Street. I lost him in the crowd."

Tekla paused. "What do you mean, 'again'?"

Oh my God, I never told her about the last time I saw him. "I forgot to tell you—I saw him once before, on New Year's Eve. He wouldn't speak to me then, and he wouldn't this time either. Tekla, he's hiding from something."

"Or someone." Tekla glowered at Sparky, who responded by licking her chin. "He's afraid to face me. I didn't want to mention it before—in case it turned you against him—but he stole some money from me."

Milo tried to keep a straight face. *Oh yeah, like the news that Jacob's a thief is the only thing keeping me from appreciating him.* "Only once? I mean—" She stopped at Tekla's pained look. "How much did he take? A lot?"

"No, just a few dollars. I figured he needed it, so I didn't worry. But now…he must be wandering around out in the cold with no place to stay. Do you think I should go to the police?"

"You mean you haven't filed that missing person report?"

"Not yet. I've had too much to do since I got back from my cousin's citizenship ceremony. I told you, I feel in my bones that he's okay, but why won't he come home?"

"I don't know. Maybe he stole from other people as well." *Or maybe…* A new thought struck her. *What if he knows something about the murders? What if he witnessed one?* "Tekla, he may be in danger."

Her friend stared at her. "Are you thinking what I'm thinking? That he may be hiding from the killer?"

"It's possible. I think you should go to the police right away. Tell them exactly what happened the day you threw him out, if he said anything or did anything that would provide a clue to his behavior."

"Do I have to tell them about the money?"

Poor Tekla. "I don't see why. And I don't think a piddling couple of dollars would be enough to keep him from a free place to crash and a willing lover."

That helped. Tekla smiled. "Okay, I'll do it. I'll let you know what they say."

A few hours later Milo closed up her studio and drove home. She fed Pinkie, mixed some tuna fish for herself, and lit the oven. Once she'd lathered a couple of slices of caraway rye bread with the tuna and slapped Swiss cheese on top, she set them in the oven to broil and went back to the living room to turn on the television. The same anchor babe as before—only this time in a slinky knit dress and bright pink lipstick—announced in a voice bordering on hysteria that there were new developments in the Doyle robbery.

"Martin, can you tell us what the police said at the press conference today?"

The camera panned to a broad back in a pink smock.

"Um…Martin?"

The back straightened, mascara held aloft in one gloved hand, and leapt stage right, revealing the reporter, lips pursed and eyes shut tight. His eyes flew open as he tore off his makeup bib, revealing sartorial resplendence unmatched by any other non-cable correspondent. Without missing a beat, he chirped, "Press conference? Actually, no I can't, Rebecca." He straightened his hyacinth Versace tie and faced the camera with what he obviously thought was a compelling smile. "I'm standing here in front of the warehouse where the police located the first stash of stolen goods. Of course, they were removed yesterday, but I'm still here in hopes of more news. Anything rather than schlep down to the police station where they held the news conference. For that, we go to my intern Jimmy. Jimmy?"

He didn't really say that, did he?

Jimmy, a bright-eyed, big-eared young college student, looked about to wet his pants. "Rebecca! Rebecca! Can you hear me?" He tapped his earpiece, almost knocking the anchor babe off her perch and revealing way too much of a fairly decent pair of legs.

"Yes, *Jimmy.*" She shook her hair out and shot a surreptitious look at the mirror on her desk. "What can you tell us?"

"Police Chief Jones announced that they had finished the appraisal on the recovered items and…Rebecca, guess what? *They're fakes.*"

Anchor babe looked up from the mirror. "What's that, Jimmy? Did you say the antiques are fakes?"

"Yes. The experts from Samson Appraisals claim that all the Chinese porcelains and a significant number of the carpets and furniture pieces are first-rate imitations of original pieces."

"*Really?*" Apparently the news was too much for Rebecca to handle alone, so she turned to her colleague. "Martin?" Instead of the magnificent Martin, however, the audience was treated to a dramatic shot of the empty warehouse. "*Martin!*"

The correspondent, now attired in a trench coat—presumably to add gravitas—hove into view, his producer whispering energetically in his ear. "Sorry about that, Rebecca. We have the same statement. We should have more information by the eleven o'clock broadcast. Martin out."

Milo clicked off the set. *Fakes.* How very strange.

Doyle must be fit to be tied. Nothing has gone his way. One happy thought intruded. *At least he can't blame Tristram for this latest fiasco. Wait a minute—or can he? Doyle had assigned Tristram to work with Ursula. If she sold Doyle antiques she knew to be forgeries...but she wouldn't risk that. Would she?* It would destroy her business if it got out that she'd knowingly or unknowingly fenced counterfeit goods. It would probably be even worse if it was unintentional, since her reputation would be destroyed as well. At any rate, Tristram wouldn't be involved in anything shady. That didn't preclude Doyle from holding him accountable, however. She frowned. *Did he say something about being an antique expert? If so...no, that's ridiculous.* Milo decided to wait for the late news before wasting any more time on speculation.

As she tucked into her second tuna melt, the telephone rang. "Milo?" The voice sounded breathless and scared.

"Tekla? What is it? What's happened?"

"It's...it's Jacob. He was here."

"Was?"

"He's gone now. Milo?" Her voice came through softly. Milo could hear the terror and the tears in it. "He...he...hit me."

"I'm coming over right now. Did he hurt you?"

"Not much. Hurry."

She took the elevator to the parking level, jumped in her car, and roared out of the lot. Tekla lived at the end of Prince Street near the King Street station. Milo took the turns at forty miles an hour, thanking God the streets were finally clear of snow, and drew up in the front of the townhouse in ten minutes. Tekla had left the door open. Milo found her on the couch, a large blue handkerchief pressed to her face.

"Oh, Milo, thank God you're here. He scared me so much."

Milo pulled a glass from the cupboard and a bottle of Stolichnaya pepper vodka from the freezer. She poured out a tot of thick clear liquid and handed it to Tekla. Without removing the handkerchief, the Russian swallowed it and handed her glass back. Milo poured again. After the second shot, Tekla's breathing slowed to a more normal pace.

Milo sat down next to her. "Better? Okay, tell me everything that happened."

"Aren't you having some? No?" Tekla dropped the cloth on the table and heaved a huge sigh. An angry red spot colored her cheek. "When I got home tonight, Jacob was waiting. Or rather, hiding—I saw his Birkenstocks peeking out from that big boxwood to the right of the door. I didn't want to scare him off so I pretended I didn't notice them. When I unlocked the door, he slipped in behind me. He wouldn't let me turn on the living room lights. I asked him where he'd been, but he refused to answer. I asked him if he was okay and he said yes, but then I asked him what he was hiding from—if he'd done something wrong—and he went ballistic. He slapped me, Milo! I couldn't believe it." Her hand flew up to the bruise on her cheek. "It shocked me so much I just stared at him. Then he poured himself a large glass of whiskey and drank it all down. After that, he started to talk. Or rather rave."

"What did he say?"

"Mainly gibberish. He complained about the government and Nazis and Japanese whalers—the usual stuff. But then he started mumbling. The only words I could make out were 'mistake' and 'shouldn't have.' "

"Did he mention any places? Names?"

Tekla shook her head. "I probed as gently as I could. I tried to sound sympathetic, but he turned on me! Then…then…oh, Milo…he pulled his bike lock—the combination one with the big steel chain—out of his backpack and started waving it around! I ran into the bathroom and locked the door."

"Did you have your cell phone?"

"No. I'd left it on the couch. I heard the front door slam. I waited fifteen minutes—I was terrified that he hadn't really left, that he lay in wait for me with his…his…chain. When I finally peeked out, I saw no sign of him, so I grabbed the phone and went back into the bathroom to call you. After I talked to you, I felt a little better and checked the house. He'd emptied my wallet and thrown it on the floor. Milo, I don't know what's going through his mind. He's gone crazy!"

Milo refrained from concurring too heartily. "We'd better go to the police. Are you sure he's gone?"

"I hope so."

"Get your coat."

****

Lieutenant Webley listened carefully to Tekla's story. Once she'd calmed down, she remembered a bit more of Jacob's rant. "He mentioned a 'colleague' who had lied to him."

"Did he give a name, even a first name?"

"No. When I asked, his eyes closed to slits and he kept darting glances around—like an animal. He mumbled that 'he'—meaning the colleague—had promised him something. That's when he pulled out the chain and started waving it around. He didn't even look at me—just screamed something like, 'The pigs are coming to get me! They're out there!' "

"I see." Webley jotted something down. "When did he first disappear?"

"He didn't disappear so much as not show up." At the policeman's quizzical look she hastily said, "Remember, Milo, I told you I threw him out? It was around two weeks before Christmas."

"Yes, I remember. You said he'd been so irrational after the city council hearing that even you couldn't handle him." Milo stopped, her eyes wide. "Wasn't that the same day I found the dead man in the tower?"

Webley consulted his notes. "The body of Randall Galt was discovered on December 16th. The city council hearing about the Torpedo Factory happened a few days before, on December 12th."

Tekla nodded. "It must have been after the twelfth then. Remember, Milo, I came into your studio and told you, didn't I?"

Milo shook her head. So much else had happened in the intervening weeks. "I can't be sure of the date."

Tekla closed her eyes. "I'd just bailed him out…again. Yes, that's it. He'd chained himself to the Burke & Herbert bank. I told him I'd had it." She hummed to herself, a habit she'd picked up whenever she had to focus on something other than large metal objects.

Webley raised his voice to drown out the sound. "We can check the arrest records. So you claim you haven't seen Mr. Stickler since mid-December, correct?"

Tekla's only answer was a low hum. Milo touched

the detective's arm. "I did. I saw him twice."

"Oh?"

"Both times were on the street. When I called to him he ran away."

"Do you remember the dates?"

"The first time was New Year's Eve."

"And the last time?"

"Yesterday."

Webley turned to Tekla. "You say he took money from you?"

She stopped humming and opened her eyes. "Yes. A couple of times."

"Well, that may explain why he didn't skip town. You'd think if someone were after him, he'd try to get out of here, but he may not be able to afford it."

Tekla raised a tearful face. "Lieutenant, the m...murders. Do you think he may have seen or overheard something that's put him in danger?"

"Maybe. One more question. Why did he have a bike lock?"

"What do you mean? For his bike, naturally." Milo hoped Webley couldn't read the thought plastered on Tekla's face—*Policemen are such idiots.*

"Stickler's been hanging around Old Town for weeks. Ms. Everhart saw him twice walking on the sidewalk. How come he wasn't riding his bike?"

The two women stared at each other. Finally Tekla said, "I don't know, Officer. When I threw him out he had it—I remember watching him ride away."

Webley said nothing but pulled out his cell phone. "Buckler? See if any bikes have shown up in the Lost and Found recently."

Milo rose. "If you're finished with us, I'd like to

take Tekla home. It's been a very traumatic night for her."

The detective waved them out. "If you do hear from him, call me. Meanwhile, Miss Spirikova, would you mind giving a full description of your friend—and of his bike—to the sergeant? Thanks."

Milo deposited Tekla at her house and made her way home. She kicked off her shoes, poured herself a whiskey, and clicked on the television. The eleven o'clock news was in full swing. Rebecca and Martin had apparently retired for the evening and a new, less-expensively coiffed reporter stood before City Hall. "Chief Jones gave a brief statement at ten-thirty to the effect that the investigation is ongoing and they are pursuing several leads. They haven't scheduled another presser yet, so we're assuming they don't have much information so far. Hang on…" The reporter broke off and fiddled with his earpiece. "Katie, I'm getting word that there may be a connection between the antique dealer who was murdered just before Christmas and the stolen antiques. Eustice von der Dieb owned the Legerdemain Gallery on the corner of Union and King in Old Town. The police have found no leads in his death. Maybe this is the breakthrough they've been hoping for. Back to you, Katie."

Milo flipped Katie off. *I never could stand her perky little voice.* She opened the curtains to the balcony. The sky was clear for once, and stars gathered in little shiny clusters like guests at a cocktail party. She sat sipping her drink and musing. So what if the police discovered that some of the antiques came from von der Dieb's store? It had nothing to do with the Torpedo Factory. A fresh idea inched its way into her brain. *If it had nothing to do with the Torpedo Factory, that lets Archie off the hook for von der Dieb's death!* She jumped up, spilling some of the drink in her lap.

She longed to call Tristram and ask him his opinion. *I can't just call him about Doyle. He might think I'm rubbing it in that he was fired.* And considering the artists' victory, voicing sympathy for the crummy way he'd been treated would smack of...what? Insensitivity? Insincerity? Schadenfreude?

*If I went further—if I told him how much I missed him, he might misinterpret my words, think I'm asking...*Her throat constricted. She coughed to relieve the tightness and gagged. Falling into a chair, she crossed her arms over her chest and began to rock. *I'm just scared. That's all it is. How do I know when I'm ready?* She didn't want to start something up and pull back again—that would definitely be the last straw for him.

A tear fell unheeded into her whiskey, hissing a little when it hit the ice. *But all I think about is Tristram.* She missed his strength, his quiet masculinity, his bad jokes. She missed his pancakes and that comfortable sense of being home when they were together. She conjured up the picture she had framed and set on the mantelpiece of her memory. Grass green eyes, ebony hair just a teensy bit too long (but that allowed that perfect curl to decorate his temple), Celtic cheekbones that gave him a slightly exotic look. *And a body...*Her brain zeroed in on the muscled chest, then moved down to the flat belly, the slim hips and...and to that masterpiece of masculine physiology. Milo caught herself just before she fell off the chair.

She left the glass in the sink and went to stare at

the cold fireplace in the living room. It had been almost a week since they parted. She scratched her head, smoothed her skirt, anything to avoid admitting the obvious: she really, really wanted him. *I want his tongue, and his fingers and his prick. I want him grinding his hips into mine and whispering dirty words in my ear. I want to feel the tension, the rising pressure, the feel of that hard rod inside me, the rhythm of mating, the sweet release. I want to see that beatific smile on his face when I've given him the best ride of his life.*

She checked the calendar. January 5th. The day before the Epiphany. That's what she needed: an epiphany. *Oh, Michael, give me a sign. Anything to help me know it's okay. Michael?*

The tap-tap of cat's feet sounded from the bedroom. Milo waited, listening.

Chapter Nine

Someone pounded on her front door.

"Milo, let me in!" Esme banged the door again. As Milo hauled herself off the couch and tottered to the front, she heard her friend talking to someone. "Yes, ma'am. I'm sorry to make such a racket. Yes, ma'am, I'll stop now. No, ma'am, there's no need to call the super. Thank you, ma'am."

Milo opened the door to find Esme bobbing and curtseying at an irate Mrs. Peale in curlers. "Sorry, Mrs. Peale. I must have dozed off." She drew her friend inside.

Esme shivered. "I hope I never get that mean in my dotage. Milo, I've been calling you all morning. Is your cell phone off?"

Milo wiped the sleep from her eyes and felt around in her pockets. Empty. She searched the sofa cushions and came up with the cell phone. Assorted lights blinked silently on it. "Sorry, I had it on mute. I must have fallen asleep. What time is it?"

"It's nine o'clock." Esme surveyed her friend with some distaste. "I think you slept in your clothes." She sniffed delicately.

"Okay, okay. I'll go take a shower." She stopped at the bedroom door. "Why are you here, anyway?"

"Did you forget Archie's preliminary hearing is today? I told you I'd give you a ride."

A little voice in her head acknowledged the truth. "I forgot. When's the hearing?"

"Ten. Hurry. I want a big show of support for Archie. Even Homer's taking off to be there."

Fifteen minutes later, they were sailing toward the courthouse in Esme's Bentley. Esme grandly waved a hand sheathed in dove gray chamois leather at the security guard and double-parked by a police car. A short discussion ensued with said guard, and Esme graciously allowed him to move her car to a "safer" location.

"I don't think I should tip him. Do you, Milo? It doesn't seem…er…seemly."

Milo suppressed a chuckle. "No, dear, you shouldn't. Save your change for the hefty parking ticket you'll get in the mail."

They found seats in the pews next to Esme's husband Homer. He pointed out the high-priced lawyer he'd engaged, the epitome of pinstriped competence. "Aloysius Tupper. Best I could get. This should be over quickly."

Instead, the day dragged on. The court had a full docket of cases, and they had to sit through several repeat drunk driving offenders, a pickpocket, and a towing company charged with removing legally parked cars and demanding cash to return them.

Esme leaned toward Milo. "You figure Al's Towing has a chance to beat the rap?"

Milo stared at her. "You've spent a total of two hours in a courtroom, and you're channeling Damon Runyon?"

"Huh?"

"Never mind. Look, there's Archie."

Two policemen half carried Archie into the courtroom from a side door. He wore a terrified expression and dark brown overalls with "ADC" on the back in large orange letters.

Homer walked up to the lawyer's desk. When he came back he whispered, "Evidently Chisholm tried to make a break for it yesterday, so they hauled him in and kept him in jail overnight. Not a good move. Tupper says this will make it tougher."

"Oh dear. Poor Archie. Running away isn't a confession of guilt. He's just frightened, I'm sure."

Milo leaned over Esme. "How did they catch him?"

"Tupper says they had a plainclothes man keeping tabs on him. They picked him up as he came out through the Torpedo Factory loading dock carrying a suitcase."

"Why wasn't he at home?"

Homer shrugged. "Dunno. Esme tells me he practically lives at the Factory. They probably tailed him there from his house."

Milo considered. "Yes, I don't suppose his going back and forth to the Torpedo Factory would raise any special suspicions."

Esme's warm voice broke in. "We should have visited him over Christmas, Milo. That would have comforted him, I'm sure."

"I told you, he refused visitors. He wouldn't even answer my calls."

"Oh, well, then. Homer's lawyer will get him off." She lapsed into contented silence.

Milo wished she could be so serene. Archie's gray face and the hands trembling in his chains troubled her.

He didn't look at all well.

The bailiff called Archie's name. He stood, swaying slightly, while the lawyers huddled around the judge, their chins almost scraping the tall desk. Five minutes later they gathered up their papers as the two sheriff's deputies led Archie back out the side door. At one point he made a feeble attempt to struggle but then sagged against one of the officers. Esme and Milo sat stunned.

Homer consulted with Tupper and came back, a grim look on his face. Esme asked in a small voice, "What happened, dear?"

Her husband patted her shoulder absently. "The prosecution has asked for a grand jury."

"That's bad?"

"It's sure not good."

Esme took out a pristine white lace handkerchief embroidered with her initials. She wiped away a tear. "When does the…the grand jury happen?"

"The court's very busy this time of year. Tupper said he'd let me know but doesn't expect it to be scheduled for at least a couple of weeks."

Milo remembered her research. "He'll be indicted, won't he?"

"You know what they say." Homer's face revealed his pessimism. "Look, ladies, I have to get back to the office. Do you need a ride? How did you get down here?"

Esme replied airily, "Oh, that nice Officer Mars took care of the Bentley for me."

Her husband gazed at her. "Esme, my love, I expect to find it in our garage tonight."

"Of course." She shook her head, baffled, as he

strode off. "Why wouldn't it be?"

Sure enough, the good Mars retrieved the car for them. When he refused a tip, Esme arched her eyebrows at Milo as if to say, "See?"

Home at last, Milo checked her email. Nothing again. Why did she persist in thinking she would hear from Tristram? He'd said very clearly that he would wait for her to contact him. She looked behind her, trying to identify the source of the unattractive growling. *Oh, um.* It was her insides reminding her she hadn't eaten anything before the hearing. She checked the refrigerator. Nothing. *Well, nothing but baby carrots, half a jar of cheap caviar, and a can of V8.* Her taste buds craved beef. She got her coat and walked the few blocks to Rustico's.

"I'll have the blue cheese burger special please." She consulted the beer list. "And how about this Blue Mountain Full Nelson pale ale?"

"How could you resist it with a name like that?" The waiter grinned.

"Think it can take me?" Milo smiled back.

"Depends. If you get fries and bacon too, probably."

"I'll take that chance."

An hour later, Milo walked back across the Parkway toward Harbor Towers, trying to hold her bulging stomach in. Bacon and beer gurgled in nauseating syncopation. She felt better though. Or more accurately, she had something else to dwell on, like when it would all be digested so she could breathe again.

She passed through the lobby and out onto the terrace. A chill wind blew down the Potomac and whistled around the pool. She made her way around the building and stared downstream. The huge and unsightly Mirant power plant obstructed her view of Old Town—and more depressingly—Tristram's building.

When she returned to the lobby, the desk clerk called her. "You have a letter, Milo."

A letter? "Thanks, Hassan." She accepted a linen-finish ivory envelope addressed in florid gold ink. Few people wrote in this day and age. *Except Michael's mother.* She checked the return address. Pearl Everhart, 1103 Casa Loco Drive, Mesa, Arizona. She opened it.

Dear Milo,

I hope you are doing well. We continue as usual. I have gotten myself mixed up in a book club which is forever suggesting boring tomes by liberal pundits. I must say I enjoyed the Bingo club more! Rock sends his best—he plays golf every day and is looking younger by the minute. We miss you, dear, as much as we miss our Michael.

Which brings me to the topic of my note. Don Kinder—Michael's old Marine buddy—called me this week to invite us to an event in Washington for Gold Star families. Rock and I can't make it, but Mr. Kinder would like to escort you. He's been deployed in Europe since Michael's death, but he told me Michael had made him promise to get in touch. His number is 202-555-5540 (that's his cell phone). Call him one way or another, will you?

All my love,

Pearl

Milo wasn't sure how she made it into her apartment and drew the bath. She woke up when she felt hot water seeping into her vagina and steam into her nostrils. *Michael. Could this be my sign? But what does it mean? And who is this Don Kinder?* Michael had never mentioned him. Maybe he knew him from boot camp. Milo had only met her husband after he'd begun Officer Candidates' School. He'd always joked about how lucky she was not to have lived through recruit training on Parris Island with him.

She let the lilac-scented water soothe her. Her thoughts drifted to her late husband. She saw him again in his uniform—straight as a telephone pole, proud as a toddler taking his first steps, his jacket unstained, the golden wings brilliant, the ribbons in perfectly aligned rows, spit-shined shoes. *Shiny shoes.* The shoes brought her full circle to Tristram. *I don't want to see this Kinder person. I don't want to talk about Michael. I want to move on.*

She sat up suddenly. "Oh, my God. This *is* my sign! This Kinder fellow's name never came up because he wasn't part of *our* world. He's from Michael's past, not mine." She fell back into the water and closed her eyes. A soft, damp nose touched hers. "Pinkie!"

The cat took a nosedive into the tub, surfacing with a screech and scrabbling on the slippery enamel. Milo caught her under the belly and heaved her out. The little cat stood on the mat and shook herself, letting the drops fly around the room. She threw her mistress a look filled with bitterness and stalked out. Milo giggled. Just then, a flash of sunlight split the curtains. A little wan, yes, but yellow. Spring sending a heads-up. Milo toweled off and padded naked to her bedroom, still giggling. Life held promise. The future looked warm. *Thank you, Michael. Or rather, Pearl.* All that was left was to put this Kinder fellow off permanently.

She had picked up the phone and was looking for Pearl's letter to get the number when it rang in her hand. "Hello?"

"Mrs. Everhart? This is Don Kinder. I'm a Marine buddy of your husband Michael's?"

"Oh. Er. Hi. I was just about to telephone you. I got Pearl's letter today. I…um…I'm afraid I can't accept your kind invitation…Um, I do appreciate it, but—"

"No, no I understand. At least my call isn't totally out of the blue. Look, Michael probably never mentioned me and I'd like to explain. Can we get together for a drink?"

No. I don't want to. I want to move on. "Sure. Where are you?"

"I'm at a hotel near the Pentagon. I can meet you in Old Town. Tonight okay?"

Something burbled in Milo's stomach, which sounded perilously like fermenting blue cheese. "Tomorrow would be better. Are you in D.C. for long?"

"I've been assigned to the Pentagon temporarily." She heard a chuckle. "I'm sure you know what that means. All right, six-thirty tomorrow…Where?"

Quiet? Or crowded? "How about Pat Troy's? It's on North Pitt Street."

"I'll find it. See you then."

Milo sat in the apartment, quiet except for Pinkie's irritable sneezes and the occasional shaking of her feathers. *He had a pleasant voice. Seemed…nice. Efficient. Not long-winded.* She sighed. *It's just a drink.* Still, she resented the inevitable hitch it would throw into her path to recovery. She'd felt so liberated just twenty minutes before—ready to take on the world. She hoped it wouldn't cause a relapse, that she wouldn't have to scratch her way back up from the abyss one more time.

****

Okay, there's no reason to dress special. Milo surveyed her jeans and pink tunic sweater, feeling guilty. *On the other hand, I don't have to look like something the cat slept on. After all, you could call this a blind date. Sort of.* Besides, she would have frozen in a dress, and Pat Troy's, a venerable Irish pub, frowned on formality.

A couple squeezed past her stool, knocking her elbow. The dark-paneled bar had barely enough room for patrons, much less furniture, with political and military memorabilia infesting most of the ceiling and all of the wall space. Pat Troy was the scion of the Republican establishment in Alexandria as well as its foremost promoter of Irish culture. He'd organized the first St. Patrick's Day Parade in Alexandria in 1981 and acted as mascot ever since. Milo watched the old man cruise the restaurant, whacking shoulders and greeting old friends. A fiddler tuned up on the tiny stage.

Milo ordered a glass of Rietvallei Estate Dry Riesling, ignoring the dirty look from the bartender. *Hey, we don't all have to order Guinness.*

"Mrs. Everhart?" She turned to find a surprisingly short man standing behind her. He wore dress blues, his hat under his arm. He stuck out the other hand. "Don Kinder. I apologize for the uniform. My meeting went late, and I didn't want to keep you."

She'd been right—he had a very pleasant voice. Sandy hair, light blue eyes, a few freckles scattered over his fair cheeks like scarecrows on a Kansas wheat field. "Please call me Milo. How did you recognize me?"

"Oh." He sat down on the next stool and hung his cap on the hook beneath the bar. "Don't tell me you're surprised that Michael shared pictures of you on Facebook?" He surveyed her appreciatively and grinned. "I must say they didn't do you justice."

The bartender came by, and Kinder ordered a pint of Smithwick's Ale. In order to put some distance between the fiddler and their conversation, they took their drinks to a table on the upper level.

"Michael told me you're an artist."

"I do needlepoint—embroidery? I hand-paint and sell the canvases as well as my own work. I have a studio at the Torpedo Factory."

"Ah, the Art Center. He mentioned that. Very interesting."

Clearly not. "Why don't you tell me when you met Michael?"

He perked up. "We were at boot camp together— Parris Island. They assigned us as buddies, and we became really close while we were there. Since I opted for MSG school—that's Marine Security Guard training—at Quantico and Michael went to OCS, we still saw each other but rarely. We lost touch after he headed out to Corpus Christi for flight training." He signaled the waitress and pointed at his empty mug. "The Marines assigned me to the U.S. embassies in Austria, France, and England. I had it pretty easy compared to what he went through."

Milo wondered how close they'd really been, given that she'd met Michael soon after boot camp and he had never mentioned a Don Kinder. "How did you reconnect?"

"On Facebook, if you can believe it! Boy, I tell you, it's a godsend for us military folks. I've been able to track down so many of my old friends. Michael and I linked up just before the USS Reagan deployed. I actually heard from him the day before he...before the accident." He put a friendly hand on her arm. "Milo, that was his last entry. He wrote about you."

She didn't trust her voice. She ordered another glass of wine, cleared her throat, and pretended to listen to the fiddler. Finally she gave it a try. "Wh...what did he say?"

"He said you'd had a big show at the Factory and that the *Washington Post* wrote it up in an article in the Style section. He talked about how talented you were and how proud he was of you. I told him they'd assigned me to Washington, and he asked me to look you up. I would have, but they sent me to Brussels instead. Before I could let him know about the change he had...well, this is the first chance I've had to contact you. I'm sorry."

"That's okay." *It doesn't really make any difference, does it?* "So you didn't actually serve with him?"

"No. But you never forget the guys you go through boot camp with. Milo, he was a good friend—loyal, decent, a guy we all depended on. And a great loss to the Marines."

That's what Colonel Murray said. "And to the nation, I know. Thanks, Don." *Why do I get the feeling this is part of a Marine widow consolation program and not a social call?*

She sipped her wine and he ordered another pint.

He'd finished that one before he asked if she wanted anything to eat. "No, thanks. I've got some work to do. I'd better get back to the studio."

He gave her a meaningful look and covered his mouth to hide the burp. "Let me walk you back to the Factory then."

As they reached the entrance, Milo finally remembered the question that had been slipping in and out of her mind. "Don, you said you were posted to embassies in Europe, right?"

"Yup. Vienna, Paris, London. Had a great life. Real downer coming to the Pentagon, I've gotta tell you."

"Were you ever inspected by an officer named Tristram Brodie?"

Kinder almost tripped over the curb. "Captain Brodie? God, yes. Toughest son of a bitch who ever ripped through the barracks. He expected perfection in everything—posture, uniform, training. One time in Vienna he made us run emergency drills for fourteen hours straight until he was satisfied." He shook his head ruefully. "He almost discharged my buddy Jonah for being thirty seconds late to duty. Real bastard."

"I see. Well, thanks for the drink and talk, Don."

"Me too. I'll give you a call sometime, shall I?" His voice was half hopeful, half pessimistic. She knew he'd sensed her lack of enthusiasm.

"Sure." She walked away quickly, hoping he wouldn't see the happy smile on her face and misinterpret it. *So Tristram's a bastard. And a perfectionist. How wonderful.* A gentle euphoria filled her heart. Her epiphany. *Thank you, Michael.*

She loped up the stairs to her studio, casting glances up and down the halls. She didn't much like being in the place late at night now. A few lights still burned in studios. As Milo gathered some materials to take home, Morgana stuck her head in.

"Hey, there. I heard about Archie. What terrible news."

"Yes, our only hope is this big-time lawyer Homer hired for him."

"That, or finding the real killer."

"Yes, that." Milo didn't want to admit that every time she dismissed Archie as the culprit, she remembered that glimpse of his face in the crowd. *His angry face.* She heard again the detective's confident voice as he laid out the case for Archie's guilt. Her suspicions must be wrong. *There must be another explanation. Maybe if I asked Archie what he was doing there...but how can I? He's in the slammer.* If the police overheard her telling him she'd seen him on the street the night of the murder, they'd just take it as more evidence.

Morgana interrupted her thoughts. "We're all planning to go to the grand jury to lend support."

"I'm not sure you can do that, Morgana. It's supposed to be closed to the public. Even the defense lawyer can't be there."

"That seems awfully unfair. What kind of a justice system is this? Sounds like the Star Chamber." She turned around to leave, muttering to herself, but paused at the door. "I almost forgot. Tekla asked me to tell you she'd seen a photography exhibit in some gallery up on Queen Street. She said you should check it out—she thinks the photographer is a friend of yours."

"Did she say who?"

"She mentioned a name but I didn't recognize it. I

175

can't remember. Sorry."

"I'll check with her tomorrow. Thanks. 'Night, Morgana."

" 'Night."

As Milo kicked off her shoes, one of the flats fell next to Pinkie, making her jump. She hissed at her mistress, clearly still out of sorts over the bathtub episode. The little cat flounced into the kitchen, but not before taking a claw to Milo's favorite chair. "Pinkie! Stop it!"

Milo followed her. She pulled a plastic bag of homemade chicken stock from the freezer and plopped it into the microwave to defrost. Meanwhile she filled a large pot with water and set it to boil. *Now where are those noodles I picked up at Balducci's?* She threw a handful of basil-flavored capellini into the boiling water, accompanied by a dollop of olive oil, and kept it at a high boil until the pasta was cooked *al dente*—just the way her Italian neighbor had taught her. Emptying the water into the sink, she put the stock, the drained noodles, and some peas into the pot and set it to simmer while she changed into a soft flannel dress and slippers. The smell of rich chicken broth filled the apartment. She cut a thick slice of marbled rye bread, slathered it with butter, and took her soup and bread to the living room.

As she ate, she stared into the fire, trying to gauge her feelings. *I should be bawling into my dinner by now.* She'd been sure that meeting someone associated with Michael would tear her apart—that it would send her into spiraling despair, incapable of doing more than leafing through tear-stained photo albums. To her surprise, she didn't feel much of anything now except hungry. She polished off the soup and turned on the news. They mentioned Archie and the grand jury but no more about the fake antiques. *No, wait, a teaser.* She hated those.

"Coming up—a possible connection between the antiques stolen from Remington Doyle's mansion in Old Town Alexandria and one of the Torpedo Factory murders? We'll talk to psychiatrist and CNN news contributor Dr. Ivram Gotarub after the break."

The local news outlets had naturally dubbed the recent crimes the "Torpedo Factory Murders." Luisa wrote outraged letters to all the television and radio stations demanding they call them the "Christmas murders." To no avail. Milo smirked at the image of the illustrious president of the Artists Cooperative thrashing around the building, buttonholing every artist she met and ordering each of them not to speak to reporters. Not that it mattered any more. Archie had been right about one thing. The crimes had lured hordes of tourists into the art center, where they snooped around the corridors pointing out potential bloodstains with grisly pleasure. Given the amount of red paint splashed on the walls and floors of the building over the past forty-odd years, the would-be detectives had a field day.

Milo waited impatiently through the ads, teasers, and buildup. Fifteen minutes later, after drearily dull segments on lost cats, lost wallets, and lost souls, she was ready to give up. As her finger bore down on the remote's power button, the ever-fashionable Rebecca materialized, this time in a low-cut mauve silk blouse and teased hair.

"Welcome back. Dr. Gotarub, a prominent psychiatrist, is here to shed some light on the latest speculation concerning the Torpedo Factory murders. Rumor has it that one of the victims may have actually committed suicide. Dr. Gotarub?"

Milo fell back into her chair, then leaned forward eagerly, fighting down an urgent prickle of hope—*not murdered? Archie could be innocent!* She turned up the volume.

A swarthy man of middle age with close-cropped white hair and a brand new lab coat lounged in the easy chair next to Rebecca. "Yes, Rebecca, the police are making noises that the first victim found in the Torpedo Factory, a Mr. Bieberson—"

"Er, I believe the man's name is von der Dieb, Eustice von der Dieb, Doctor," an obviously uncomfortable Rebecca interrupted. "And...er...we've been told he was the *second* victim."

The good doctor remained unruffled. "Eustice you say? Oh, well, whatever. I don't need much more information than his name to indicate depression and suicidal tendencies. The police investigation will bear me out, I'm sure."

"Doctor, the police are saying the stomach wound that killed von der Dieb came from a sharp object—a letter opener or pair of scissors. Could it have been self-inflicted?"

"Certainly, certainly. I saw the pictures in the newspaper. From the angle of the wound, he could easily have stabbed himself."

His interviewer nodded sagely, almost as if she understood what he was talking about. "I'm sure you've also heard the reports that many of the antiques stolen from the multimillionaire entrepreneur Remington Doyle were purchased through von der Dieb's store,

Legerdemain. They have discovered that some of the antiques were replicas—well-made forgeries. Do you think that could have anything to do with his suicide?"

The good doctor's mouth dropped open. A blank look emptied his face of its customary smugness. "Reports? Fake antiques? I don't..." He recovered quickly, however, and blustered his way through, impressing both Milo and Rebecca. "No, no, my dear. Any one event by itself won't cause suicidal thoughts—they only arise from clinical depression, which can be effectively treated with drugs. Now, the tranquilizer I've had the most success with..."

Click. Milo didn't want to hear another infomercial for overmedicating Americans. *At least it kept me from obsessing about Michael. Or Tristram.* She headed to her bedroom, pulled on a T-shirt and pajama bottoms, and joined Pinkie under the covers. The cat graciously moved over half an inch. *Bed and work. Let's stick with that for awhile. No more thinking.*

Asleep in minutes, she dreamed she wandered the streets of an unfamiliar European town. Rain pelted her, trickling down her neck and into the gutters. Goosebumps rose on her arms, and she looked down to find she wore only a flimsy negligee, rendered nearly transparent by the rain. Her honeymoon gown. She scanned the vicinity, searching for a bit of shelter from the cold. A tall spiked fence screened a compound, dark and lifeless. Pausing before a shield attached to the iron fence, she read "Embassy of the United States." She peered through the gates. Suddenly a white face loomed out of the night and leered at her. After the pounding in her ears slowed, she stepped toward it. The face, all freckles and empty blue eyes, stared silently at her chest. As she pulled the thin material close across her breasts, the face disappeared, only to be replaced by another. Tristram. His eyes rolled over her without recognition, and he waved a hand dismissively.

"Please move along, miss. There's nothing to see here. No dead bodies."

She backed away, too mystified to speak, and turned to run. Instead she slammed into a creature that crouched behind her, covered in shabby gray rags. It grabbed her arm, opened its tobacco-stained mouth, and emitted a spine-tingling wail. "Don't listen to the Marine! Dead bodies everywhere! I've seen 'em!" She looked from the cringing beggar to Tristram, who took a stone from his pocket and pitched it at the creature. It hit him in the forehead and knocked him flat. As he lay on his back in the gutter, raindrops pinging off his mud-splattered forehead, she recognized him. *Jacob.*

Chapter Ten

"Are you ready, Milo? We're late. Sparky's appointment at Barksalot Dog Spa is for eleven forty-five."

Milo sighed and put her paintbrush down. "Honestly, Tekla, I know your life revolves around that mutt, but does mine have to?"

"If you come with me, I'll spring for lunch."

Stall if you can. "Where?"

"How about Bistrot Lafayette? I love their mussels in white wine and garlic. They're running a special on duck confit, and I know that's one of your favorites."

Milo choked on her coffee. "Not on your life. Michael took me there for my birthday a couple of years ago. I had the steak tartare and was sick as a dog for three days. You won't catch me eating there again."

"Oh yeah, I'd forgotten. It has such a nice reputation too. I've never had a bad meal there myself."

"That's because you have an iron stomach due to a childhood diet of borscht and vodka."

Tekla bridled. "My mother was an excellent cook. In fact she had…" She counted on her fingers. "…at least nineteen different versions of borscht." She stuck out her chin. "The villagers often spoke of her way with cabbage."

"Yes, her reputation spread even to the known world." At Tekla's expression Milo hastily suggested,

181

"How about Hank's Oyster Bar?"

"Yummy, but a hike from Barksalot, don't you think?"

"Okay, okay. Overwood? That's only three blocks away."

"Done. Get your coat."

The day did not disappoint them since they were expecting cold, dreary, misty January weather. They delivered Sparky into the sturdy, enthusiastic arms of "Miss Cleo," trudged down Queen, and turned right on Lee Street. They climbed the steps into a welcoming but empty restaurant.

"At least we don't have to worry about getting a table," boomed Tekla. From their mournful reaction, the staff of Overwood did not share her appreciation of the barren room.

The waiter led them to a booth next to a roaring fire. Milo leaned toward it, warming her face. "This is nice, Tekla. I'm glad you made me come."

"You've buried yourself in work this past week, Milo. I'm worried about you."

"Well, what about you? Since Jacob disappeared, you've been more Russian than ever."

That made her friend smile. "I'll take that as a compliment. But you're right. It's been very upsetting. The police have found no trace of him."

"That's understandable, since he has nothing to trace—no bank account, no apartment, no job. Say, did they ever find his bicycle?"

"I don't think so. He never reported it stolen."

"Yes, but Lieutenant Webley instructed the police to search for it."

The waiter brought glasses of wine. "The Louis

Jadot Gevrey Chambertin '07 you requested."

Tekla sipped. "Thank you, it's excellent." She turned back to Milo. "Anyway, even if the police found the bike, how would they contact Jacob?"

"And how would they know it belonged to him if he didn't report it? You're right. Jacob has made himself amazingly anonymous."

Tekla wiped a tear away and blew her nose. "Just what he wanted. The perfect cipher. He can't harm the environment because he barely uses it. Oh, Milo, I hope he's all right."

The waiter set down their steaks with a flourish, and they cheerfully dug in. "I suppose I should have had the salad," said Milo between bites of juicy ribeye.

"Why? Salad sounds so unsatisfying on a day like this. Besides, you always eat a big lunch."

"And not much dinner. True. Why can't they come up with a hearty salad though? One that doesn't sound quite so wussy? I mean, what real woman would order"—she read from the menu—" 'Tomato stuffed with non-fat cottage cheese on a bed of sliced celery, dressing on the side, crouton upon request'?" She took a generous bite of garlic mashed potatoes and an impressive gulp of wine. "*One* crouton? I ask you!"

"Amen. A salad should have three kinds of meat, cheese, eggs...and maybe anchovies." Tekla signaled the waiter. "Another glass of the Gevrey-Chambertin please." She glanced at Milo's glass. "You?"

Milo nodded. "Do they make wine in Russia?"

Tekla guffawed. "It's too cold to make whoopie, much less wine. Why do you think I liked Jacob's rubber gloves?" As Milo concentrated on not spitting up her wine, Tekla went on dreamily. "Vodka. That's the thing on a winter day." She shook herself like a cat. "Hey, waiter, belay that order. Bring me a Stoli!"

After that, lunch took a turn for the jolly.

As they wove unsteadily back toward the dog spa, Tekla paused to pull up a woolen stocking. When she straightened, she threw an arm out, whacking Milo in precisely the worst spot after a heavy meal.

"*Ooph*. What the…?"

"Milo, this is the studio I noticed the other day. Did Morgana mention it?"

"Studio? Oh, you mean the photograph gallery. Yes, she did. I'd forgotten." Milo looked up at the sign. "Olde Towne Galleree? They can't be serious."

"Rise above the name, dearie. You might want to check out the current exhibit." She winked.

Milo dutifully entered the tiny shop. Pictures crowded each other, some on the walls, some in glass cases, some pinned to easels.

Tekla moved to the back of the store. "Come and look."

Milo followed her. A space had been cleared on the counter for three large framed photographs. The small white card taped to the glass indicated they were the work of an up-and-coming local man named—Milo bent closer—Tristram Brodie.

"Oh my God, Tekla, they're Tristram's!"

From the back room, they heard the rustling of a newspaper and a spoon scraping a plate. Tekla called, "Hello?"

A scratchy voice squeaked, "Be there in a jiff. Just finishing my lunch." The two women shrugged. Evidently, the proprietor didn't go for the hard sell.

Tekla picked up the first photograph. "All three are

of the waterfront and lower Old Town. Take a look. Don't you find it intriguing?"

The grainy black and white photograph showed the marina in front of the Torpedo Factory. Tristram had done something to give the surface an antique wash. The sky was dark, and a few dots of light flickered from the riverboat moored at the far dock. In their refracted glow, the boats appeared to dip and sway. A lone figure wearing a hooded sweatshirt leaned into the back of a launch at the far end of the dock, too far away to make out his face.

"Yes. It's like the cover of a mystery novel." Milo held the photo up to the fluorescent light. "It almost has a texture to it, doesn't it?"

"I like the sepia tones. Reminds me of a nineteenth-century daguerreotype."

Milo moved on to the next shot. She recognized the passageway between the waterfront and the southern end of Union Street known as the Strand. Old buildings leaned in over a street flooded with melted snow. Far up the alley, a lone pedestrian headed away from the camera. "Isn't that the same man who's in the first picture?"

Tekla peered at it. "Can't tell. It could be. Maybe Tristram took the photographs in sequence. Let's see if he's dated them." She turned the third photograph over. "It just says 'Old Town, December.' "

Milo took it from her. "That's Windmill Hill—across from Tristram's house. He must have been shooting the scenes on his way home." The angle of the shot came from the river looking up toward Lee Street. Parks and playing fields rose in terraces up the hill. Beside a low stone wall near the top, a hooded figure lay supine on a bench.

Tekla peered at the figure. "It's the same fellow, isn't it?"

"Seems to be. Do you think Tristram included him on purpose? Or was it coincidence?"

"Must have been pure chance. Otherwise he would have given the series a title like, " 'Bum in Old Town,' or 'The Last Living Inhabitant of Old Town.' " Tekla chuckled.

"Still, it's odd. Wonder why this guy turns up in all the photos?"

"Yeah, who would be wandering around at midnight in the snow and sleeping on a park bench?"

The two women stopped and stared at each other. "*Jacob.*"

At that moment a man wearing a shabby sweater vest and ancient corduroys appeared, preceded by the scent of pipe tobacco. He wiped his mouth with a napkin. "Now, how may I help you ladies?"

After a whispered debate, Milo spoke. "Yes. Thank you. We'd like to inquire about these photographs by…" She pretended to look at the card. "Tristram Brodie?"

"Interesting, aren't they?" He tamped a pinch of tobacco into the bowl of his pipe and puffed, releasing another wisp of aromatic smoke. "He brought them in last week. I was happy to give them pride of place. He has talent, don't you think?"

"Oh, yes."

"Yes." *Can we sound any dumber?* "Er, how much does he want for them?"

The old man shook his head sadly. "I'm afraid they're sold. A lady came in yesterday and bought them all."

"Lady?" Milo ignored the sinking feeling with difficulty. "What did she look like?"

"Quite tall, dark-haired. Rather…How shall I put it? Imposing?"

Ursula. "And she bought them all? Did she leave a card?"

"No, but I have the receipt here somewhere…" He fumbled on a cluttered desk.

"It's all right," said Milo hastily. "Did she say when she would come by to pick them up?"

"In the next couple of days. Would you like me to say anything to her?"

"No. No!" Milo swallowed. "Could you do us a favor though? We'd like someone else to see them before the…buyer…takes them. If we send him by this afternoon, can you help him?"

"Sure. I'll be here." He gestured around the tiny spot, hinting heavily that it doubled as home.

****

"Now, Lieutenant, you will just go look at the photographs without identifying yourself, right?"

"Why shouldn't I?"

Milo couldn't put a finger on what worried her, but it had to do with Tristram. *What if he knew who his subject was? If he did, why didn't he turn Jacob in to the police?* But that didn't make sense. After all, he'd taken the pictures in December, and the police didn't start looking for Jacob until he attacked Tekla in January. Tristram had no way of knowing any of that. She concentrated on the detective's voice.

"If this mysterious figure is the missing Mr. Stickler, I'll want to talk to the photographer. You say

187

you know him?"

Before Milo could stop her, Tekla piped up. "Yes, he's that fellow who works for Doyle, the pig who wanted to put his box store in the Factory. What's his name, Milo?"

"Tristram Brodie."

"What? You'll have to speak up. His name is—?"

"Tristram Brodie. He's a partner with Zeller, Schwartz, and Katz—a law firm in Old Town. He represented Doyle before the city council." *And here it comes.*

"So he worked for your competition?"

Tekla jumped up and paced the detective's miniature office. "And Jacob's! He—Mr. Stickler—had a proposal before the council as well. He wanted to throw the artists out and force them to use recyclables or destroy their work after presenting it."

Webley replied mildly, "From what I understand, Stickler's plan didn't have much of a chance."

Tekla shook it off. "We all heard the rumors that Doyle didn't tolerate any rivals no matter how weak, and Brodie was his right-hand man. Doyle may have sent him to harass Jacob."

"Tekla!" *The traitor!*

"I can't see Doyle's minions taking someone out unless they were a serious contender."

Milo relaxed when she caught the twinkle in Webley's eye. *Thank God he's not stupid. Or a conspiracy theorist.*

Tekla's eyes lit up. "Take someone out? Is he some kind of gangster?"

"Not at all. But he's not known for playing softball either."

A light bulb went off. Milo raised her voice. "Anyway, *Tekla*, Tristram's been fired. Or rather, Doyle fired his firm. He doesn't have any skin in the game anymore."

Tekla gave Milo a severe look. "Skin? We don't want to get into *that* here, now do we?" She jerked her head in Webley's direction. "In front of the you-know-what?" She looked from one perplexed face to the other. "What?"

Milo floundered on. "Besides, at the time he took those photos, the city council hadn't made its decision yet. Right?"

Tekla waved her hand dismissively. "We don't know when he took them."

I am going to kill her. Right here.

Webley interrupted the glaring match. "Let me take a look at the pictures anyway. I'll compare them with the digital photo of Stickler you gave me. Now, you think you know who bought them?"

Milo tore her eyes from Tekla's glittering ebony ones. *Why does my best friend have to be a Russian?* "We're not sure. The description was pretty vague—a tall brunette." If the police learned of the connection between Ursula and Tristram, they might decide they were accomplices. *Another notch in the noose tightening around him. Wait, that doesn't sound right...*

"But, Milo, you said it had to be Ursula Baines. Who else would snap up those pictures so quickly?"

Sigh. "There are plenty of tall brunettes in the greater metropolitan area, Tekla. I'll bet there's more than one woman out there with an eye for talent."

That shut her up. *Finally.*

Webley took his hat off the old-fashioned coat tree.

"Okay, ladies. I'll visit the gallery. Even though I suspect this is a wild goose chase." He gestured for the women to precede him out the door. "Why don't you two just relax? Do some artwork or something. The police can handle this." Milo turned, ready with a snarky reply, but caught the smile on the detective's face just in time.

Tekla took Webley's advice, but Milo thought it prudent to go home.

The cat and the phone interrupted her much-needed nap. "Pinkie, get off me. Ouch! Yes? Hello?"

"Milo? Bill Webley here. I've just been discussing the Brodie photos with Ms. Baines. She happened to come into the shop as I was admiring them. She's graciously allowed me to take them home…on loan…so the wife can see them. I'm thinking the figure may be her brother-in-law Colin, who disappeared before Christmas. If she agrees, we'll take them to the police. It could be a lead in the case."

"Oh, er, yes." *Wow, what a great cover story!*

"Miss Baines says the photographer is a good friend of hers. She says that's why she's buying up all his pictures. In hopes of jump-starting him in his career."

"I see." *Yeah, right. The cow.*

"She tells me she has a decorating business and will be able to showcase his work for free. At any rate, I wanted to let you know since you had expressed interest in purchasing them too. Unfortunately, Miss Baines says she won't sell them."

I'll bet she won't. This is her hook into him. "Thanks for letting me know…Bill."

Milo pushed some pillows behind her head and sat

up on the bed. Grudgingly she recalled Ursula's doting attention to Tristram. With the husband von der Dieb—if he ever was her husband—out of the way, she had every right to go after Tristram. *If Ursula were looking to land him, then she could hardly be his accomplice in crime. And what would she be an accomplice to, anyway?* Milo couldn't see any linkage among the cast of characters—Tristram, Doyle, Jacob, Ursula—not to mention Archie. Ursula and Tristram both depended on Doyle for their business, but Jacob...*Well, Jacob lives in his own little world.* He couldn't have known any of them, and he didn't constitute a threat to any of them. Not really. Likewise Archie. Something itched the back of her mind. She got up and splashed water on her face. *Six o'clock already!* She'd better eat something.

She ordered Peking duck from the Happy Family Garden and pulled out the paper bag of leftover tubes of soy sauce, duck sauce, and mustard from her cupboard. As she dumped them into a basket, she considered. *Wait. Jacob may not be a threat to Doyle, but Doyle is a threat to him.* Again, it all came back to Doyle. Why hadn't she mentioned her suspicions to the police yet? *Because I'm afraid Tristram is mixed up in it.* Once again, she saw his face, wreathed in desire and bejeweled with Christmas-green eyes. A tsunami of emotion welled up from her heart and spilled out of her pores. She wiped her forehead with damp palms. *What is this feeling? It can't be. No. No. Oh God, I miss him. I can't hold off any longer. I don't care about anything else.*

She picked up the phone and dialed. Busy signal. She waited a minute and dialed again. This time the phone kept ringing. Finally an answering machine came on.

"Tristram? It's me. I'm coming over."

She pulled on a jacket, took a last gulp of whiskey, and headed out the door.

****

"Tristram! Open up!" Milo waited ten seconds and pounded again. *I know he's in there. I can smell him.* "Tristram!" She heard a step.

"Coming!" Tristram opened the door, his jacket pulled onto one arm. "Milo!"

He didn't act very hospitable, but then she hadn't exactly given him a heads-up. *I tried to.* She stepped around him into the living room. "I need to talk to you." The coat finally caught her attention. "Were you going out?"

A low growl came from behind him. Yum-yum peeked between Tristram's legs. When he saw Milo, he zipped out and jumped on her, barking happily.

"So much for my guard dog." Tristram bent down and ruffled the little terrier's ears. "Yes, I'm on my way to meet someone, but I have a couple of minutes. I see you're already in. What's up?"

He seemed…not cold…but indifferent. *He's already forgotten me.* She felt an embarrassing urge to cry. She took the chair he indicated, a rather spindly maple Windsor chair. The choice wasn't lost on her. *He's being careful to stay at a distance.* He dropped his jacket on the floor. Yum-yum immediately lay down on it, crossed his paws, and looked up at them both expectantly. Tristram stood before her.

"I…I thought you were only babysitting the dog." She darted glances here and there, checking for Ursula spoor.

192

"I was. Ursula came back from Brazil a couple of days ago. I'm on my way to return Yum-yum to his mistress." He held up the leash and a shoebox of toys as proof.

"Oh. I see." Milo tried desperately to recall what she came for. *Yum-yum. Ursula. Leashes. What the hell?*

Tristram must have decided to take pity on her. "I'll call Ursula and tell her I'm delayed. Want a drink or coffee? I'm afraid I don't have much to eat in the house. We had planned to go out to dinner."

Oh my God, it's dinnertime. Wait a minute. Wasn't I—? Oh, shit, the Peking duck. "I'm sorry, I didn't notice the time." She pushed herself off the chair. "Look, we can talk tomorrow. It's just…it's just that so many things have been happening and I thought…I wanted to…talk them over with you." *Pathetic enough, Milo?*

Tristram said nothing but dialed a number. "Ursula? Look, something's come up and I can't meet you…Yum-yum? He can stay with me—I'll bring him round to your place tomorrow…Pick him up? No! Er, I'm at the office and the meeting's about to start…Yes, of course Yum-yum is with me. This is a dog-friendly office…Okay. See you tomorrow."

Milo didn't dare look at him. Her thoughts were so jumbled at this point that she only knew one thing for sure—whatever she said would sound addlepated. *Is he? Are they? Is she? Who's on first?* She slowly became aware that Tristram had taken her coat, slipped her boots off, and put a glass of whiskey in her hand. She took a sip.

"Jack Daniels green label okay with you?"

She nodded. "It's better than the black label, don't you think?"

"I do."

"So I guess we have one thing in common..." *Soooo lame.*

He laughed, his pearly whites glinting in the flickering light. "Indeed."

"Er, Tristram? Did you light a candle?"

He went into the dining room where two tall white candles set in a beautiful baroque silver candelabrum glowed on a carved cherry wood bar. "Of course. It's happy hour. I always light candles at happy hour. Don't you?"

"Not when I'm alone."

"Ah, but I'm not. You're here." She must have appeared bewildered, for he added, "I lit them when I made your drink." He poured himself one and came back to the living room. "Now, sit. Tell me what's on your mind."

This time she took the dark red microfiber sofa, just in case he wanted to sit next to her. Instead, he pulled a straight chair out from the desk and sat down backwards in it. After a minute of silence, it popped into her head that he expected her to speak.

"I hear Mr. Doyle fired your firm."

"Yes."

"And blamed everything on you."

"Yes."

"Are you...has it...hurt your career?"

"You mean that one of the richest clients Zeller, Schwartz, and Katz have ever acquired trashed my reputation in public? Nah."

Milo couldn't tell if he meant to be serious or

flippant. "Can you do anything about it?"

Tristram took a sip of whiskey and set the glass down on a small table. "Not much. My only defense is the truth. And the fact that everyone knows Doyle does this to people."

Doyle. "Tristram, I've been thinking."

He leaned toward her, a sudden sparkle in his emerald eyes. "Yes?"

"You know the murders? In the Torpedo Factory? I'm still wondering whether Doyle could have done them."

"Huh?" He leaned back and almost fell off the chair. "*Doyle*? What the hell are you talking about?"

I'd better lay this out carefully. "See, Jacob's proposal actually had a chance, and the other corpse may have committed suicide, but he sold Doyle the fake antiques. And the *other* corpse, the second one—I mean the first one. No, I mean…well anyway, he was going to recommend against the box store. So…"

"Whoa! Back up. None of this makes any sense at all. For one thing, I'm pretty sure corpses can't commit suicide. Let's take it from the top. First of all, who is Jacob?"

"Jacob. Jacob Stickler. Tekla's boyfriend. Or he was. Till he disappeared." Even Milo knew her exposition lacked cogency. *But is it punchy enough? Or am I?*

"Look, this isn't getting us anywhere. Hang on." Tristram went to the kitchen and came back with a plate of stone ground wheat thins and a round of Brillat Savarin cheese. "Eat."

Milo dutifully finished off five crackers slathered in cheese, two chunks of Granny Smith apples, and her

Jack Daniels. Tristram poured her another.

"Okay, better? Now, why don't you start from the beginning?"

The food had revived her brain cells, and this time Milo, portraying a lifelike facsimile of an intelligent woman, related her thought process more lucidly. When she finished, Tristram frowned.

Staring over her head at the mantelpiece, he said slowly, "So, you're postulating that Doyle killed them both?"

"I...I don't know." Once she finally laid it all out, it sounded rather far-fetched. "He's the only one with a possible motive for both murders."

"Do you think he killed Jacob?"

Milo thought back. "If he did, it had to have been in the last week. I saw Jacob around January fourth on the street, the day before he threatened Tekla."

"Wait a minute. Threatened Tekla? How?"

"With a bicycle chain. Or rather, a bicycle lock. With a chain."

"But what for?"

"I don't know. He's just nuts." Her lip quivered. Every bone in her body felt ready to dissolve into a molten pool of exhaustion. "Tristram, I'm so tired. It's all too much for me." She looked at him.

A minute later, a strong, comforting masculine presence enveloped her. The dog licked her toes, diverting her attention from Tristram's lips, so he lifted her and took her upstairs. He kicked the bedroom door shut, abandoning Yum-yum to mewl on the other side. Words interspersed with the kisses as she unbuttoned his shirt.

"Milo, Milo, are you? I mean, are you sure?"

"Yes. Tristram. Tristram? I—"

"I don't want to rush you. I'm—"

How to put this? "Shut up and make love to me."

The magic words.

****

She made her way in from the parking garage to find the lobby lit up like a disco. A police car stood at the main entrance, its revolving roof light sending fiery beams in all directions. *Déjà vu all over again.* The desk clerk stood by the elevators, his expression a mix of hostility and trepidation. "Oh, thank God you're home, Mrs. Everhart. The police are looking for you. The residents are terribly upset."

Milo felt in her pocket for her cell phone. It stared back at her blankly. *The battery must be dead.* "I'm sorry, Hassan. Are they waiting out there?" She waved a hand over her shoulder.

"Yes, ma'am. Here comes one of them now."

She turned to see Sergeant Buckler heading toward her. "Ms. Everhart? Glad we found you. Can you come down to the station? We picked up Jacob Stickler. He won't call a lawyer. We've been told he'll only talk to you. Sorry it's so late."

"Do I have time to…er…freshen up?"

" 'Fraid not. We can't book him until we've gotten statements."

She started to follow him out, thanking her stars she'd showered at Tristram's, when Hassan called out. "Mrs. Everhart! I almost forgot! Happy Family Garden delivered your dinner. Since you were out, I had them leave it here. Do you still want it?"

Milo, whose stomach had only recently explained to her that it required more than five cheese crackers and two shots of whiskey to be obliging, thought she'd never heard such wonderful words. She stepped back and held her hand out. "Thanks *so* much, Hassan. I'm starving!"

The desk clerk handed her the paper bag and said, "That will be twenty-five dollars. Plus tip."

She scrabbled in her purse, muttering non-sweet nothings under her breath, and came up with a twenty and a ten. Hassan took it with a nod but without offering change.

"Ms. Everhart? Are you coming?"

"Yes, yes."

As she got in the car, someone scooted over. She had opened her mouth to apologize when she recognized her seatmate. "Tekla!"

Her friend huddled under an enormous fur coat that smelled of wood smoke and cedar. "Thank God you've come, Milo."

"What are you doing here? Sergeant Buckler said Jacob would only talk to me."

"I told them that. I doubt whether Jacob will talk to anybody at this point, but it was the only way I could think to get them to pick you up. I need you with me."

"Where is he? At the police station?"

Tekla pointed out the rear window. "He's in that other squad car. Milo? I…I turned him in."

Milo quelled the alarm that threatened to cut off her windpipe and took a deep breath. "Tell me what happened."

Tekla nodded toward the policeman at the wheel. "Do you think it's all right? I mean…"

"Of course. You're going to have to tell them everything eventually."

"Okay. Well, you remember those photographs of Jacob?"

Oh no. I never told Tristram that Ursula bought them. Unless he knows already. In the passion of their recent encounter, she'd forgotten entirely about Ursula. Jealousy sparked, but she set it on the back burner. It wouldn't do to let that distract her from poor Tekla's predicament. "Photographs. Yes."

"Well, I decided to follow their path myself tonight. I walked down Union to the park—by the way, the sign called it Marina Park—"

"That's because they want to renovate the entire waterfront, and they want a fancier name."

"Oh. How come you called it Windmill Hill? There's nothing but a playground there."

"Guess."

Tekla rolled her eyes. "Just tell me."

"A wind-powered water mill stood there in the nineteenth century. Duh."

"Fascinating. Anyway, I turned on Wilkes but ended up in an underground tunnel that spit me out on Royal. It was very strange."

"There used to be tracks there. That's where the old Orange and Alexandria railroad made the turn west to a roundhouse on Duke and Henry Streets. Remember the roundabout we walk to? It's part of the same line."

"Oh. That's been gone since the last century too, though, right? Since when did you get so interested in local history?" Apparently Tekla didn't expect an answer and went on without pausing. "Anyway, I got myself turned around and climbed back up to Lee Street and the top of the park. The ground was really sloppy, but luckily I didn't have to walk far. Guess who I found sleeping on a park bench?"

"Jacob."

Tekla nodded miserably. A tear rolled down her cheek. "I only wanted to talk to him. I tapped him gently and spoke softly, and you know how hard that is for me." Milo nodded sympathetically. Tekla's deep voice had been known to carry from one end of the Torpedo Factory to the other when she was in a rage. "He leapt up and started waving that stupid bicycle chain around his head and screaming at me."

"What did you do?"

"I ran back to Lee Street. Providence came to my aid, Milo. A police car happened to be cruising up Wilkes. I flagged him down, and they arrested Jacob."

"Why didn't you go straight to the police station?"

"I told you. I need you with me. The officer understood." She leaned forward to pat the driver's shoulder affectionately.

When the squad car pulled up in front of the station, Webley stood on the sidewalk. "I hear you found him. Well done." Milo refrained from a snide remark about police work. As they followed him inside, they heard the sounds of a struggle coming from the other car. Webley led them to a small room and placed two large cups on the table in front of them. "Coffee. Now, let's hear it."

Milo opened the bag with her dinner and dipped a finger into the plum sauce. At Webley's disapproving frown, she closed it with a sigh. "What about Jacob? Don't I need to talk to him?"

"We have him in a holding cell. You can see him after our chat."

"But what about reading him his rights?"

Webley stared at Milo as though she'd sprouted two extra heads. "What do you mean? He's been read his rights. First thing we do when we arrest someone."

"Oh. I thought. Um…"

Tekla patted her knee and whispered, "Thanks, dear."

The detective turned to Tekla. "Well?"

Tekla told her story fairly easily this time. The rehearsal in the car had smoothed out the edginess. Webley took notes.

"And how come you're here, Ms. Everhart?"

Tekla jumped in. "I asked your sergeant to bring her. I need her with me."

"*Hmm.* Okay. Are you willing to press charges, Ms. Spirikova?"

"Charges? What does that mean? Will he go to prison right away? You won't hurt him, will you? Where do you send your prisoners?" Her rich alto rose another octave.

The other two threw questioning glances at each other before understanding bloomed. "Tekla is from Russia, Lieutenant. She's not familiar with the American justice system."

Webley reassured the poor woman that police did not torture prisoners in the United States. He even explained the Miranda rule to her. "Which brings me to the charges. Considering the earlier incident, we'll have to charge him with two counts of assault. Did he actually hit you?"

"Oh, no. Jacob wouldn't hurt a fly. He just waved it menacingly at me. I wasn't scared."

The absurdity of this statement went unchallenged, although Milo could see a corner of Webley's mouth turn up. "All right, no battery then. Do you want to see him?"

Both women cried, "No!"

"Okay. You're free to go. Would you like a lift back to your homes?"

"Yes, please." Milo finished the coffee—a testament to her thirst rather than the station percolator—and stood. "Thanks, Lieutenant. I hope I never see you again."

He shook his head and grinned. "I have an awful feeling you will."

Chapter Eleven

"Mimi, we've got to stop meeting like this." Tristram nuzzled Milo's neck and tickled her belly button.

"We do?" She smiled up at him. She loved his pet name for her. He'd said Milo was a mouthful, and he'd rather use his mouth for other purposes with regard to her. It seemed reasonable.

"Yes. My office mates have been wondering where I am. And when I do come in, they avoid me. Could it be because I'm wandering around the halls with this stupid grin on my face? That is, when I'm not whistling 'Happy Days?' "

"The political tune or the sitcom theme?"

"Sitcom?"

"Oh, that's right. You were in the Marines. No time for television."

"Nope. No time for shallow distractions." Tristram stretched lazily, kicking off the covers so she could appreciate the full effect of his muscular, lust-provoking body. Which she did. "I was too busy destroying corporals' careers for coming to inspection in lusterless boots."

Don Kinder. "That reminds me. I met another Marine the other day. An old buddy of...of...Michael's." *That wasn't too hard.* She felt Tristram tense beside her. She wanted to tell him it was all right, but first she had to catch her breath. *One, two, three. Okay.* "He said he'd been posted as a guard at several embassies in Europe. He knew you."

All but one part of his hard body relaxed. "What's his name?"

"Don. Don Kinder."

"Kinder...I knew a Master Gunnery Sergeant Kinder—I think I inspected his security guard in Vienna. Good man."

Milo debated whether to continue the conversation or allow herself to be distracted by the pulsing penis currently batting against her thigh. *Let him wait just a couple more seconds.* "He seemed nice. Drank too much beer."

Instead of the satisfying exhibition of jealousy she hoped for, she got a chuckle. "That's what happens when you're stationed in Vienna. You get used to guzzling a lot more beer than is considered proper here. I have fond memories of *ein gutes Österreichische Bier.*"

All right. Fine. I can see I have to take a hand. So she did. One finger crept down her thigh unobtrusively and walked itself over to the still bobbing cock. She tickled the tip then drew her finger down the shaft to his balls. He said nothing, but from the deafening stillness, she knew he concentrated all his synapses on her finger. *He's not even breathing.* She added three more fingers to the mix, two on each side, squeezing and tugging. Tristram arched his back and stared at the ceiling, pretending he hadn't noticed. *Oh yeah? We'll see how long that lasts.* She ran her palms down to the root and bowed over his abdomen. Her tongue flicked out, barely brushing the crown, licking up the drop of semen that had escaped the hole.

Tristram let out a soft "*Uhhhh.*"

Milo smiled. *I've got him.* She kept a tight hold on him and began to lick up and down, squeezing gently whenever she reached the top and releasing as her fingers slid down the shaft.

Tristram writhed. "Milo, Milo. Don't—"

She pulled away. "Don't what?"

He grabbed the back of her head and urged her back down. "Stop. Don't stop. God, you make me crazy." She obediently began to suck. He pressed into her, molding her lips. She could feel the pent-up pressure growing. Finally he shouted, "I'm coming, I'm coming!" They both heard a yowl and a bang as Pinkie hit the floor.

Milo rolled onto her back and started to giggle. "Poor Pinkie. This is not what she bargained for when she signed on."

Tristram straddled her, an arm on either side of her face. "She'll get used to it. At least she doesn't stare at us like the dog does."

"Speaking of, have you returned Yum-yum yet?"

"Uh uh. I've been too busy. Besides, I like having him around. He's so cute and fluffy."

"I'm not enough for you?"

"Well, you're cute. But you're not fluffy."

"I suppose I could wear a pink satin bed jacket and have my hair permed. Would that help?"

He dropped his head and kissed her hungrily. "No. I don't want you fluffy. I want you naked. And I want you now." He kissed her neck and started down the path that led to orgasm. Milo lay back, soaking in the sensation. He reached her vagina and, lips still on clitoris, inserted a finger and rolled it around. She raised her hips to get closer. Taking one last taste, he raised a face suffused with desire. He murmured, "More?"

"More."

He inserted one more finger. She didn't know whether to react or lie there and revel in the glorious, slow-moving ascent to climax. He kept pressing in and out, in and out, his fingers palpating the soft inner flesh. She felt deliciously stuffed, like a warm yeast roll wrapped around a nub of melting butter. The pungent scent of sex filled her lungs. *Oh baby, oh baby, gimme more. Take me there.* Her body took over, and she bucked uncontrollably.

As she ground against the pulsating fingers, she could hear him whispering, "Come on, baby, come to me, let it go, let it out. I want you to come till the stars burst." The words—echoing her own thoughts—dragged her to a height of passion she'd never known. Her body lifted off the bed and she drove herself onto his fingers, losing all control and demanding satisfaction. While she dangled in mid-air, panting, praying for the last step over the edge, he pulled the fingers out.

"Oh, my God. Tristram! *Arrgggh.* I'm so close. Let me finish. Please, honey, *please.*" In answer, he thrust her back on the bed and let his thick, hard, long prick find its harbor. He began to pump, staring into her face, love and desire etched in it. She met him, and they rode the crest like surfers, embracing the churning waves before finally rolling over and over in the soft sand. She lay, sated and complete. As she savored the peace, she rolled on her side. Tristram had fallen fast asleep.

****

"Two days. Archie's grand jury is in two days. I'm as jittery as a chick with spring fever."

"Esme, remember, I told you. We aren't allowed to be there. And it's not going to be fun for anyone."

"I know. I just want it over with so we can get on with defending him."

"You're assuming they'll indict him."

Esme arched her eyebrows. "You know as well as I do how easy that is to do. Weren't you listening to Homer?"

Milo knew from experience the futility of reminding Esme that she—Milo—and not Homer, had explained the indictment process to her. "Yes, of course, Esme. Thank God we have Homer." She set her mug down on the work table. The square of canvas stretched on the easel before her bore just the outline of a head. To one side lay the pencil drawing she'd made of Tristram. She couldn't decide whether she wanted to do a full color portrait or just black and white. Black and white didn't do justice to the vivid Persian yarns, nor to his eyes. She picked up a tube of pthalo green and squirted some on her palette. "I just wish they'd find the real killer before Archie has to go through any more of this. Even if he's acquitted—"

"As he will be of course."

Esme looked so adorable with her arms akimbo and her long gray braid swinging with confidence. Milo wondered again how someone with the financial means to wear designer clothes every day and have anything done to her body she wanted—cosmetically at least—would insist on wearing unbecoming broomstick skirts and an old-fashioned plait in her natural hair color.

Still, even at sixty, her face remained arresting. How often had they been walking together and someone would stop mid-stride as Esme passed, marveling at her smooth, baby soft skin, regal cheekbones, and brilliant hazel eyes. Tekla often said Esme reminded her of a Renaissance portrait—" 'Venus in Winter,' something like that."

"Of course he'll be acquitted, but you saw him in court at the hearing. This whole affair will take its toll on him. He's always seemed a bit fragile to me."

"Fragile? Archie Chisholm? He's the toughest nut I know. After all, who else could be married to a building and still be the dominant partner?"

"Not to mention ruling over a brood of almost two hundred oddball artists," Milo said with a laugh.

Esme picked up the box of paints beside Milo. "I can't believe you use these acrylics. The colors are so…flat."

"I told you—they're better for stitch-painting on Congress cloth. It's a totally different surface from your primed linen."

Her friend ignored her, messing around with the tubes until Milo pushed the tray out of her reach. "You know," Esme mused, "it's not really that funny. I wonder whether the worst part of all this for Archie *is* that he's cut off from the Factory. It's got to be agony for him not to be here managing every little thing."

Milo added a smidgen of yellow to the green swirled on her tablet. "You're right. This place is his whole life. That's why Detective Webley believes he killed Galt and von der Dieb. To defend his Factory."

"Really? But where's his motive? What threat could an antique dealer and a bureaucrat possibly pose to the Factory?"

"Webley's theory is that both victims were conspiring or involved somehow in replacing the art center and that Archie found out about it."

"But Eustice had no connection to the Factory! His shop isn't even in the same building!"

"Yes, but it's on the same block. Remember, Mayor Carstairs said there were several proposals out there. Maybe von der Dieb had hatched a plan to partner with the box store."

"Then what about this Galt fellow? Wasn't he an aide to Dottie?"

"Her chief of staff. I heard that he'd talked Dundicut into recommending the city approve Jacob's proposal."

"That's absurd. No one took that weirdo's idea seriously, certainly not Dottie."

"*Shhh.* Here comes Tekla."

The towering Russian stuck her head in, long silver filigree earrings jingling. "How's the portrait coming?"

Milo hastily threw a sheet over the easel. "Okay."

Esme looked from one to the other, pausing at Milo's blush. "Ah ha. This is your young man, isn't it? Show me!"

Milo dutifully uncovered Tristram, and Esme examined it, head cocked. "I've seen him someplace before. Where? Who is he?"

Tekla jumped in before Milo could make up a plausible lie. "Tristram Brodie. Lately minion to the infamous Remington Doyle, former scion of Old Town."

"That's right—I saw him at the council meetings." She checked the palette. "You need a darker green for the eyes. I remember them as arrestingly Irish." She let the adjectives roll off her tongue like warm caramel.

Milo pulled the sheet back over the portrait. "Thanks for your advice. Are we on for lunch, then?"

"Yes, but wait. You hadn't finished explaining why the police think Archie is the murderer."

"I only know what they told me when they arrested him. The detective had mapped out the method and execution. He's still working on motive."

"But he actually thinks Archie is capable of murder?"

"To protect his beloved Factory? Yes." Milo felt her tears well up and noted glistening eyes all around. "Right."

They walked up King Street. For once, the streets were clear of slush, but the sky was matte white, and the weather channel predicted more snow. At Washington they turned right into the little French bistro Le Refuge. The hostess took their coats, stooping a little under the weight.

"Sooo, how's that global warming working out for you?" Tekla chanted for the hundredth time.

"Fine, Tekla. Take it up with your boyfriend." The words slipped out before Milo could stop them. "I'm so sorry, sweetie. I wasn't thinking."

Tekla shook her head. "I'm not going to let it bother me today. I'm too hungry. Give me the mushroom omelet, Jackie? And…lessee, a glass of Meursault—the Gouttes d'Or '05, please."

Esme ordered onion soup and tea. "What's this about Jacob? Is he still in jail?"

"Yes," said Milo. "The judge felt he could be a danger to himself, and maybe to Tekla, so they're keeping him incarcerated until the hearing."

Tekla took a swig of wine. "It's for the best. Where else would he stay? Not with me! He's got no money. He even lost his bicycle."

"So he did lose it. How?"

"Oh, he left it at the park and somebody swiped it. It hasn't turned up yet. I don't think he owns anything else."

Milo couldn't resist. "At any rate, he won't be needing his bicycle chain then."

Even Tekla laughed. The tittering subsided long enough to dig into the good French country fare. Milo had her usual, Dover sole lightly sautéed with butter and lemon. It always reminded her of traveling through Europe with her parents. She could still feel the cool breeze fanning her thirteen-year-old cheeks as the white cliffs loomed into view from the deck of the Calais ferry. The small restaurant on the ship cooked up the freshest fish, the most perfect potatoes, and the juiciest tomatoes she'd eaten in her young life. She often wondered why American mass transportation couldn't offer such delightful fare. *Maybe because here you can't throw a line overboard and bring up lunch still wiggling on the hook.*

****

"How did the ladies' lunch go?"

"Ha ha. Shut up and eat your burger." Milo slapped a large, juicy hamburger onto Tristram's bun. "We talked about Archie. Webley claims he killed both Galt and von der Dieb."

"What makes you so sure he's wrong?"

"We just know. He's not capable of it. Even though I saw him that night."

"That's not dispositive. You told me he'd left just before you. He could have turned back when he heard the police sirens."

"I wish, but no. It took me about five minutes to get up to the tower. After I found the body and ran out, it took me another ten minutes to find my phone, call 911, and get downstairs. It was pitch black in there, remember. The police didn't arrive at the scene for another five minutes or so. And then they kept me for another hour. Sergeant Buckler didn't take me home until after midnight. What had Archie been doing all that time?"

"Maybe he'd gone out for a drink."

"He doesn't drink."

"A walk?"

"At midnight? In the snow?"

"Okay, so you tell me."

"I don't know." Milo spooned ketchup, mustard, and relish on top of the lettuce, tomatoes, onion, and avocado smothering her own burger. She cocked a meaningful eye at Tristram's unadorned patty. "Nothing green on that?

"Only if there's mold."

"Typical."

"I'd ask for an explanation of that remark, but we're discussing something infinitely more interesting than my eating habits. I repeat, what then do you suggest Archie was doing on the sidewalk?"

"Perhaps he came back to make sure I left the building."

"Then why did he run away when you saw him?"

While Tristram waited patiently, Milo took a huge bite of hamburger to give herself time to marshal

Archie's defense. "I don't know that either. But it's not because he killed anyone."

"Okay." Tristram wiped a river of juice from his chin and tasted his beer. "This is good. What is it?"

"A microbrew from Maine. Geary's Pale Ale. A few years ago you could only get it in Maine, but now it's distributed everywhere. Not bad, huh?"

"It's good, but it would taste better in Maine." He sighed.

"You've been?"

"My family had a cottage up there. Midcoast."

"Camden?"

"Naw—too ritzy for our blood. Rockland. My great-uncle had a lobster business. Spent my summers hauling traps for him. That was my alternate career choice. If the Marines didn't work out."

"Really? I thought it was juvie."

He laughed. "Did I tell you that? It's true…sort of. I got in all sorts of trouble as a kid. My record almost did me in when a guy tried to frame me for breaking and entering. The perp confessed, but even so, I almost didn't graduate high school. Uncle Mason came down to Poughkeepsie and literally stood in the courthouse door until the District Attorney wiped the slate clean. Then he dragged my ass to the recruiting office. He and the Marines saved me."

Milo remembered the look of nostalgic fear on Don's face when he mentioned Tristram. "You may have saved a few Marines yourself."

"Hey, I was a tough bastard, but any soldier who thinks guarding embassies is a cushy job gets a hard lesson fast. Think Beirut, El Salvador, Nairobi, Kabul."

Milo wanted to ask more, but Tristram took a last

bite and pushed his plate away. "Gotta get back to work, love."

"Now? It's seven o'clock!"

"I know. New client. Higginbotham wants to expand his store on King Street, and I have a presentation before the city council in less than a week."

"Higginbotham? Which store is his?"

"You know it—La Volupté. The adult toy store."

Milo burst out laughing. "Oh dear, I'd love to see the mayor's face when you bring it up. How delicious."

"We're expecting hordes of outraged little old ladies trailed by their hubbies, the latter banking on a really detailed slide presentation."

As Tristram pulled on his coat, he called, "We'll finish the discussion tomorrow, okay? I'm still waiting to hear your explanation, Mimi m'dear. If Archie's innocent, you'll have to convince the police that Doyle is the culprit. Might want to be thinking about that."

****

"Oh, Milo, good. I was looking for you."

Milo looked around wildly for a hole to jump into before Luisa could grab a piece of her shoulder. Too late. "What do you need, Luisa?"

"There's a meeting of the Archives Committee on Friday—surely you received the notice?" Milo shook her head. Luisa bit off a mean-spirited reference to the temporary office manager's origins. "You did go through those records in the tower, didn't you? Are they in good enough order to allow us to put something together for the council?"

Oh, no. In all the excitement she'd forgotten all about them. Milo peeked at Luisa's pinched face. She'd need a better excuse than that. "Er, of course. I've made a couple of passes, but I want to check through them once more to make sure. We don't want you or the committee to waste any of your precious time, now do we?" She ran off gaily and tripped up the stairs to the Friends' office.

As she passed Morgana, her friend stopped her. "You're not going up to the tower, are you? Doesn't it give you the willies?"

Milo shook her off. "We have to go on with our lives, Morgana. I'm surprised at you."

The other woman shivered, her bracelets jingling. "Don't see why. You wouldn't catch me going up there—I hear you can still see the bloodstains on the carpet. And besides," she nodded knowingly, "they haven't caught the killer yet. For all we know he could still be up there, his body picked clean by those vultures."

"Thanks for the image, Morgana." Milo shook off the uneasiness her friend had revived as she continued up the back stairs to the tower.

From the other side of the fire door, she could hear the printer clacking. *Someone's inside.* She gulped twice and told herself it had to be Penelope Matthews, the executive director of the Friends. She used the room now and then to print out forms and correspondence. Milo opened the door.

"Oh, hi, Penny."

The woman, a youthful fifty-ish blonde with striking lavender eyes, turned quickly. "Milo! You startled me!"

"Sorry." Milo gestured toward the cabinets. "I need to go through some of these boxes of papers for Luisa.

Don't mind me."

"That's okay. Since the murders, we're all a bit jittery. I'm surprised you'll even come up here!"

She's worse than Morgana. "Thanks for reminding me."

"At least they finally got the blood out of the carpet." She surveyed the large bleached square in the middle of the room. "I wish the cooperative would spring for a new one—this is no better than the red splotch."

"Penny? Would you do me a favor?"

"Sure."

"Stop talking about it?"

The woman backed up a step. "I'm sorry, Milo. I didn't mean to upset you. I spend so much time alone, sometimes I find myself thinking out loud."

"I thought you had a boyfriend? Don't you see him?"

Penelope shook her head. "Not for a year." A film of tears blurred her beautiful eyes. "I discovered the hard way that he's incapable of real affection. I didn't want much, but it was more than he could ever give anyone. He's happier sitting in bars leering at girls half his age and mooching beers off suckers." She turned back to the printer with a sniffle.

Milo decided to make a project out of Penelope. She deserved better than that jerk. *After all, now that I'm deliriously happy, I should help others to reach nirvana as well, shouldn't I?* "You need to get out then, meet someone else. Why don't you and I go out for a drink soon? Carlyle Grand in Shirlington is always a good bet for meeting new people."

Penelope wiped her nose. "I should be angry with

you for treating me like a basket case, but I'm not. I admit it—I'd love to go out. Spending day after day in my little study staring at the birdfeeders gets pretty old."

"Great." Milo opened one of the cabinets and pulled out the box she'd organized on her first visit two weeks before. She went through the file cabinet as well and pulled a few more papers out. When she came to the cabinet that held the two safes, she paused. "I'd forgotten about these. Penelope, can you help me?"

Together, they heaved the boxes onto the table. Milo tried to open the first. "Locked. Oh, right—I could only get into one of them." She flipped the clasp on the second one. An empty case greeted her surprised face. "That's funny. I only took out a couple of files—now what did I do with them? And what happened to the rest?" She scrabbled around among the piles on the bookshelves. "I don't see any of them."

"What kind of papers were they?"

"Oh, miscellaneous financial papers. Purchase records. Invoices. I don't know if they were from an old show or belonged to an artist who's long gone. They didn't make much sense."

"Maybe the janitor threw them out."

"No, I must have put them somewhere."

Penny shrugged her shoulders. "It's probably not important."

"Probably not." Milo gazed thoughtfully at the locked box. "Still, perhaps I should take this one down to my studio. I can ask Archie—I mean the temp—to pry it open."

"It's awfully heavy. Can you manage it?"

Milo tried to lift it. "I don't think I can get it

downstairs myself. Do you mind taking one end?"

"Not at all."

Lugging the box between them, they negotiated the steep stairs to the third floor and carried the safe down the corridor to Milo's studio. They let it fall with a resounding thud on the cement floor by her desk.

"Oh, look! Here are the files!" Milo picked up the two manila folders marked *Leach* and *Kang-xi*. "I remember now. They were invoices for some ceramics."

"Juliana Moss is a potter. Maybe she can decipher the mystery."

"I'll ask her. Thanks, Penny."

Penelope waited for her breath to catch up with her then headed back to the tower, calling out, "Don't forget! Carlyle Grand soon!"

Milo took out a screwdriver, inserted it into a slot in the safe, and tried to turn it. *Nothing. Probably needs a key, but where's the keyhole?* She was kicking the side when Tekla came to a screeching halt outside her door.

"Milo! Come! Now!" She spun around and threw herself back down the hall, her heels clattering on the iron stairs.

Milo grabbed her purse and coat and went after her. Tekla had reached the parking garage across the street from the Factory when Milo caught up with her. "What is it?"

"Jacob. It's Jacob." She jerked her head, shaking tears off like a wet cat.

"What about him?"

Tekla found her car, an ancient Fiat, and they hopped in. She turned the ignition, but the engine only sputtered feebly. Milo waited with a resignation born of past experience. A few expletives later, Tekla got out and lifted the hood, slamming it back into place with an irritated grunt. "Okay." The engine spurted alive, and they backed out, suffering only one slight scrape from a concrete column in the process.

Once they were safely out of the garage, Milo assumed it would be okay to ask a question. "Where are we going?"

"Politsiya."

A horrible thought struck Milo. "Tekla, Jacob didn't...hurt himself, did he?"

"What? No." She swerved around an enormous SUV with Georgia plates attempting to park. When the man honked at her, Tekla screeched, "Gaia ravager!" threw him the finger, and roared on down Duke Street.

She didn't speak again, which was fine with Milo, until they reached the station. Tekla pulled the key out and left the car in front of the "Police Cars Only" sign. At that moment the rain that had been threatening all day took its cue and poured down in one vast sheet. Together they ran inside.

"Officer, vere it da plennik?"

Tekla's accent had thickened to the point where neither the desk sergeant nor Milo had a clue what she said. Luckily Lieutenant Webley appeared from a side door.

"Ladies, this way." They went into the same small brown room where Milo had given her statement the night Archie was arrested. "I'm glad you could come. Mr. Stickler's been asking for you, Ms. Spirikova."

Tekla drew back, her eyes liquid with apprehension. "I don't want to see him. This time he will kill me. You have to protect me!"

"It's okay." The detective's voice softened. "We'll be with you. He can't hurt anyone." He went to the door, opened it, and called to someone.

They stood listening to the shuffling of shackled feet, accompanied by a wheezing sound, probably a sign that Jacob's post-nasal drip had returned. He came in, a sheriff's deputy on either side of him. When he saw the women he slumped, dragging his guards almost to the ground. They sat him on a straight-backed chair and stood back.

Jacob stared at the floor. In the lengthening silence, the wheezing became more pronounced.

Finally the detective said, "Mr. Stickler, you wanted to see Miss Spirikova. What did you want to tell her?"

"*Mmph.*"

Tekla made an involuntary movement toward him, but Webley held her back. "Ms. Spirikova, Mr. Stickler confessed to the murder of Randall Galt fifteen minutes ago. He has made a statement. His lawyer is on his way. Due to Mr. Stickler's extreme agitation, we thought it appropriate to bring you in, hoping you can keep him calm until Mr. Tupper arrives."

"Tupper!"

Before Milo had time to wonder how Jacob could afford the most high-priced lawyer in town, Webley said, "One of your colleagues—an Esme Leventhal—called to say she had hired Tupper."

"How did she know about all this?"

He shook his head. "Beats me. You people all seem to know what's going on before I even get a chance to put out an APB."

Someone knocked on the door, and one of the guards escorted the expensively shod and suited Aloysius Tupper into the room. He waved a regal, beringed hand at the group and sat down across from his client. Webley ushered the women out.

When they had settled in his office, Milo turned to the detective. "What did Jacob say? Why did he kill Galt?"

"I'm not at liberty to let you see his confession, but I think it's all right to tell you this much. Stickler claims it was an accident, that he and Galt had an argument. Galt keeps…kept…his Boston Whaler at the marina across from the Factory. Stickler met him there the night of December 16th to discuss strategy. Or so he says."

"Strategy? You mean about the city council's plans for the Torpedo Factory?"

Webley nodded. "I think you know Galt was Councilwoman Dottie Dundicut's chief of staff. According to Stickler, he'd convinced Galt to support his—I think he called it performance art—idea. About nine o'clock that night, Galt called and asked Stickler to meet him at his boat. At this point in his narrative, Stickler became hysterical. We gathered from his ravings that Galt told him he'd been unable to convince his boss to vote for Stickler's proposal. Stickler admits he became enraged and hit Galt with his bicycle chain."

"Urk." They both looked at Tekla, whose hands barely covered her open mouth. "The same…same chain he…?"

"Yes. When we arrested him, we sent the chain to the lab. They found blood stains on it that matched Galt's. We were about to charge him when he confessed."

"But how did he...How...?" Milo felt more and more confused.

"How did he get the body up to the tower?"

"Yes. Archie and I were both in the building. We would have heard something."

"We're still trying to get the full story out of him, but he must have carried the body in while you were calling the police. That would explain the blood stains on the stairs. You probably just missed each other."

Milo's head began to spin. Tekla had lapsed into silence broken only by low hiccups.

"Okay, but then what did he do with the first body?"

"Good question. When we asked him, he just stared at us blankly. I can't tell whether he'd blotted the memory out or if he even knows there was a second body. Or rather, a first body. Maybe he found von der Dieb in the tower and killed him too, or maybe von der Dieb had been removed by the time Stickler arrived with Galt's corpse."

"This is crazy. If he didn't kill the antique dealer, who did? And if someone else did, that makes"—Milo stopped to count on her fingers—"at least six people in the Factory at the same time. How come nobody ever crossed paths?"

Webley shrugged. "We still consider Chisholm the prime suspect in the von der Dieb murder. That makes only five people to account for."

"No!"

"Now, Ms. Everhart..."

Tekla mumbled something.

Milo asked gently, "Tekla, would you like some

coffee or something?"

Webley flicked a finger at the desk sergeant, who filled a plastic cup from a pot on the file cabinet. When he brought it to her, she gazed up at him tearfully. "Do you happen to haf any wodka to go in it?"

The big man tittered, his voice surprisingly high. "Sorry, lady."

Milo waited until she put the cup down. "What did you say, Tekla?"

"Jacob couldn't have killed the first man."

"Why not?"

"Because Milo told me the first man had been stabbed in the stomach. Jacob didn't own a knife."

Webley rubbed his chin. "Could have been a letter opener, something he found there. I'll check with the lab, see if they found the murder weapon."

"There's one other little thing, Officer." The Russian woman clearly found it difficult to contradict a policeman. "He'd have to have killed the first man first, then gone down, had the argument, and killed the second man later. Why would he do that?"

Silence. Milo had an ancillary thought. "And if that's how it occurred, how could he have gotten past me twice?"

The lawyer knocked on the office door and came in. He didn't look happy. "Mr. Stickler wants to make a full confession and throw himself on the mercy of the court. He has refused my services. There's nothing more I can do." He pulled out his cell phone and walked out, leaving the door open.

Another door opened, and the guards came out with Jacob. He still wouldn't raise his eyes to Tekla, but as he passed he muttered, "Sorry, love. Sorry." She put out a pleading hand, her face crushed with misery, but they had turned down a hall and Jacob didn't see her.

Milo turned to Webley. "What happens now?"

"We go through the usual procedure. He'll stay in prison until the hearing."

"No, I mean, what happens to Archie?"

"Archie? You mean Chisholm?"

She resisted the urge to retort, "How many Archies do you currently have in jail?" and asked, "If he didn't kill Galt, what happens to him?"

"Those charges will be dropped, but he still has the von der Dieb murder to answer to."

"Can I see him?"

Webley looked at his watch. "Visiting hours at the detention center will be over in twenty minutes. I'll make a call and see if we can get you in."

Milo collected Tekla and they ran out into the rain. Sergeant Buckler bundled them into his squad car, turned on the siren, and sped the few yards to the detention center. Under any other circumstances Milo would have been enchanted. *Make way! Make way for the princesses!* They reached the side door, and the sergeant escorted them inside.

A policewoman sat behind a sliding glass window, talking on a telephone. She saw them and slid open the window. "You Milo Everhart and Tekla Spirikova?"

They nodded.

She listened to the receiver a minute then hung up. "I'm sorry. Lieutenant Webley did call, but I'm afraid we can't let you see the prisoner."

Milo glanced around for a clock and noticed the waiting room lacked any decoration or reading material. Not even an official notice graced the walls. She finally remembered to check her own watch. "It's only three-forty-five. Don't we have fifteen more minutes before visiting hours are over?"

"You do, but the prisoner is unavailable right now."

Sergeant Buckler leaned in. "Gladys, what's the problem?"

She looked from one face to another. "That was the ward officer on the horn. The prisoner Chisholm has been taken to the infirmary. When Derek went to fetch him for you, he found him hanging from the ceiling light in his cell. Looks like he tried to commit suicide. I'm so sorry."

Chapter Twelve

"Milo, Milo! Calm down and tell me everything."

"It's Archie. He tried to kill himself. Are you coming? Tristram? Are you coming?"

"I'm on my way. Are you home or at the jail?"

"Home. Tekla went straight home, and Sergeant Buckler dropped me here. Oh, Tristram, they wouldn't let us see him. He's in the infirmary. When will you get here?"

"I'll be there in five minutes."

She couldn't talk anymore. She didn't even have the strength to tell him she was hanging up. She pulled the wingbacked chair over to the balcony door and stared out over the dreary landscape. Far below her on the terraces, bits of gray snow interspersed with bits of yellow snow, melting slowly under the slanting drizzle. She couldn't see the water for the mish-mash of logs, cans, plastic toys, and dead ducks jammed together like leftover vomit from the river's intestines. She curled up in the chair under her grandmother's quilt and took another belt of iced vodka. The thick, cold liquid burned her throat. Tekla had pulled it from her glove compartment and pressed it into her hand before she drove away. "You'll need this."

The box by her door buzzed. "Ms. Everhart? Mr. Brodie is here."

"Send him up, Hassan. Thank you."

And there he stood, his heavy overcoat sparkling with rain, wrapped in a woolen scarf the color of tourmaline, holding out a bottle of Stolichnaya. "I thought you might need this."

Milo's laugh sounded unnatural coming from such a raspy throat. She held up the pint bottle Tekla had given her and preceded Tristram into the kitchen. She brought out another of her tiny crystal vodka glasses, encased in a silver filigree holder. "Tekla gave me these for a wedding present." She filled the glasses, and they went to sit facing the gray sky.

"Well?"

Milo told him about Jacob's confession, Webley's contention that Archie was still guilty of the von der Dieb murder, and the final sprint to the detention center. "They said he would survive, but I don't know what that means."

"You mean, you don't know whether there will be any permanent damage?"

She nodded miserably. "We should have insisted on seeing him before today. We should have marched en masse over to that stupid jail and showed Archie we believed in him. He must have felt so alone."

Tristram put an arm around her. She was thankful he seemed to know enough not to dismiss her regret with trite words of sympathy. After a minute he murmured, "Well, at least they postponed the grand jury. Perhaps the real murderer will be identified between now and then." He tasted the vodka and grimaced. "This is strong stuff."

Milo locked her eyes on his and downed her glass in one gulp. "No sipping. Wimp."

He chuckled and dipped a dainty finger into his

glass and sucked it, his tongue licking slowly up and down the finger until Milo grabbed his hand. He set the glass down. "Do you think Archie knew about Stickler?"

"You mean that Jacob murdered Galt? Or about his confession?"

"Good question. I meant about the confession, but it's possible he suspects, or knows, something about the murder itself."

"It's funny you should ask that. Tekla and I both assumed Jacob went underground because he'd witnessed something and thought the killer was after him. I guess we were wrong." She drew the quilt up over both of them and said slowly, "If Archie knew something that would exonerate him, why didn't he tell the police? Why allow the police to charge him with a murder he didn't commit? Even if he didn't know anything about the murder, but knew Jacob had confessed, why try to kill himself?"

"Why indeed. Did he know Stickler personally?"

"Everyone knew Jacob. He lived with Tekla, you know, and showed up at every Factory event that served free food." She closed her eyes, thinking about the past. "In a way, he really was a lost soul. No one took him seriously. That had to grate on him."

"Sounds to me as though he took himself seriously enough to make up for it."

Milo started to laugh but caught herself. "It isn't funny. His loony ideology drove him to murder."

"Are you sure? Maybe he had another motive?"

Milo stared at Tristram. "Like what?"

"I don't know. You told me he was...er...highly sexed. Could he have...?"

Milo threw his arm off. She could imagine Tekla's shocked face at such a suggestion. "How could you even *think*...No. Jacob has a lot of quirks, but he is definitely heterosexual. You don't know him. He's extremely emotional about the environment—almost pathological. He might kill a person who came between him and his Gaia. But I think only *accidentally.*"

"I see." He took another sip of vodka and filled Milo's glass. "What about Archie then? Is he capable of murder to protect his art center?"

"It's possible. He has no life outside of it." She smiled. "We all tease him that he's dug out a cave somewhere under the foundations."

"He has no family?"

She shook her head. "Not that he ever mentioned. I mean, he *must* have a parent or two."

"Well, perhaps the police can locate them. I have another question. If he loved the building enough to kill for it, why try to kill himself?"

She shivered and pulled his arm around her again. "Maybe he missed it too much."

He nuzzled her neck. "I missed you too. All day."

She settled deeper into his arms. When she looked up into his eyes, they were damp. "What's the matter?"

"Nothing. I...Milo, you know how I feel about you."

It struck her that up to now he'd never actually told her how he felt. "Do I?" She hoped that didn't come out as too arch.

He kissed her nose. "I'm in love with you, you little idiot. You know it."

A knot of fear blocked her throat. She'd been so happy with him over the last couple of weeks.

Everything felt perfect. *I thought I was ready. What am I afraid of now?*

"You're not saying anything, Mimi."

It came out in a rush. "I'm scared, Tristram. What happens if I give in and you…you…"

"Leave you?"

"No." Her tears threatened. "No, it's not that. I don't want to…what if I had to live without you…what if I let myself love you and you—"

"Die? Like Michael?"

She nodded dumbly. "I can't go through that again, Tristram. I'm not strong enough."

He stood up. "Now look here. You're being ridiculous. It's not like I'm going off to battle or something. Very few lawyers—at least corporate lawyers—face more than an angry client in their careers. I admit Doyle is a pretty mean son of a bitch, but—" Despite her misery, she giggled as he continued. "*But* I have survived worse. Now, are you going to marry me or not?"

She choked on the laugh. "What?"

"You heard me." He stood, clearly making a stab at casual indifference, hands in pockets, lips pursed to whistle. Only his eyes betrayed his hope and fear.

How can I reject him again? If I did, it would be permanent. Am I willing to risk never seeing him again? Never to hold him close, our bodies tightly woven? Her lips seemed to be glued together—she couldn't get a word out edgewise. Finally she whispered, "Tristram…"

His hands came out of the pockets, white-knuckled. "I see."

"No! It's—"

He raised one fist and scanned the room wildly as though searching for a wall to punch through.

"No! Tristram—"

"Enough." He grabbed his coat and, before she could get out of the chair, the door slammed.

Her final "no" echoed in the empty room. "I mean, yes."

****

A rough tongue on her cheek woke her. She jumped up quickly, and Pinkie fell to the floor with an angry whump. Milo looked down at the wet stain on her new cashmere sweater. She sniffed. *Vodka.* Stumbling to the bedroom, she shed the remains of the night's revels on the way. *I must have fallen asleep. I didn't get a chance to call him. He's going to think...oh no.*

She retraced her steps, shaking assorted articles of clothing for her cell phone. It fell out of the jeans pocket, knocked the edge of the coffee table, and skidded under the sofa. She went down on her knees and reached in, but Pinkie got there first. Milo watched a disembodied paw curl around the phone and gently push it away from her grasping fingers. The cat swept it out onto the floor and sent it skittering toward the kitchen. Not to be outdone, Milo did a kayak roll, caught Pinkie by the tail, crawled over her, and grabbed the phone.

She lay there panting for a minute, the cat glowering at her, then dialed Tristram's number. It went immediately to voice mail. She dialed his office. A pert voice came on. "You have reached the offices of Zeller, Schwartz, and Katz. The office is closed now. Please leave a name and number and a member of our support staff will return your call. Thank you!" *Click.* Milo noticed the alarm clock blinking. 6:00 AM. *Oh.*

She might as well shower and get something to eat.

As she licked the last bit of egg from her plate, the phone rang. She leapt for it. "Tristram?"

"Milo? No, this is Luisa. I know it's early, but I wanted to remind you of the Archives Committee meeting this evening. You said you were going to put the papers together?"

Papers. "Yes, I have them sorted into a box. I'll bring them down today. Say, Luisa, do you know anything about two strong boxes that were in one of the cabinets in the tower?"

"Strong boxes? You mean like safes? No. The Artists Cooperative only stores old papers up there. Did you ask Penelope? The Friends use the space more than we do."

"Penelope didn't know anything about them either. I wonder how they got there."

"Well, people have dumped stuff up there for years. It could be anything. Maybe love letters from some office romance." She managed to convey her disapproval—or was it envy?—even through the phone.

"*Hmm.* Well, I found some files in one of them that mentioned antique ceramics."

"Why don't you ask Juliana? She's a potter."

"I meant to—I'd forgotten about it until now." *Gee, I must have had other things on my mind.* "I'll see you later." *I'd better go take care of those papers for Luisa now.* After that she could concentrate on more important matters.

Since the Factory didn't open until nine o'clock, the front doors were still locked, but the janitors usually left the door in the south entrance open while they cleaned both the art center and the corner building. As she passed Legerdemain, she noticed the CLOSED sign remained on the door. *I wonder what will happen to it now?* Maybe the city would buy the property. Thank God it wasn't big enough for a box store, or they'd have to contend with Doyle all over again.

She climbed the stairs to the third floor, opened the steel door that led to the tower, and started up. She stopped as she always did to gaze through the great window down to the waterfront. Not a soul braved the damp wind. The boats pitched in the choppy water, straining against the ropes. She wondered idly which one had been Galt's. Wait, it must be the one at the end of the dock—the one in Tristram's photograph of Jacob. She imagined the scene—midnight, a meeting on the boat, Galt explaining that he hadn't been able to convince Dottie Dundicut to vote for Jacob's plan. Then Jacob, in a towering rage, lifting his bicycle chain and smashing it down on Galt's head.

He must have hauled the body up here without anyone seeing or hearing anything. *So where was Jacob when I brought the police upstairs and we found Galt's body?* She trudged up the last few steps and pulled the key to the tower door out of her pocket. Not until she put her hand on the knob did she realize it was ajar. *Penny must have forgotten to lock it.* She pushed it open.

A woman, her back to the door, was dragging boxes out of the cabinets and cursing angrily. "Where the hell is it?"

Milo stood, uncertain. The door banged shut. The woman froze and turned. *Ursula.*

Both women burst out, "What are you doing here?"

Ursula recovered first. She peered at Milo. "Don't I know you?"

"No. Or, yes. I think we met once." Milo hardly expected the exalted Ursula to remember her. *No way could I forget the big hair and stiletto heels, though.* Or the crimson mouth and matching purse.

"I see. Well. Do you work here?"

Milo tried not to bristle. "I have a studio here. I'm Milo Everhart."

"Milo? Wait, you're not…are you a friend of Tristram Brodie's?" She managed to put the question on a par with, "When did you stop beating your wife?"

"I know him." *No need to go into detail just now.* "May I ask why you're up here?"

A momentary embarrassment crossed Ursula's professionally made-up face. "I…er…I came to pick up some papers that were left here for me."

"Papers? Here in the Torpedo Factory?"

"Yes. My late…my ex…husband kept them here. With the permission of the archaeology museum."

Just a little too glib. "Really? This space belongs to the Friends of the Torpedo Factory. The Archaeology Center is downstairs. It's not supposed to store anything here."

Ursula shrugged and commented airily, "That's not my affair. Eustice told me he had an agreement with them." Milo had to admit Ursula could hold herself together admirably.

"Eustice? Eustice von der Dieb? Was he your husband?" *Let's hear your excuse, Ursula.*

"Ex. Now late. I'm sure you've heard he died. Even though we were divorced, we remained close, and I've been…er…designated his executor. I'm trying to clear up some of his effects."

Milo allowed the relief to flood through her. Ex. Divorced. So Tristram didn't have an affair with a married woman. *I knew he wouldn't...couldn't, do such a thing.* Her simultaneous distrust of and loyalty to Tristram didn't strike her as inconsistent. In any case, the news hardly altered her opinion of Ursula. *Still a nasty piece of work—and anyway, there's something fishy in her story.*

"You're looking for some papers? Maybe I can help you."

"There were...Eustice said there were two safe boxes in one of the cabinets. They had some...business files in them. I can only find one."

She must be the one who emptied the open safe. "That's because I took the other one downstairs. No one knew who they belonged to."

Ursula took a step toward Milo. An angry flush showed even under the artificially creamy complexion. "What gave you the right to take it? They're *mine.* Did you open it?"

Milo could feel the tension even across the room. *Why are the boxes hers all of a sudden? What's putting her in such a tizzy?* "Yes I opened it," she lied. The invoices from the other box came to mind. "I found files. On ceramics. Valuable antiques. I was going to ask one of our artists about them."

The other woman rose to her full height, her head almost grazing the fluorescent fixture, her features distorted in a snarl. "Oh, you *were.* That would have been a very stupid idea."

Something in her tone spelled imminent danger. Milo kept her face calm. "I hadn't gotten around to it yet, though. Look, why don't we go down to my studio, and you can have the box?"

Ursula took another step toward Milo. "You've already opened it. It's too late." The narrow worktable stood between them, folders and scissors and pens strewn across it. Before Milo could move, Ursula snatched up a pair of scissors and rounded the table. Milo backed away. Now Ursula stood between her and the stairs.

"What are you doing? Ursula, stop!" She took a step toward the door to the roof. Even a temporary escape route would be better than nothing.

The other woman's face had gone from red to livid purple. She shrieked, "You bitch! You stole Tristram, and now you want to destroy me!"

"What are you talking about?" *Play for time.* "I don't understand."

The woman studied Milo and apparently decided a little indulgence was in order, for she lowered her voice a notch. *I wish she'd put down the scissors though.*

"I guess I can tell you. It's not like you'll be around to spill the beans."

Milo swallowed hard. "S…sure."

Ursula's thin smile failed to reassure her. "Eustice wanted to stop. He said we were in over our heads, that the bastard wasn't the type we were used to. We couldn't handle him like we could the old dames. Then when Doyle demanded an appraisal, Eustice insisted we destroy the evidence and get out. If they found out Doyle's antiques were all fakes, they'd start looking into our other clients' collections. He said the jig was up." A tear welled up in a strikingly blue eye, but she flicked it away. Milo wondered irrelevantly if she wore colored lenses. "I had no choice."

"Choice?"

"I had to kill him. Poor Eustice. Getting cold feet at this date. Bad move." She shook her head with real regret. "I do miss him, you know. We were quite close."

Milo tried to appear engrossed in the unbosoming of Ursula's problems, while one hand curled behind her to turn the knob on the door. She knew from experience that it took a mighty push to budge the heavy panel. Maybe if she leaned forward to build some momentum then bashed into it with her whole body, it would open. No need to think beyond that. *Except that… except that Ursula may have done this before. She must have killed von der Dieb here. She must have been hiding here when I came in, and moved his body out to the roof after I ran out to call the police.*

Ursula's eyes narrowed. "What are you doing?" She raised the scissors over her head and pointed them at her victim.

"Nothing."

"Back away from the door."

Milo obeyed.

Ursula lowered her weapon but kept the blades open in front of her. A dark stain marred the shine.

Milo pointed. "Did you kill him with those?"

Ursula stared at them absently. "Oh yes. These are my favorite scissors. I keep them in my purse. They come in very handy in the decorating business."

No wonder they didn't find the murder weapon. She took it with her—in case she needed to kill again. Milo's knees buckled. *She's going to kill me.*

Meanwhile, Ursula had moved to the roof door and

heaved it open. Holding the scissors waist high, she gestured outside. "This is as good a place as any. I doubt if the police will look in the same spot twice." She laughed. "If you're lucky, the vultures have moved on." She stuck her head out and surveyed the roof. "Once you're disposed of, I can grab the box from your studio. Where is it, by the way? Oh, never mind, I'll find it. And be on my way. With sales skills like mine, I'm sure I can set up shop elsewhere. Maybe Beverly Hills…"

Momentarily distracted, she closed the scissors. Milo lunged for them, but Ursula had eight inches and thirty pounds on her and quickly pinned her to the wall. The sun sent a pale beam into the room. Ursula checked the window. "All right, time to get this over with before people start coming into the building."

Milo began to writhe, hoping Ursula would lose her grip. The scissors inched closer to her abdomen. *Her target of choice.*

As if she'd read her thoughts, Ursula snickered. "Yes, the stomach bleeds out so quickly. Only takes a minute or so. And it's so satisfactorily gory, don't you think?"

Milo opened her mouth to scream, but before she could make a sound all hell broke loose. The door to the stairwell burst open, and men came pouring in. Ursula took a flying leap toward the roof, but Sergeant Buckler caught her in midair. While he held her, kicking and drooling, Webley cuffed her. The first to reach Milo had very familiar hands and blazing emerald eyes.

As the police led Ursula, still raving about Beverly Hills, downstairs, Milo watched as if in a dream. She awoke to the sound of a deep, rich voice.

"Milo? Come here." Tristram helped her to a chair. He touched her face and her hands, felt her neck, picked up one foot after the other, and only stopped when she kissed the top of his head.

"I'm not hurt. You got here right on time."

He looked up through ebony curls and grinned. "They taught us to be punctual in the Marines."

Milo thought of the open scissors and Ursula's open, scarlet-lipped mouth. "Tristram, she was going to kill me."

"I know, love. She killed von der Dieb."

"I know." She closed her eyes, but opened them quickly. "Wait a minute! How did you know?"

"You're not going to like it."

"Try me."

"The precious Doyle."

"Mr. Meany Pants?"

"Yup. If it weren't for his obnoxious personality, the police wouldn't have solved the case. Remember the appraisal? He was so pissed to discover that the antiques for which he'd shelled out millions were knock-offs, he hired a private detective. It didn't take a rocket scientist to trace them to Ursula. She and von der Dieb had a nice little scam going. He'd get the merchandise through a Chinese connection, and she'd sell them to her clients. Most of those clients were too dumb or too rich—"

"Or too cowed?"

"Maybe. She can be rather intimidating, can't she? Anyway, nobody questioned the most sought-after decorator in Old Town. Until Doyle."

She remembered the fringe jacket and the snarky expression on the entrepreneur's face. "He's not the sort to take kindly to being snookered, is he?"

"Uh uh. Once he brought the scam to the attention of the police, they collected evidence from the houses of many of our finest citizens. Who are more than willing to press charges. Now."

"But why would she do it? She had a thriving business. Legerdemain is in a perfect location. We all assumed it was doing well."

"I don't know about that. From what I gathered, von der Dieb had filed preliminary papers for bankruptcy. If it weren't for the money he and Ursula collected from their victims, they would have gone under long ago."

Milo cast her mind back. "That makes sense now. When the store closed, Tekla and Esme assumed the inventory would be auctioned and were all gaga about picking up some good deals. I didn't focus on it at the time, but the pieces they were interested in had been on display for years."

"Ah."

"Ursula told me he wanted out, that he was afraid they'd get caught. That's why she killed him."

"I wouldn't put it past Ursula to have been blackmailing him. If her trade in fake antiques were uncovered, she'd lose everything. Not just her source of income, but her professional reputation."

Milo mused, "And if she thought he planned to skedaddle, she'd feel she had no choice but to kill him."

Tristram stood. "You look beat. It's time I took you back." He shot a questioning glance at Webley, who gave him a thumbs-up.

Milo pushed her aching body off the chair with some reluctance. "Okay." She let him take her hand and lead her down the stairs. As they passed the empty gift shop in the lobby, she stopped. "There's one good thing that will come out of all this mess."

Tristram kissed her. "I hope so."

She shook her head. "I didn't mean that." When his lips set in a grim line she pecked his cheek. "There will be plenty of time for that when we get home."

"Home?"

"Home." After she recovered from possibly the best kiss she'd ever had, she resumed a little breathlessly. "No, I mean, Archie is off the hook. They'll have to let him go now."

"That's right." Tristram grinned. "Poor Lieutenant Webley. He had such a nice clean case—one murderer, one motive, one opportunity. Too bad he had two bodies."

Chapter Thirteen

The caterwauling woke them up. Pinkie sat at the end of the bed, tail swishing angrily. The sun beat through the open curtains, showing off a beautiful, almost-spring dawn. The air smelled soft, like bath foam or cotton balls. Pinkie yowled again.

"You feed her."

"She's your cat."

Milo sat up straight, the sheet falling from her breasts. Tristram shot up a lazy arm and cupped one of them. She peeled him off reluctantly. "Hey, what about *your* cat?"

"Atticus? He's all right. He's an alley cat, remember? He can last for days on a single sardine carcass."

"Okay, then where is Yum-yum?" She couldn't help it—she'd grown fond of the little tuft of hair. He'd at least get them out of the house once a day. Otherwise…"You didn't…no!"

"No, Mimi, my pet. Yum-yum, like Atticus, has acquired squatter's rights. Right now he's probably depositing dog hair on my suede couch." Tristram heaved himself out of bed. "I'd best go and let him out." He looked down at her. "Don't you think it's about time we had a female there to look after us?"

She tried to keep her eyes on his, but they kept trailing down his pecs to that flat stomach—*I hate him*—and on to the rest of his parts. "You know, you have really nice legs for a guy." It was the only thing she could think to say that wouldn't get her in trouble. The kind of trouble she liked, but still…

He struck a pose. "Got them from my mother."

"Really? How's she getting around then?"

"Ha ha." He headed toward the bathroom, giving her yet another angle to admire. "I'll be out in a jiffy. Pour me a coffee, would you, love?"

Milo rose and found the black satin teddy she'd enticed him with the night before. After an anchovy pizza and a couple of beers, she'd felt much more lively and thought she would try seducing *him* for a change. She wasn't sure which part of the scheme worked best, but it did very well. She smiled to herself, feeling comfortable and serene. *All's right with the world.* They'd decided to save more discussion of the recent events until later that day. Tristram still had his presentation to the city, and she…she had a secret task ahead of her. She made coffee and yet another attempt at whistling.

Tristram came in, pulling his pants up and buttoning the top. She loved it that he wore buttons rather than a zipper—it made taking them off so much more of an adventure.

"What was that racket?"

"Whistling. Why?"

"Really?" He took the mug of coffee from her, spread his legs wide, and belted out the tune to "Oh, What a Beautiful Morning." "*That's* whistling."

"Stuff it."

"I wish I had time," he grinned. "I've gotta run. Wish me luck with the city council."

"Don't forget Yum-yum."

"I won't." He kissed her and left.

An hour later, Milo walked up the steps of the Torpedo Factory. *How come it looks just the same, as though nothing exciting ever happens here?*

"Milo?" A familiar voice called from the bowels of a Bentley parked illegally at the fire hydrant. "There you are. You're late. We've got to get to the detention center!"

"What's happened, Esme?"

"Happened? Nothing. I just thought you'd want to go visit Archie. The doctor said he is doing well, but they want to keep him a couple more days."

"Can't they release him to a real hospital?"

Esme looked at her as though she were daft. "Why would they do that? He might escape."

Milo realized that the events of the night before were not yet public knowledge. "He doesn't have to. They should have dropped the charges by now."

"What on earth do you mean?" Esme's voice rose with anticipation. "This sounds like good news. Tell me."

Milo related Ursula's confession and attempted murder while Esme negotiated Old Town's streets. As they turned onto Mill Road, Esme said, "You'd better let the others know. And soon. Poor Tekla. Jacob may be a loss, but at least we'll have our Archie back."

"I will. After we see Archie."

They signed in at the window and followed a guard to the infirmary. Archie slept peacefully in a bed at the end of the ward. Aloysius Tupper stood at the foot.

Tupper raised a hand to his lips and whispered, "Just dropped off."

"He knows?"

"He knows."

"Is he…is he relieved?"

For the second time that morning, someone looked at Milo as though she were dimwitted. She could tell he longed to say "Well, *duh,*" but felt it would undermine his well-manicured dignity.

"Yes. The doctors don't want him moved just yet, but all the papers are signed. He's free to go."

The two women looked down at the sleeping man. His neck was bandaged and his face still puffy and bruised. In repose he looked older, and very tired.

Esme put out a hand to touch his cheek but pulled it back. "He'll be so much happier when he's back at the Factory."

Milo nodded.

Archie opened one eye. "Hello, ladies."

"Hello, Archie."

"Welcome back, Archie."

He closed his eyes for a second then opened them. "I can't believe it's over," he whispered.

****

"Archie's back! Archie's back!" Artists mobbed him as he walked through the front door into the Torpedo Factory. Tourists gathered in small groups on either side, trying not to gawk. One fat fellow with a broad Boston accent told his children, "That's the man they thought murdered two people right here in the Torpedo Factory." The two little girls clutched each other and giggled nervously.

Archie took the attention in stride, wading through the well-wishers to get to his information desk. His studied indifference finally bore fruit as people began to peel off. At last only Milo remained. Archie peered at his computer, his face inches from the screen, clearly hoping she'd go away.

"Archie, I have a question."

"I'm fine. I have a lot of catching up to do, Milo. I can't believe the mess that temp left this place in. Where did Luisa find him, anyway?"

"This is a question about the night of the murders."

He stopped breathing. His nostrils closed and his ears turned red. "Is this necessary?"

"Yes. For my own peace of mind, Archie."

He sat back and folded his arms. "All right, what is it?"

Milo took a deep breath. "You walked out in front of me."

Archie moved restlessly, like a fox about to be released while the hounds bay in bloodthirsty anticipation. "We walked out together."

"No. Remember, I'd forgotten to get those papers from the tower. You went on down the hall."

"Okay. So what?"

"Well, after I found the corpse and called the police, I…I saw you. On the sidewalk outside. Archie, what were you doing there?"

He looked puzzled. "Going home, I guess. I stopped to see what all the hoopla was about."

He's not making this any easier. "But you should have been long gone by then. I'd been inside with the police for almost two hours."

"Oh." He leaned forward and started tapping on the keyboard.

"Archie! What were you doing there? I have to know. I never told Lieutenant Webley. It's…it's the only reason I thought the police might be right—that you were the killer."

He didn't look at her, but a blush rose from his collar up to his ears and showed through the sparse hairs on the crown of his head. "Okay, but if you tell anyone—*anyone*—I'll...I'll throw out all your mail and tell your customers you've left the country."

A glimmer of hope kindled with his embarrassment. *It can't be too bad then. A girlfriend?*

Archie continued to stare at his keyboard. In a voice she could barely hear he murmured, "You guys have teased me for years about how much time I spend here. You and Morgana are the worst—spreading rumors that I must live in the building. Well."

"Well, what?"

"I do."

Milo gasped. "Where?"

"Never you mind. The Torpedo Factory has secrets best left to professionals. I aim to keep it that way."

"But, Archie—"

"No buts. Before you ask, yes, I do have family. Cousins in Omaha and a sister in Maui. I haven't spoken to my mother in fifteen years. And no, I don't live in a cave—my place is actually quite snug." He clicked something on the computer. "End of conversation."

Milo stood there a moment longer for show, then backed off and trudged up the stairs to her studio. *I'll begin the search tomorrow. Starting with the roof.*

****

"So, Archie was actually coming home when you saw him on the sidewalk." Tristram signaled to Tony for another drink.

"Yes. Now one more time, swear."

"I swear I won't tell another soul that Archie Chisholm lives with a life-size plastic replica of his mother in the cellars under the Torpedo Factory, playing his organ all night and dreaming of bringing a bride home to Mummy."

"Good. You can snigger all you want, just so long as you keep mum." They waited until Tony had set down the drinks and, despairing of hearing anything juicy, stalked off.

Milo took an appreciative sip. "What's funny is Archie did have an elaborate alibi in case I caught him going back into the Factory. It just didn't include murder."

They were silent, musing over the many things they had yet to discuss. Milo opted for a flea flicker. "How did the presentation go with the City?"

"What? Oh, fine. Higginbotham has agreed not to expand La Volupté in exchange for a tax break."

"A tax break? I don't understand."

"He'll receive a significant charitable deduction for donating 'holiday' attire to the city for its parades." He grinned wickedly. "Like Kelly-green pasties and miniskirts for the lassies who escort city dignitaries on Saint Patty's Day."

"Let me guess—and fur-trimmed Santa bikinis for the Scottish Walk?"

"How'd you know?"

"Well, phooey. I was going to buy one of those." Milo batted her eyes at Tony as he handed them menus. He jumped back in mock dismay.

Tristram ignored him. "You know, I think those are on sale. Why don't we walk down and—"

"Later. So do you want to hear Webley's explanation of how the bodies got where they ended up or not?"

"When I figure out the syntax in that last sentence, I'll listen."

She stuck her tongue out at him. "Okay. First body: Eustice von der Dieb, antique dealer. Say, did you know 'Dieb' means thief in German? Morgana told me."

"Life is one big irony, isn't it?"

"We never dreamed the name actually defined the man. He sure got what he deserved. And I don't mean a divorce from Ursula Baines. By the way, I'm glad she cleared *that* little mystery up."

"I can't believe you thought I'd date a married woman."

"Okay, so Esme got it wrong. At any rate"—she blew Tristram a kiss—"I feel better."

"We were talking about von der Dieb. How did he get in the tower?"

"I'll tell you in a minute. Let's back it up a bit. See, he and Ursula kept their second set of books in the tower. The files in the strong boxes were proof of the fencing operation. They had forgers on their payroll who produced the copies of Chinese porcelains and pottery, which they then sold to Doyle and their other clients. He and Ursula had gone up there that night to go over the books—that's probably why I found one of the strong boxes unlocked. What with one thing and another—"

"You mean the murder and you and Jacob and the other body and then the police?"

"Exactly. She didn't have a chance to lock it again.

The police cordoned off the tower for a few days—"

"And don't forget, she went to Brazil for a fortnight too."

"That's right. She probably waited for the uproar to die down as well. She must have emptied the first box, but I'm guessing someone interrupted her. She couldn't return until the night she tried to kill me. She expected to find both boxes in the cabinet."

"Hold on,. You haven't explained what happened the night of the murders yet."

"Well, if you'd stop interrupting." She pouted until he stuck a straw between her lips.

Tony's head appeared between them. "What'll you have?"

Tristram ordered for both of them, then leaned his elbows on the table. "Go on."

"That night—December 16th—von der Dieb told her he was going to declare bankruptcy and skip town. She flew off the handle and stabbed him with her scissors."

"So she's standing there with bloody scissors, and he's face down on the floor. Then what?"

"She hears me coming up the stairs. She quickly puts his hat back on—"

"Why?"

"I dunno. I guess so whoever walked in wouldn't immediately identify him."

Tristram mused. "Seems an odd thing to do."

"*Anyhoo.*" Milo told herself not to be cross with him. "May I continue, please?"

"Sure, sure." Tristram signaled Tony for another drink and settled back.

"Where was I? Oh, yes. She hears me coming,

turns out the lights, and runs out on the roof. I scream and run back down the stairs. Once I'm gone, she reenters the tower room and pulls the body outside."

"Surely she must have known the police would search the roof?"

"Of course, but she figures it will take a while for me to get hold of the cops and even longer for them to get up to the tower. She did actually have about twenty minutes. She starts to drag von der Dieb toward the next building, thinking to hide him behind one of the parapet walls—"

"How do they know that?"

"They followed a trail in the pebbles covering the roof. The marks ended abruptly right in the center."

"Shades of Agatha Christie—the footprints that go nowhere. So how did she manage it?"

"About a yard from where the marks ended are some flagstones, set there so service people don't walk on the pebbles. A ladder lay next to the big furnace unit. She left Eustice on the ground, retrieved the ladder, then backtracked with the body to the tower. She set the ladder up against the tower wall, lifted Eustice up, and dumped him over onto the tower roof. Then she huddled next to him while the search went on below her."

"How did she manage to hoist a dead weight ten feet up the side of a building?"

Milo smirked. "It shouldn't have been too difficult for a woman as…sturdy…as Ursula. Plus, according to Esme, Eustice was a scrawny little guy."

"What about the ladder?"

"She knocked it away."

Tristram cupped his chin, musing. "She must have

had to stay out there in the cold for hours. Poor thing."

"Yes, poor thing. Really." Milo hoped her voice dripped with sufficient sarcasm.

"Wait a minute. How did she get out of the Factory?"

"Same way she got in—she had a key to the building. She told me Eustice had an agreement with the Archaeology Center—I assumed at the time she lied, but maybe not. Maybe he'd wangled a key from them."

"But didn't the police remain on guard all night? They must have stationed men at the doors."

"I asked Webley that same question. He said they assumed the culprit had escaped, so they were only interested in suspects coming into the building, not leaving it."

Tony brought soup bowls and a plate of steaming cornbread. The smell of chili and cheese filled the little booth. As Milo poured half an ounce of Tabasco sauce into her bowl, Tristram watched with chagrin and took a preemptive swallow of his beer. While she slathered butter on a chunk of cornbread he took the floor.

"Okay, let's recap. The intrepid Milo goes downstairs to let the police in. During said intermission, Ursula escorts her ex up to the tower room roof. Milo returns to the tower with the police, only to discover a different corpse has taken up residence. So tell me, oh clever one, how did Randall Galt arrive in the tower?"

"Here we come to the really weird part. More like a Marx Brothers movie than Agatha Christie I think."

"Except that we're talking about murder."

"Yes, yes. You can be such a nitpicker." She smiled fondly at him. "You know Jacob killed Randall

Galt on Galt's boat in the marina, right?"

"Yes. Stove 'is 'ead in wif a blunt instrument, he did."

Milo gave him a disapproving stare before continuing. "Even at that late hour, he knew he had to hide it somewhere, or someone—the harbormaster at least—would be sure to see it the next morning."

"Why didn't he just toss it in the water?"

"Too much ice. He was afraid Galt would land on a floe and he wouldn't be able to reach him before he floated out to the river. So he hauled him inside the Factory."

"Weren't the doors locked?"

"Not the back one. Archie hadn't done his rounds yet. He and I were still talking in my studio at that point." The steam started to dissipate on Milo's chili. If she raised her voice, maybe she could finish her narrative before Tristram could get in another question. "He dragged the body onto the freight elevator."

"How come you didn't see it then?"

Milo reluctantly put down the lovely spoonful of indigestion. "Because I didn't take the elevator. I walked down with Archie. I was halfway down the main hall when I remembered the files and turned around. It's quicker to take the main stairs than to go through the automatic doors and around the corner to the elevator. I never saw him. He told Webley when the elevator started to open on the third floor he heard me scream. There's a partition at the back of the elevator. He hid behind that until I'd passed it on my way downstairs."

"But the police didn't find any blood in the elevator. Nor outside on the waterfront, if I recall the newspaper accounts correctly. Only on the stairs."

"Jacob told the police he'd covered Galt's head with his backpack. It fell off on the stairs."

"You know, if Jacob hadn't confessed, the police still would have charged Archie with murder."

"Why?" Milo didn't mean to wail, but couldn't hide the desperation Tristram's words gave her.

"Because they didn't know Galt was killed in the boat. There was no blood trail from there to the Factory."

Milo paused. "Yes. But still, it would have been nearly impossible for Archie to go out the side entrance, zip around to the marina, meet Galt, bash his head in, and get the body back up to the tower before I came back with the police."

"Especially having already killed von der Dieb a few minutes earlier and salted his body away." Tristram took a tentative bite of his chili, followed hastily by a snort of beer. "What's hard to believe is that, with all the close calls, no one ran into anyone else. But if your scenario is correct…" He drew back at Milo's expression. "Just kidding. *Since* your narrative is correct, the murders must have occurred at the same time. Ergo, two murderers."

"I hadn't thought of that. Yes." She shivered. "Kismet?"

Tristram blew her a kiss. "More like the Furies. But you were explaining how Jacob did his sleight of corpse."

"When he heard me go down the main stairs, he carted Galt out of the elevator and up to the tower room, dumped him, and ran down to the third floor. There's a little-used stairwell on the north side of the building. He took it and escaped through the loading dock. After that he only had to turn right, away from the main entrance and the police, slip back around to the waterfront, run down toward the Strand, circle around and make it back to Prince Street and Tekla's house before the police entered the building. He missed us by maybe two minutes."

"He couldn't have planned it that way. Just dumb luck."

"Or maybe he knew exactly what he was doing." A thought struck her. "Say, we have proof that that's how it happened, don't we?"

"What do you mean?"

"Your photographs. You must have taken them that night. They showed Jacob at the boat, and running up the Strand—"

"And sleeping on the bench in the park. If he went back to Tekla's, that photograph doesn't fit."

"*Hmm*. Do you remember when you took the pictures?"

"N...no. Wait, let me check my phone." He pulled out the smartphone and touched the screen. "December...16th, did you say?" He shook his head. "Nope. I worked late that night. In fact, I remember being relieved that Ursula broke our date."

Milo curled her lip. "Too busy cleaning the blood off her Jason Wu jacket, I suppose."

"Don't be catty. Lessee...I'll pull up any stored photos...Yup, December 17. Shots of the way home. And Jacob."

"What the hell was he doing? Returning to the scene of the crime? That's insane."

"Maybe not. Perhaps he retraced his footsteps to

see if he'd left any evidence. He must've been a bit...er...flustered after killing Galt. By the next night, he'd calmed down enough to go back over the scene methodically."

"They say the mind focuses amazingly in the midst of a crisis."

"I don't know about Stickler, but it sure focused mine." Tristram took Milo's left hand and kissed the ring that encircled it. A beautiful pear-shaped ruby nestling amid six diamonds sparkled in the candlelight. "I thought I'd lost you before you even belonged to me."

She smiled at him, her eyes blurred with tears. "My hero."

"Milo." Tristram's face became grave. "You wouldn't marry me because you were afraid I'd die and abandon you like Michael did. That night you almost turned the tables on me. So I figure we're even."

She kissed him gently. "Me too."

****

"I can't believe it. Where did it go?" Milo darted to and fro, pulling out canvases and riffling through sheets of drawings.

"Where did what go?"

"My portrait of Tristram. I can't find either the sketch or the canvas I'd started." She threw up her hands in frustration and stared at the mess. "I wanted to finish it before the wedding."

"You know," observed Esme, "I hate to say this, but a needlepoint portrait is a little too...er...sissified."

"I know, Esme. And I would agree, but that's all I know how to do!"

"Couldn't you just give him the sketch? I rather

liked it."

"No! Black and white doesn't do him justice."

"You mean doesn't do his eyes justice."

"This conversation isn't helping, Esme."

Tekla popped her head in. Morgana zipped around her and trotted over to the worktable. She wore an exotic assortment of scarves and belts, her orange hair covered by a beaded turban. "Well? Have you given it to her?"

Esme ran a finger across her lips and goggled at Morgana. "Thanks for ruining the surprise."

"Surprise?" Milo looked from one to the other of her friends. "What?"

Tekla's head disappeared and reappeared holding a frame. She turned it around to show Milo. "This."

Milo gazed at a portrait of Tristram in oils. It captured not just his eyes, but his essence. She gazed at Esme. "I'd forgotten what a wonderful painter you are. Thank you."

Esme bowed her head. "This is my wedding present to you." Then she danced a little jig, her gray braid bobbing up and down. "Now you'll have to find something else to give your groom."

Milo grinned. "Oh, I'll think of something."

A word about the author...

Although M. S. Spencer has lived in Chicago, Boston, New York, France, Morocco, Turkey, Egypt, and England, the last thirty years have been spent mostly in Washington, D.C. as a librarian, Congressional staff assistant, speechwriter, editor, birdwatcher, kayaker, policy wonk, non-profit director, and parent. Once she escaped academia, she worked for the U.S. Senate, the U.S. Department of the Interior, in several library systems, both public and academic, and at the Torpedo Factory Art Center. She holds a BA from Vassar College, a Diploma in Arabic Studies from the American University in Cairo, and Masters in Anthropology and in Library Science from the University of Chicago. All of this tends to insinuate itself into her works.

Ms. Spencer has two fabulous grown children and an incredible granddaughter. She divides her time between the Gulf coast of Florida and a tiny village in Maine.

http://mssspencertalespinner.blogspot.com
https://www.facebook.com/msspencerromance
www.twitter.com/msspencerauthor

~*~

Other M. S. Spencer titles
available from The Wild Rose Press, Inc.:
*THE MASON'S MARK: LOVE AND DEATH
IN THE TOWER
THE PENHALLOW TRAIN INCIDENT
WHIRLWIND ROMANCE*

www.ingramcontent.com/pod-product-compliance
Lightning Source LLC
Chambersburg PA
CBHW070333260626
47160CB00003B/1034